The Secrets That Shape Us

by

W. L. Brooks

The McKay Series, Book 2

The Secrets That Shape Us

Cover Art by *RJ Morris*

The Wild Rose Press, Inc.
PO Box 708
Adams Basin, NY 14410-0708
Visit us at www.thewildrosepress.com

Publishing History
First Crimson Rose Edition, 2018
Print ISBN 978-1-5092-2210-0
Digital ISBN 978-1-5092-2211-7

The McKay Series, Book 2
Published in the United States of America

Disgusted with her pity party, Casey had decided to leave when a man walked in the door. Not a pig! Nope, this one had class written all over him. Unfortunately, she didn't do class; she preferred dirty, edgy, and unencumbered.

Too bad; he was a hottie. She couldn't tell the color of his eyes, but his dark brown hair looked salon styled, and he carried himself in a professional manner. He wore a gray pin-striped suit with a gray shirt and tie, but his body didn't scream desk job.

It was hotter than hell outside, and the man had on a suit jacket? Casey snorted. Class or stupidity?

He leaned in to ask the bartender something, and his forehead pinched when the other man pointed to her.

Wait a minute! Why was he pointing at her? What had she done? Oh, crap. Could he be a lawyer? No, she hadn't gotten into any fights recently…well, there was the guy who grabbed her ass but—nah, it couldn't be that. Knowing his eyes were focused on her, she paid special attention to the label on her beer bottle while keeping tabs on the man out of the corner of her eye.

Also available by W. L. Brooks from
The Wild Rose Press...

Between Death and Destiny

After a near fatal accident, Reegan McGrath is warned
never to come back to Willows Bluff. For years she
stayed away despite the haunting nightmares. Now,
with her grandmother dying, Reegan returns to find an
evolving second sight, a man she is fated to fall in love
with, and an overwhelming reaction to an old foe.

Let the Dead Lie
The McKay Series, Book One

Former FBI sharpshooter Emmit McKay likes to keep a
handle on things. But nothing can prepare him for the
battles coming to his small hometown.

Savannah Walker takes over as principal of the school
Emmit's daughters attend. But her intimacy with the
family stirs up rumors and unearths secrets.

Savannah and Emmit cannot deny the chemistry which
draws them together, but the closer they get, the more
dangerous the stakes become. When a murderer is
hidden amongst you, you can't let the dead lie.

Dedication

To my brothers for encouraging this anxiety-riddled, somewhat neurotic author. Your support means more than I can say. Thank you!

Chapter One

His brother was a dead man. He was going to die a slow and painful death. And, for good measure, Ryan Keller would even throw in a nice long lecture on the merits of responsibility.

Ryan had asked his older brother to do him a small favor. Though, technically, it wasn't even a favor he was asking for. No, he was asking Jake to do his damn job! He should have known better. Jake had always been a loose cannon, never playing by the rules, and doing what he wanted when he wanted.

Must be nice, not having any real responsibilities or anyone to answer to. He had simply asked his brother to meet with a prospective client. When was the last time he'd asked him to do anything? Jake had dropped the ball, and now Ryan had to fix it—again.

The Keller brothers owned a private detective agency called Sleuths, and even though Jake was consistently absent, they were doing quite well. Ryan shook his head. If he hadn't been finishing up another case, he would have taken the meeting himself and been spared the drama, but he had been right in the thick of things when the woman called.

What was her first name? Ryan drummed his fingers against the steering wheel. Alexandra. That was it. Alexandra McKay had heard about their agency from a guest staying at her bed and breakfast. Usually he did a thorough background on new clients, but he'd been previously engaged and hadn't had the time; he was going into this with less information than normal.

What he did know was that Ms. McKay owned and operated a bed and breakfast in the small town of Blue Creek. She needed to find someone and had called their agency for assistance. Which was all well and good, but Ryan had made the mistake of asking Jake to go in his stead.

He didn't know why he had been surprised when he received a phone call from Ms. McKay—a *displeased* Ms. McKay. She had informed him Jake had not only missed the meeting but also hadn't called to let her know he wasn't coming. She'd reminded Ryan it was bad business practice not to meet with potential clients, not to mention rude.

Now here he was driving to the mountains of North Carolina to see Ms. McKay. She had been more than understanding about the situation with his brother, but she hadn't been as forthcoming with information pertinent to her own case. In fact, she'd been downright evasive, which was strange, but he wouldn't complain. He was thankful she was giving Sleuths another chance. In his line of work, reputation was key, and he had assured her he would be there and be prompt.

Ryan passed the Welcome to Blue Creek sign around noon. He had an hour and a half to spare before he was scheduled to meet Ms. McKay, so he decided to stop for a bite to eat. He drove around the town square, and two things caught his attention: two buildings, standing side by side, with the same name.

One read McKay's Hardware and the other, McKay's. The first building was obvious in its function, and the second appeared to be a diner. His stomach growled, and he pulled into an empty space right in front. The traditional vibe struck him when he first opened the door. The stainless-steel countertops looked like they'd recently been buffed, and the red vinyl-topped seats shone. The eating area was open and friendly with fresh flowers on every table. There was a jukebox in the corner, and a delicious aroma wafted through the air.

Behind the counter, a petite blonde woman took orders. Her T-shirt was blue with the name of the diner written across the back. Ryan would bet if you straightened out the riot of curls touching her shoulders, they would reach the middle of her back.

Someone smacked him upside the head. He spun around and peered down at the person responsible. The look on the young woman's face made Ryan want to confess to whatever she thought he'd done. She was short, but he was well over six feet, and she had the coldest blue-green eyes he'd ever had the misfortune of seeing. Her high cheekbones were flushed, and her bow-shaped lips were pursed. She would have been beautiful if she would stop poking him.

"If you don't quit ogling my sister"—she poked him again—"I'm gonna arrest your sorry ass!"

"Your sister?" Ryan sputtered. He was by no means a man who frightened easily, but this woman—he supposed she was a girl—made him rather uncomfortable. Thinking how his brother would laugh his ass off if he witnessed Ryan's reaction made him stand straighter.

"The blonde behind the counter is my sister," she said, pointing at the other woman. "Hey, Charlie, you don't like it when people ogle you, do you?"

The blonde gave him a once-over and grinned. "Honestly, little sister, who am I to complain if this handsome gentleman wants to ogle me? Welcome to McKay's. I'm Charlie." She came around the counter to shake his hand. She gestured toward her sister. "That's Fletcher. Don't mind her. She likes to intimidate men because she can. And you are? Other than handsome, I mean," Charlie said, winking as a blush swept up her cheeks.

He ignored the desire to straighten his tie. "Ryan Keller. Nice to meet you both. Ah, sorry about—"

"It's okay, really," Charlie said. "Are you here on business or pleasure, Mr. Keller?"

"Business. Actually, you might be a relative of the woman I'm meeting. Alexandra?"

"She's our sister. What kind of business?" Fletcher asked, crossing slender arms over her overalls and drawing Ryan's attention to a couple of nasty cuts marring her flesh. She caught him staring, pulled her sleeve down, narrowed her eyes, and repeated the question.

"That's between your sister and myself, but I'm a private investigator," Ryan said, then jumped back when the girl started shouting.

"That prissy bitch! She's gonna try and find Casey. I told her not to go sticking her pert nose where it wasn't wanted, but does she listen to me? No! Not Miss the-world-works-for-Alexandra-fucking-McKay. Pops and Ma know where Casey is, but she has—"

"That's three dollars, Fletcher!" Charlie hollered, holding up a blue mason jar labeled *Pay for Profanity*. "And one dollar for the 'ass' you used earlier. Don't think I'd let one slip."

"Ass is a slang term for gluteus maximus, which is part of the human anatomy, so it doesn't count!"

Charlie raised an eyebrow and extended the arm holding the jar.

Fletcher took a few deep breaths, put in four ones, and stomped out of the diner.

"Finish eating, folks, and be thankful she doesn't carry her sidearm when she's not on duty," Charlie said, making the patrons laugh.

"She…uh…carries a weapon?" Ryan asked, a bit unsettled.

"All deputies carry one," she said, making her way back around the counter. She motioned for him to take a seat on one of the stools. "Would you like something to eat? Today's lunch special is the roast beef sandwich."

Ryan sat, but his attention was drawn to the front window of the diner and the young woman getting into her truck. "She's a deputy? She's a child."

Charlie cleared her throat and pointed to the menu.

"Sorry. Yes, roast beef sounds fine, thank you."

"It'll be a minute on the sandwich. Yes, she's a deputy. She's twenty-three, but I'm twenty-four and run this place." She shrugged. "So what does that say about either of us?" Instead of waiting for a reply, she plunked a cup of coffee in front of him and walked off.

An older man came up behind him and patted him on the shoulder. "Don't let the age fool you, boy. A body learns real quick not to judge a McKay by her cover. And if you want to know who put a gun in Fletcher's hand and named her deputy, that would be me. Name's Jasper Hart, *Sheriff* Jasper Hart." The man stuck out his wrinkled hand. "I've been the law in these here parts for nearly thirty years."

The man's booming voice didn't fit his small frame. The sheriff wore a tan uniform with his badge shining on his chest. His hair was gray and cut military short. His face was friendly, but his eyes were hard and flashing with impatience. Realizing his rudeness, Ryan shook the sheriff's hand.

"Ryan Keller, private investigator."

The sheriff dropped his hand like he'd been stung. "A PI, huh? I don't know how I feel about PIs, truth be told."

"Now, Jasper, don't start," Charlie said as she laid a napkin and flatware in front of Ryan.

"It's fine," Ryan assured her. "I'm used to it." Not all law enforcement officials appreciated his profession.

"See there? He's used to it," the sheriff said, moving his plate and cup to take the empty seat next to Ryan.

"That's no excuse," she said, on her way to refill someone's drink.

"You been a private investigator long?"

Ryan fixed his coffee to his liking. "Yes, several years."

The sheriff eyed Ryan over his mug. "You like the work?"

"I do. I like to help people."

Charlie put a plate of something delicious in front of him. "Here you go!"

"This looks great. Thanks!" he said, and she winked at him. Ryan savored his first bite and paid close attention to the conversation between Hart and the woman.

"How long 'til your parents come home, Charlie?" the sheriff asked her.

"A few more days, at least. School doesn't start for Jebb until late August. I know they need a relaxing vacation, but then again, Jasper…who doesn't."

"You might have something there, girl. I'll sure be glad when your dad gets back. I can't stand that fella he hired."

"Jasper Hart! How can you talk about Clay like that? He's your cousin."

"He was Laura's cousin, God rest her soul," Jasper whispered. "That's why I can talk about him like that. If your dad don't hurry back soon, he ain't gonna have a store left. Nobody wants to deal with Clay; he's a bitter old man. See now, look what you did, missy, ruined my lunch." The sheriff pushed his plate away, then turned to Ryan. "And you! You've gone and upset my deputy, boy. Do you know what she's like when she's mad? Let's just say no one in Blue Creek is gonna want to talk to you after this."

"I certainly had no intention—"

"Now I gotta go find my deputy and try to calm her down," the sheriff said, getting up and putting a few bills on the counter. "Something's always setting her off these days, and I'm having a hard time—"

"Jasper," Charlie whispered. Something passed between the two, and Ryan couldn't help thinking there was more going on.

The sheriff cleared his throat. "Hormones—female hormones are my worst enemy! See you tomorrow, Charlie." He walked out the door after saying good-bye to some of the other customers.

The sheriff's words had been loaded; Ryan wanted

to ask Charlie about their true meaning. He also wanted to ask about Fletcher, but the look on Charlie's face had him saving his breath. She wouldn't be divulging any secrets. With a sigh, he contented himself with finishing his lunch.

"That hit the spot," Ryan said after he cleared his plate. "I haven't had a decent meal in quite a while."

"I'm glad you enjoyed it," Charlie said, taking his dish away. "What time are you supposed to meet Alexandra?"

He checked his watch. "I should probably go now."

"I wouldn't be late if I were you." She smiled. "Alexandra abhors tardiness."

"Thanks, I'll keep that in mind."

****

The house was immense and secluded. There was a large back porch, part of which was closed in, and a garage across from the main house with stairs leading to what Ryan assumed was an apartment. He parked his vehicle in the parking area, gathered his briefcase, and walked to the front door. The place was called Granny Vaughn's, but Alexandra McKay ran it. Should he knock? Shrugging, he opened the door and entered; it was a bed and breakfast after all.

The front hall looked like it had been remodeled to accommodate the enormous front desk, which took up the majority of the room. The wood was solid oak, stained dark rather than light, and it gave the room an elegance which Ryan appreciated. He smiled when he rang the small brass bell.

"Right on time," a rich, feminine voice said from behind him. "Mr. Keller, I presume?"

Ryan turned and stared, he knew he did, but who in

his right mind wouldn't? If you took her hair out of its tight bun, she would be the exact image of the mermaid who had graced the cover of his grandmother's favorite fairy tale. The deep blue of her eyes reminded him of the ocean, which only added to the mental image. He couldn't look away. She lifted a slim red brow.

Ryan blinked a couple times, then held out his hand. "Yes, Ryan Keller, and you would be Ms. McKay." She nodded and took his hand. Hers was cool and all business, like the suit she wore. She let go of his hand and led him to a large office. He waited for her to take her seat before he sat in one of the empty chairs in front of the Queen Anne desk.

"I heard you met my sisters. I hope Fletcher didn't give you too hard a time. She's off today, so I know she didn't attempt to incapacitate you," Alex said, her lips quirking.

"What they say about small towns is true then; everybody knows everyone's business." Ryan shook his head and took a moment to study the woman in front of him. She was young; it had taken him a minute to get past the air of sophistication to see the youth beneath.

"What is it? You're staring at me and not in a flattering way."

"How old are you?" he blurted.

She narrowed her eyes and sat back in her chair. "I'm twenty-four. And before you ask, no, Charlie and I are not twins." She leaned forward. "How old are you?"

"I didn't mean to offend you." She and her sister were the same age but not twins? Ryan stored the information to review at a later time.

"You didn't, Ryan. May I call you Ryan?"

He ignored the desire to tug at his tie. "Yes, of

course."

"I didn't find your question offensive. I do take the implication that my age makes me inexperienced or inferior to my elders offensive. I will have you know I am well educated and more than capable of my chosen career. You're not dealing with a child, Mr. Keller, I assure you." Alexandra inclined her head. "Now, all things being equal, how old are you?"

"I'll apologize again, Ms. McKay. I'm thirty-two, and people make that same assumption about me." And it rankled.

"It *is* rather upsetting, is it not? How about we get down to business?"

Ryan opened his briefcase and pulled out a pen and pad, then straightened in his seat. "Yes, let's begin."

Chapter Two

Casey McKay was not having a good day. In fact, she was having a shitty day. She'd gotten fired. Fired! She sighed...again. She didn't work well with upper management types. She had never been good with authority; her parents could attest to that.

She missed her folks and her little brother Jebb, the Bullfrog. It had been four months since their last visit, and she could tell the separation was wearing on them. Of course, Jebb told her how their mother would cry after every trip, then Pops would go and build her something special to cheer her up.

Casey touched the tiny wrench earring in her left ear; she had received the earrings as a gift from her mother years ago. They were her favorite, and she never wore anything else.

The old question rose in her mind once again: what would have happened if Savannah Walker hadn't come to Blue Creek? Would she still be talking to her sisters? Who knew. Maybe some questions were better off unanswered.

Here she was, no job and no family. Yep, life sucked. She lifted her finger to the bartender to order another beer. He put the bottle down in front of her and winked. She rolled her eyes; men were pigs. Unfortunately, women didn't do it for her.

She hadn't been back to Blue Creek since

uncovering a monumental secret two of her sisters had been keeping. Betrayal was ugly, no matter what form it took. Casey had left the only real home she had ever known and never looked back. Well, not really. Okay, sometimes. Shit! Casey took a swig of beer. She should at least be honest with herself. She did think about it…a lot.

Six years ago, she had taken the money she'd been saving for a new truck and leased her first apartment. She had dropped out of college and begun taking classes at a trade school instead. With her skills and knowledge about all things automotive, getting her certificate had been child's play.

She had always loved working on anything with an engine. She had a natural talent, so finding work had been a piece of cake. Staying employed, however, proved more difficult.

Okay, maybe she had a teeny, tiny temper. Casey didn't take well to people telling her how to do her job when she usually did it better than said party. She worked with men mostly, the pigs, and they didn't know how to accept a woman in their penis-dominated domain. Well, too damn bad.

She shook her head and killed her beer. Just because she had a vagina didn't mean she was incapable of rebuilding an engine. She said those exact words to her boss this morning, and he fired her. Penis envy, her ass!

She relented a bit. Not all of the guys had been jerks. In fact, a couple of her male coworkers had befriended her, and they were the ones she would miss. She tried to keep her distance from people for this very reason. Things happen, people leave or betray you, and nothing was permanent. Why bother getting close to anyone?

Disgusted with her self-pity, Casey was about to leave when a man walked in the door. Not a pig! Nope, this one had class written all over him. Unfortunately, she didn't do class; she preferred dirty, edgy, and unencumbered.

Too bad; he was a hottie. His dark brown hair was styled and precise. She couldn't tell the color of his eyes, but he was tall and carried himself in a professional manner. He was wearing a gray pin-striped suit with a gray shirt and tie, but his body didn't scream desk job.

It was hotter than hell outside, and the man had on a suit jacket? Casey snorted. Class or stupidity?

He leaned in to ask the bartender something, and his forehead pinched when the other man pointed to her.

Wait a minute! Why was he pointing at her? What had she done? Oh, crap. Was the guy a lawyer? She hadn't gotten into any fights recently…well, there was the guy who grabbed her ass but—nah, it couldn't be that. Knowing she was being watched, she paid special attention to the label on her beer while keeping tabs on the man out of the corner of her eye.

****

Ryan thanked the barkeep. Was it his imagination, or was this the easiest find in his entire career? With a shake of his head, he approached his quarry. "Casey McKay?"

"I hope so. I'm wearing her underwear," she said without meeting his eyes.

Ryan contained his smile and stuck out his hand.

"Name's Ryan Keller. I'm a private investigator." He shook her hand briskly. If the other McKay sisters were beautiful, this one was stunning in a you-can't-touch-this sort of way. Her clothes were baggy, but he could see the outline of ample breasts. Her braided black hair reached the middle of her back, and her eyes were—he'd never encountered someone with violet eyes before. He straightened his jacket; he was losing his professionalism.

"Who sent you, Ryan?" Casey asked half turning in her seat, her tone bored.

"You have to promise to hear me out first." Alexandra had warned him her sibling had a temper and wouldn't appreciate his meddling.

"Those other McKay girls sent you, didn't they? Well, I don't want any." She laid money on the bar and started walking out.

Ryan followed her to her truck. He had to admire the shiny red machine. "Nice wheels," he said.

"Yeah." She laughed. "And what is it you drive, Mr. Ryan Keller, private dick?"

He pointed in the direction of his luxury SUV, and her mouth dropped open.

"Holy shit." Her eyes raked up and down his frame. "That is not the kind of machine I associate with private dicks."

"Yes, well." Ryan tugged at his collar. "It's my personal vehicle. If I'm on a stakeout, I drive something more inconspicuous. Or incognito, if you prefer."

She put her hands on her hips. "What do I have to do for you to let me drive this beauty?"

"You have to hear me out." He had lost his mind. He hadn't even let his brother drive his baby. Now he

14

was going to let this woman—this stranger—drive it? She made a noise in her throat and switched from foot to foot before nodding. He handed her his keys, and she made a run for it. He jumped in the passenger side next to her.

"Oh, baby," she whispered and caressed the dash with her fingertips. She started the engine, and Ryan would swear she moaned. "Talk," she told him as she pulled out of the parking space.

"Your sister, Alexandra, hired me to find you. She wants you to come home." He buckled his seatbelt and mentally apologized to his vehicle.

Casey snorted. "What's in it for her? Alex always has a game plan. The deceptive witch."

"None that I could see. She wrote a note telling you someone named Ward Jessup passed away a few months ago, and the old garage is for sale. She said the asking price is pathetic, but the place is dilapidated. You'd have a lot of work to do to fix it up—if you were game, of course." He sat back, studying her in the darkness and admiring her technique behind the wheel.

"Of course," she sneered. "It's a dare! That little bitch has issued a dare. Wait a minute. She wrote me a note? Which you read? Isn't that invasion of privacy?"

He held his palms up. "She didn't tell me not to read it. In fact, she didn't even seal it."

It had taken only a couple of hours to find her. He had wanted more background information on the family than Alexandra had been willing to give, so he had walked around town and talked to the locals for an hour. He learned a lot about the McKay sisters, like the fact they were all adopted by Emmit McKay. He'd also found out about a mysterious rift between the sisters that had kept Casey away for six years.

After obtaining some backstory, he asked a friend to run a search of DMV records for an address. Usually he would have done it himself, but his code for the database wasn't working. He was almost certain his brother had something to do with that.

Stopping at an intersection, Casey asked, "How'd she look?"

"Who?" He frowned. "Alexandra?"

She nodded, then hit the gas when the light turned green.

"She looked well. In fact, all your sisters—"

"You met the others?"

"By accident. I stopped in the diner and met Charlie, who is very sweet. Of course, Alexandra is all business. Did you know she runs a bed and breakfast?"

Casey shook her head. "Whenever my parents come to visit, the subject of my sisters is off limits." She pulled back into the bar's parking lot, switched off the ignition, and shifted in her seat to face him. "So to answer your question, no, I didn't know." She drummed her fingers on the steering wheel. "A bed and breakfast in Blue Creek? Alexandra probably makes it work. My sister has a head for business, always has. She's a shark," Casey said, though Ryan was sure she musing out loud more than she was talking to him. "Does Charlie run the diner?"

"It seems that way. Best meal I've had in a while," he admitted. He had an urge to comfort her, which was not only ridiculous but also unprofessional. She would probably disable him.

Casey gazed out the windshield. "And Fletcher?"

"She's a sheriff's deputy." He didn't mention his

run-in with the young woman.

"Is she?" Casey handed him his keys and hopped out of the vehicle.

Ryan took a deep breath of the warm night air and followed Casey to her truck.

She wanted him to believe she was unaffected, but that wasn't the case. Though she was unaware, her reactions gave her away. She had inadvertently rubbed her chest—right over her heart—when she asked about her sisters. It didn't matter whether she admitted it to him or even to herself, but she cared. And she was hell bent on leaving. Ryan grabbed the door of the truck before she could shut both him and the truth out.

"Yes, your little sister is a deputy. Do you want to know the impression I get from your sisters? What some of the locals said?"

She shook her head, but he didn't let go of the door.

"Charlie is a sweet woman, and she genuinely cares about people. She likes everything to be happy, even when she's not." He gestured toward his face. "You can see it in her eyes. The people I spoke to love her and would give her the shirt off their back if she asked. Alexandra is well liked, but she's shrewd and somewhat cold. She cares about two things: her family and the bed and breakfast. She runs her life like a business, but most people respect her."

Casey growled. "Shut up!"

He put his entire body in the way of the door when she tried to shut it. He didn't know why he was going out of his way for these people, but he couldn't seem to stop himself. Casey could pretend she didn't want to hear about this, but he had seen the truth in her eyes, if only for a second.

"Then there's Fletcher. I was in her company for about two minutes. I'm six foot two and outweigh her by almost hundred pounds, and she intimidates me. Casey, you're going to listen to me because I'm not finished!" he shouted when she shoved at him. He couldn't explain it, but something in him knew Fletcher might be the key to make her listen. He wouldn't sugarcoat it either. "People are wary of her, which is probably not a bad thing given her job of choice, but she doesn't have any friends. This woman told me, and I quote, 'That little McKay girl has lost her soul. Haven't seen her smile in months.' That's what people think. They make jokes to cover the worry. I heard Charlie do it with my own ears!" He wasn't prepared when she twisted in her seat, swung out her legs, then used her feet to push him, hard. He landed on the pavement.

Casey got out of her truck and stood over him. Was it anger or pain causing her to shake?

"You're a liar. And I hate liars!" Casey spat, then stomped back to her truck.

She sped away, and he waited for her taillights to disappear before rolling onto his stomach. He got off the ground, hissing at the tear in his jacket. The woman had laid him flat.

****

What had happened to her sisters? Casey tried to get a hold of her emotions. Charlie hadn't changed; she had always been the person everyone loved. Shrewd was Alexandra to a T, but no one would have called her cold. Prissy? Absolutely. Alexandra wrote the book. But cold? Never.

Casey curled up in a ball on her couch in her small apartment. The one-bedroom had been her residence for the past year. The area wasn't the greatest, and the place was a bit shabby, but the rent was cheap. Sure, she could afford nicer, bigger, better, but it was clean and she preferred to save her money. She remembered what it was like to go without, and she didn't want to ever be in that position again. Nor did she want her father to feel obligated to her financially. Not that he ever would! Her pops wanted her to have the best—wanted all of them to have the best. Emmit McKay was the greatest man she had ever known. She loved her parents more than life. And her sisters…how did she feel when it came to them?

What about Fletcher? Casey wouldn't believe Ryan Keller. Couldn't. Fletcher was full of life. People had been drawn to her *because* she was such a free spirit. She had always been a kind of comic relief, grinning at one stupid thing or another. Her little sister had a heart bigger than the mountains; for someone to say she had no soul was ridiculous. No, Mr. Keller—private dick—wanted to get paid. She wasn't going to fall for his ploy, and she wasn't going to Blue Creek. And that was that.

****

"I tried, Alexandra. I've got the bruises to prove it," Ryan said the next afternoon, massaging his shoulder. His stomach knotted when the cool mask Alexandra wore slipped for a split second. It had been temporary, but he had seen defeat. "I *am* sorry."

"I hadn't honestly thought she'd come." She looked up at him. "I'd hoped. Naively, of course."

Alexandra exhaled a shaky breath, and Ryan

couldn't ignore the pain in her eyes. "What can I do?"

"Get Casey back for me. By force if…" She shook her head. "Never mind. I guess Charlie and I will have to call our parents."

"What's happened, if you don't mind me asking?" Ryan was overwhelmed by feelings of failure. He had let his client down, and it was Casey McKay's fault. Damn the woman.

"Fletcher quit her job. Words cannot express how deeply my sister loved her career, so you can imagine the implications. She's gone to ground."

"Gone to ground?" What the hell did that mean? Why the hell did he care?

"It means she's gone into the woods. No one will be able to find her unless she wants them to. She's always had a knack for hiding. Fletcher's at the end of her rope, Ryan. Charlie and I are afraid…"

He shifted to the edge of his seat. "Please, go on."

She took a breath. "In the last six months, Fletcher's changed; she has always been a fighter, but now she's given up. She doesn't seem to care about anything or anyone."

"I see, and you think Casey could make the difference."

"Yes. When we were children, Fletcher was Casey's shadow—she was her everything. Then we, Fletcher and I, uncovered a secret and never told our sisters. When Casey found out, she left and hasn't talked to us since. Fletcher didn't speak for two months afterward; she just sat there." Alexandra got up from her chair and faced the window. After a moment, she turned back around and rested her back against the glass.

"Our mother couldn't take it anymore and broke down in front of her. The tears woke Fletcher up, and in no time she was back to normal again. Then, several months ago, she started changing. It was little things at first…then it was as though the light went out of her, and something else took its place. Now she's gone to ground, and no one even knows where to begin to look for her."

"What about the local police?"

"Unfortunately, when people need to find someone around here, it's Fletcher they call. She can live off the land for months, but we don't think she plans on coming back."

Ryan stared at her for a moment, his heart in his throat. "I don't know what to say to that. What about your other sister? What does she say?"

"Charlie has a nasty habit of avoiding the reality of the situation. She treats life like a movie sometimes. You and I know better," Alexandra said and opened the top drawer of her desk; she pulled out a small box and handed it to Ryan.

"What's this?" Ryan opened the lid and found a round white-gold locket inside.

"Go back to Casey," she said, then motioned to what he held in his hands. "Give her that and repeat what I've told you. If she still doesn't agree to come, then tell her the next time she sees our father she can apologize because Fletcher will probably be dead."

"Alexandra, I'm a private investigator, not a family counselor. I'm not cut out for this sort of thing." He tried to give the box back, but she closed her hands around his.

"Please, I'll pay anything. I would do it myself, but

I can't leave right now."

Her eyes pleaded with him, but Ryan shook his head. This was too much. "I—"

"What if it was your brother?"

Chapter Three

Alexandra McKay was good. Ryan met his reflection in the rearview mirror. "And you, my friend, are a sucker." He wasn't a total bastard. He had felt for Alexandra, and her sister too, but he hadn't wanted to get involved. Then she had gone and pulled the oldest trick in the book. The what-if-it-it-was-your-brother ploy.

Chump that he was, Ryan had fallen for it. Now he was about to face a pissed-off woman who wasn't prone to listening to reason. He would probably leave here with more bruises than he had arrived with.

With a sigh, he took the stairs in the apartment complex two at a time. The building wasn't falling apart, but it was the next best thing. He had a feeling Casey could afford better, but she was perverse.

Why was he doing this? He could turn around and never look back. But if something happened to that girl, how would he look at himself again? Damn it. He knocked and waited. Violet eyes flashed. The door would have slammed in his face if he hadn't shoved his booted foot against the frame.

"Just five minutes, please. I promised your sneaky sister." He was relieved when she opened the door wider. His body was extremely grateful. The woman was practically naked. She was wearing only a tiny purple tank top and matching short shorts. Her skin was a dusky hue, and her long dark hair touched the middle of her back. She was exceptional.

"You said talk," she said and rolled her eyes, but she let him in. "I don't sleep with suits."

He closed the door behind him. "That's a shame," Ryan said before he could stop himself.

"You know, with the luxury ride and fancy clothes, I'd never guess you were a private investigator," Casey said with her head cocked to one side. She pointed to his shoes. "A PI who wears handcrafted Italian leather boots? I mean, come on."

"Not that it's any of your business, but it's family money. After my grandparents died, they—"

"Sorry. My grandparents are gone too," Casey said with a tight smile. She sat on the couch with a sigh. "Four minutes left."

Ryan gave a curt nod. "Short and to the point. Is that how you want to do this?"

She inclined her head.

"Alexandra tried to hide her reaction when I told her you weren't coming. But I saw the pain in her eyes—"

"Don't be fool. If you saw anything, it's because she wanted you to see it."

Ryan ignored her. "She and Charlie are afraid Fletcher is going to hurt herself."

"Get out!" Casey shouted, jumping up and going to the door. "Just leave. I don't know how much she's paying you, and I don't really care so long as you go."

He grabbed her arm. She brought back her fist, but he caught it. "Look, she told me to tell you Fletcher's gone to ground. She quit her job and went into the woods."

He let Casey go when she went slack. She sat back down, ready to listen. This "going to ground" meant something. He straightened his jacket; now they were getting somewhere.

Taking the box out of his pocket, he said, "Alexandra found this on the porch of the B and B." He handed her the locket.

She stared at it for a long time, then looked at him, and his breath caught in his throat. Her eyes were a sea of purple.

"It's Fletcher's. She never takes it off," she whispered, then squeezed the bridge of her nose for a moment. "To be honest, I thought you were lying to me at the bar, or at the very least stretching the truth. You know, saying whatever you could to make sure I went back and you got paid."

Ryan sat down across from her. "I wouldn't do that."

"I get that now. I was lying to myself because *I* didn't want what you were telling me to be true." She took a breath. "Fletcher's going to kill herself?"

"Alexandra didn't come right out and say it, but that's the impression I got."

"Fletch was the most annoying kid," she said with a small smile. "Always doing something to piss me off. It was usually opening her mouth. She couldn't tell a lie, as long as you asked the right question. She loved life. Loved me." Casey turned the locket over in her hands, reading the inscription he'd seen there. She touched the earring in her ear. "Our mother gave this to Fletcher years ago."

Ryan didn't know what to say; he could only stare at the torrent of emotions playing across Casey's face.

She sat up straighter and rubbed her hands over her face. After a moment, her eyes met his. "I'll go."

He released the breath he hadn't known he was holding and stood.

"Are you going back?" she asked.

"To Blue Creek?"

"Yeah?"

"No, I've finished my job."

"I know I don't know you, and I've been anything but nice," she said with smirk. "But do you think you would, you know…could you, um…oh, this sucks," she mumbled. "Could you come with me? I haven't been home in six years."

"I…I—"

"I know my parents and little brother are out of town, and I could use someone on my side. Someone to help with the search and, of course, moral support would be nice."

Ryan didn't know what to say. In a million years, he never would have expected this.

"I can pay you."

"Isn't *that* insulting?" He rested his back against the door. He was owed some free time, and he did want to help. Damn his grandfather for making him honorable. "I'll go with you, but you don't have to pay me." He was shocked and his body much obliged when she gave him a tight hug and thanked him.

****

Casey passed the Welcome to Blue Creek sign and was caught off guard by her memories. She had been five when Emmit McKay and his wife adopted them. As they drove away from the home for orphaned and abandoned children, she had been afraid to believe it was real. She, Alex, and Fletcher were legally sisters; they were a family with a mom and dad.

They had sat in the back of the SUV and been in awe of the mountains. None of them had ever seen so much green before. Casey had eaten up every word her new dad told them as they came into town and he pointed out his hardware store, Ida Mae's diner, and the house they would live in. A real home with a bedroom all her own.

They had taken the same drive after Charlie was adopted, only Pops had let her be the one to point out where things were. It had meant so much that he— Casey shook her head to rid herself of the memories before the tears could come. She had fallen in love with Blue Creek the moment she saw it. Shame encroached on her thoughts, but she wouldn't let it sink in. Couldn't.

She parked her truck in the parking lot behind the family hardware store. Things hadn't changed too much. She had loved this place. Loved the McKay name being so big. Casey looked in the rearview mirror as Ryan got out of his fancy ride. He was a sweetheart, in an uppity-suit kind of way.

They had talked a bit when they'd stopped to eat on the drive over. He told her about his brother Jake, who sounded more like Casey's type—the bad boy personified. It was fun listening to Ryan talk about his brother. Day and night; just like she and Alex were.

She had told him about her jobs—all thirty-six of them—and she was surprised when he didn't comment on her inability to stay employed. In her experience, people like him loved telling people like her what their problems were. Their conversation had been nothing more than small talk, but it had comforted her.

She turned when he took her arm. He was a gentleman, polite and controlled. It would be annoying if she didn't find it cute.

"Ready?" he asked as they came around the corner toward the diner's entrance.

She took a deep breath. "As I'll ever be."

He held the door open for her, and she walked in on shaky legs. She zeroed in on her sister, who was carrying an order to someone's table. God, Charlie had gotten beautiful. The baby fat was gone, and she'd grown into her eyes. Those big brown irises landed on Casey, and her sister dropped the tray. Food crashed to the floor, going everywhere. Everything stopped, and Charlie stood staring at her.

"C-Casey," she whispered, but every patron turned in Casey's direction.

"Jeez, Charlie, you never used to be that clumsy," Casey said smiling a bit. Ryan nudged her forward, and that was all Casey needed.

They met somewhere in the middle and took a minute to look each other. Casey blinked away the wetness in her eyes; then she was in Charlie's arms. They held on to one another in a fierce embrace.

"Isn't this a precious moment?" Alex said, and both sisters turned.

Casey let go of Charlie, who was smiling and crying, and walked over to Alex. Her sister had always been the best-looking of all of them, and it still held true. Alexandra McKay was and always would be bewitchingly beautiful. Damn her.

Casey nodded. "Alexandra." She didn't know what else to say. This was the sister who had hid things from

28

her. This was also the sister who had saved their lives. The first person Casey had ever let herself care about, her first friend, first family. Ryan came to stand behind her, and Alex raised one brow; Casey had always been annoyed by that particular facial expression.

"I swear to God, and anyone else who's listening, if you two don't get over the past right this second, I'm gonna start telling everyone your dirtiest secrets," Charlie announced with her hands on her hips.

"She'll do it too," Casey said.

Alex nodded. "I know." Her sister swallowed her pride and took the first step, then another. Casey closed her eyes as Alex's arms came around her.

"I'm so, so sorry, Casey," she whispered.

Casey nodded into her sister's hair. Alex still smelled like expensive perfume, where Charlie smelled like cookies. She squeezed her sister hard, not wanting to let go. Then she remembered they weren't alone and pulled away. Casey turned to find Sheriff Jasper Hart looking at her, tears in his old eyes.

"Jasper?" she said. He looked older than she knew him to be. Worry etched his features, and wasn't that a change.

"Blue Creek better watch out; Casey McKay is back in town," he said gruffly and surprised Casey by hugging her. "We kept it real quiet about Fletcher, but we can't find her," he whispered in her ear. Emotions threatened to overwhelm her, but Jasper patted her back, gave her a moment, then stepped away.

"Wasn't sure I'd ever see the day you'd come back here...but I'm sure glad I'm seeing it now," someone said before Casey looked up. But she didn't need to, she'd know that voice anywhere. It was deep, rich like molasses, and belonged to a huge African-American man named Tiny. She was off her feet and in his arms before she knew it.

"Oh, Tiny." Casey squeezed his neck. "I missed you," she said and kissed his cheek before he set her down on her feet. She smacked his bulging bicep. "What are you still doing here?"

Tiny Wellington had been cooking at the diner for as long as Casey could remember. He had been the diner's secret weapon since Ida Mae had owned the place before them. He had to be in his late fifties, but you couldn't tell looking at him. Tiny's nose was crooked, and his front tooth was gold. Mementos, he would say, from his boxing days. His tattoos were from his time in the marines, and his heart was bigger than the Smokies.

"Where else would you want me to be, shug?" Tiny asked.

Casey shook her head and laughed. "I can't think of anywhere."

"Thought that's what you'd say." With a wink, he turned back to the kitchen.

Casey moved closer to where her sisters stood with Ryan. "Tiny looks good."

"The man doesn't change," Charlie said, then turned to Ryan. "We can't thank you enough for bringing Casey back."

"Will you be staying long or are you leaving now?" Alexandra asked.

"He's staying," Casey said, looking between her sisters to gauge their reaction. "I think we'll stay at the parents' house, unless anyone has any complaints."

"I do, actually," Ryan said, and Casey glared at

him. "I should probably stay at the B and B."

"You most certainly will not!" Charlie said. "No offense, Alexandra, but family friends stay at the parents' house. That said, I need to get back to work. You people need to leave and stop distracting me!" She shooed them away.

"Mother hen has spoken," Alex said. "You may as well go home and get comfortable. Ryan can stay in Jebb's room or...or Fletcher's." She floated away. Casey didn't understand how her sister moved like that.

"Let's go get settled in, and then head to the B and B. Where is it anyway?"

"It's at, and named, Granny Vaughn's," Charlie said as she brought out a broom and mop.

Casey couldn't stop her grin. Sadie Madison Vaughn had been both their grandmother and friend. "She would have eaten that up with a spoon," Casey said. She sighed and headed for the door. "You can follow me, Keller. And shake a leg!"

****

Casey could not ignore the joy that shot straight to her heart as she pulled into the driveway of her childhood home. The house was a monstrous log cabin which sat in the middle of the twenty acres of land her family owned. She parked her truck and hopped out, taking a deep breath of mountain air. God, she had missed this.

"Beautiful, isn't it?" she asked Ryan, who was staring open-mouthed.

"Breathtaking." Smiling, he retrieved his suitcase from the back of his vehicle.

"Do you always keep a packed bag with you?" she asked, grabbing her own pack from the passenger seat.

"In my line of work, I'd be a fool not to."

She nodded. "Well, come on then."

"Did your family build the house?"

"Great-great-grandfather McKay built the original structure over a hundred years ago. Both my father and his father added onto it," Casey explained as she opened the door. Stepping inside, she stopped short.

He touched her shoulder. "Are you all right?"

"I will be," she said with a small smile. "It smells the same. The diner did too. Smell the same, I mean. Come on, I'll show you to your room."

Knowing Ryan was behind her kept Casey from letting her pesky emotions take over, and there were plenty. Being inside this house again—she couldn't explain the peace it brought her. Her eyes prickled when she headed up to the second floor. They'd called it the "lion's den" when they were little. She went to her old room first, hit the light, and sucked in a breath; it was exactly how she had left it.

From the curtains to the carpet, everything was some shade of purple. The quilt on her bed had been made by Grandma McKay, and all the wood furnishings had been made by her father. Photographs were taped to the walls in different collages she had made over the years. She loved this room.

She cleared her throat. "You can stay here."

Ryan grinned. "Colorful." He put his suitcase on the bed and turned to her. "Are you sure you're all right?"

"Just tired," she said, glad when he let her lie slide. She'd never had a boy in her room before, much less a man, but she kept the thought to herself. "You can use the bathroom down the hall."

She ignored his thanks and went into the room across the way. The walls were blue, the quilt green, and the furniture was also beautifully crafted by her father. She set her things on top of the desk, then turned to find Ryan in the hall peering in.

"This is Fletcher's room."

"I see."

"It was never this neat. Out of the four of us girls, she was the biggest slob. It used to piss Alex off to no end." Casey shook her head. Now, the room was empty...lifeless.

Shaking off a chill, her eyes landed on a black trash bag in the corner. Curious, she went to investigate. Her heart jumped to her throat when she looked inside. "Oh, shit!"

"Did you find something?" Ryan asked. He squatted down to check out the bag's contents.

"Yeah." Casey swallowed and showed him the tapes.

"The labels all say *Murder, She Wrote.*" He shuffled through them. "Is this supposed to be a private joke?"

"You'd think it was, but it's a hell of a bad sign." She sat down and studied Ryan. He had taken off his tie and jacket, leaving him in gray slacks and a white tailored shirt. She looked at her own jeans and T-shirt, then back at him; did he have to be so put together?

She didn't know why, but she felt like she could trust him. The tapes weren't a big secret. "Fletcher's birth name was Jamie," she began, then rolled her eyes. "She thought the name was a sissy name. Sissy was the worst thing you could call my little sister. She watched this show since before she could talk." He didn't get it.

If you didn't know her sister, you wouldn't. "Do you remember the main character's name?"

"Yes, my grandparents adored that show," he explained, then paused when he understood. "No?"

"Oh, it's so silly, I know, but that's Fletcher…or was. She wouldn't answer to anything else, so Pops had her name legally changed. You can't tell anyone though."

"My lips are sealed." He moved his fingers across his mouth to seal the deal, then grinned.

She smiled. "You can laugh before you pass out." He did laugh, and to her surprise she liked the sound. It was deep, real, and not perfect or controlled like the rest of him.

"Once when we were kids, the VCR ate one of her tapes, and she was devastated. It took her a week before she'd talk to any of us." Casey put the items back and stood, avoiding the hand Ryan offered. Fletcher had a few pictures up, which made Casey smile. Ryan was going over her sister's things, probably trying to get an idea of who Fletcher really was.

"Did Alex tell you Fletcher's crazy smart?"

"No, she didn't mention it."

"Well, she is. I'm the oldest and graduated first, but my sisters didn't want to be left behind when I went to college. They each took tests and extra classes so we all graduated together. Fletcher, being Fletcher, hadn't told anyone how easy school was for her. She got in fights most of the time; she even beat my record of going to the principal's office."

"Now, *that* I can see."

Casey chuckled. "Teachers never noticed how smart she was. They thought she was a juvenile delinquent. And just like that"—Casey snapped her fingers—"she took the tests to graduate and aced all of them."

"She sounds like an amazing person; however, not like the one I met."

"It's my fault. It's so clear to me now, you know." She sat down on Fletcher's bed. "If I had been—"

"You haven't been here two hours, and you're already reprising your big sister role," Alex said from the doorway. "Protector and martyr."

"How long have you been standing there?" Casey asked.

"Long enough." Alex sighed. "It was my fault, actually. I made Fletcher promise to keep the truth of what we found from everyone. So if those events are the cause of this, then it wasn't your fault or hers. It was mine." She sat down next to Casey.

"I'll leave you two alone," Ryan said and he left the room.

"It's not anyone's fault, Alex," Casey said. "The secret you two hid—the truth of it—was too much for me on too many levels. I can admit I've never been real good with feelings…"

Alex smirked. "Do tell."

Casey snorted. "Yeah, well, what can I say?"

"You don't need to explain yourself to me."

"I'll never forgive myself if something happens to her."

"Well, that makes two of us."

"Three," Charlie added coming into the room. Casey smiled when Charlie joined them on the bed. This was how they used to be, but it didn't feel right without Fletcher.

"Who let you out?" Alex asked.

Charlie smirked. "Tiny told me the only place I needed to be right now was with my sisters. He's worried about Fletcher too."

"Do the parents know what's going on with her?" Casey asked.

"Not this part of it. We're hoping we can find her ourselves. They went on this vacation as sort of a refusal-to-face-reality thing. They didn't want to see what was right in front of them. Denial at its finest," Alex said and shot Charlie a look as she shifted the skirt of her dress.

"None of us wanted to see it," Charlie said. "Even Jasper turned a blind eye, and you know how he adores her."

"Really?" Casey remembered Fletcher going to see Jasper every time they'd come home for breaks, but she figured it had been to annoy the man. Her sister had always had a knack for driving the sheriff to distraction.

"Yeah, Jasper's wife died a few years back."

Casey ducked her head. Mrs. Hart had always been warm and welcoming to them. "Laura was a sweet woman."

"She was indeed," Alex said.

"They never did have children, did they?" Casey asked.

Charlie shook her head. "Laura couldn't, and it's a shame too."

"I remember them having a big extended family, right?"

"Yes, but the family is Laura's, and Jasper doesn't particularly care for any of them. He and Fletcher mesh well. So, needless to say, Jasper's taking this hard.

When Fletcher started acting peculiar, he noticed but decided not to press the issue. And, honestly, no one wanted to," Alex said.

"Now we face it head on, but we do it together," Casey said. And, like they did when they were younger, her sisters nodded.

****

The bitch was back! Excellent. Everything was coming together as planned. "Four McKay bitches sitting in a tree, K-I-L-L-I-N-G. First falls one, then falls three; next comes death and tragedy…"

Chapter Four

Casey sat on the porch swing her father had made for her mother on the day Jebbediah was born. Casey called him Bullfrog because Jebbediah sounded so much like Jeremiah—and "Jeremiah was a bullfrog." Casey smiled thinking of her brother; he was hitting puberty now, and the girls had better hold on to their hearts.

When her parents had first brought Jebb home, it had made all of them crazy with worry—everyone but their mother, who could handle anything. Casey had followed her around so she could learn all the secrets of taking care of an infant. The first time they left him in her care she had been speechless; knowing how much her parents trusted her had meant the world.

Both her parents loved and trusted her, always would too, even after she left with no explanation. She knew she had hurt her mother more than Pops; he understood. Emmit McKay knew the pain secrets can cause better than anyone, and he didn't even know what Casey knew.

It was getting warmer as the morning wore on. Casey turned toward the outskirts of the forest; the McKay home was right on its edge. The woods were deep, running up the mountain, and almost encircling Blue Creek.

Could she find her sister in there? Would she find

Fletcher in time? Time, as they say, was such a fragile thing; she had wasted six years, and if she didn't find Fletcher soon, she wouldn't be able to make up for it. Casey couldn't live with that.

"Would you like a cup of coffee?" Ryan asked, hovering in the doorway. He was wearing a white dress shirt with brown slacks, and his incredible green eyes were studying her.

"Yeah, that sounds great."

He smiled, handed her a cup, and sat next to her.

She took a sip and closed her eyes. "This is really good."

"Thank you, but I can't take the credit. Charlie made it."

"Figures," Casey said and smirked. "She was always good at making coffee, but Alex's is even better. When we were kids, we took turns in the kitchen, but Charlie cooked the most. We would trade chores just to get her to make the meals. Even when Pops married Ma, Charlie still took charge of the kitchen."

"I didn't realize you had a stepmother."

Casey looked down at her bare feet. "She's my mother in every way that counts. No one could be better than Savannah McKay. She's the strongest woman I know; she had to be, getting involved with us. The people of Blue Creek thought she was crazy, but that didn't stop her. Nothing can when she sets her mind to it."

"She sounds remarkable," Ryan said.

Casey smiled. "She moved here to be the new principal of our school. The first day we met, my sisters had gotten into a fight with Marylou Thomas; I found out and went to the office to investigate. She told me my sisters were none of my concern. No one told me my sisters weren't my business, so I threw her coffee mug against the wall; it shattered everywhere. Piss and vinegar, that was me. But I got to stay with my sisters."

Ryan laughed. "What did she do to you? Punishment-wise, I mean."

"I got two days out-of-school suspension. Pops grounded me for two weeks, which was worse." Casey shrugged and sipped her coffee eyeing him over the rim. "You know, you're going to need some different clothes to wear in the woods. Pops might have something that would fit you."

Ryan shook his head. "I did some shopping last night while you and your sisters got reacquainted. Lucky for me your town comes equipped with a Target and a Wal-Mart."

"It does?" she asked with a pinched brow. "That's new, the Target anyway. We got the Wal-Mart when I was sixteen. It was a *big* to-do. I wonder who sold off their land?"

"The Thomas family did," Charlie said from the porch door. "They were in a bad way financially. Marylou's ex had taken her for all she was worth."

"No prenuptial agreement?" Ryan asked.

Charlie shook her head. "She was only eighteen when she got married, but by twenty-one, she was divorced, and her family was on the verge of bankruptcy."

"Who the hell would marry her?" Casey wanted to know. Marylou Thomas was a pest. A pink, pansy, pretentious pest.

"Do you remember the Randles?" Charlie asked,

smiling when Ryan got up so she could sit next to Casey.

"Yeah, they had two boys and a girl, right?" Casey asked as Ryan pulled over one of the rocking chairs and took a seat. "It was Daemon, Rick, and Dana, if I'm remembering correctly."

"Yep, Marylou married Rick; he was a few years older than us and oh, so charming."

"He married her and took everything she had. Yeah"—Casey snorted—"a real prince."

Charlie shrugged. "He had everyone in town eating out of the palm of his hand. Then he left the Thomases with next to nothing. Rick's older brother, Daemon, tried to make amends by finding buyers for the land they were forced to sell."

"I bet that put old Ian Thomas's boxers in a bunch," Casey said fighting a smile. There was no love lost between the McKays and the Thomases.

"Mr. Thomas wouldn't accept his help; then he had a heart attack and died. Mrs. Thomas's only option was to go to Daemon," she explained. "He made sure they got the best deal possible. Then, presto, they had their money again, and the Randles were accepted back into the community. It's sad. I feel sorry for Daemon. He's married now, and his wife's a witch. Did you get all that, Ryan?"

"I think so," Ryan said looking sheepish. "You don't feel bad for this Marylou woman, though?"

"No, she got what she deserved."

"Charlie! As much as I agree with the sentiment, that's not something you'd say. Is there more to this?" Casey eyed her sister.

"Isn't there always with Marylou?" She chuckled.

"Nothing to worry about or bring up, really."

"What happened to Rick?" Ryan asked.

"He used the money he got from the Thomases to buy and furnish a big, fancy apartment in the city. He was killed when the place was robbed. Some called it poetic justice." Charlie shivered and walked back into the house.

"Did you get the feeling she was leaving something out?" Casey asked Ryan after the screen door shut.

"Perhaps," he said.

Casey pursed her lips, then pushed up her glasses.

"I like your glasses."

"I wear my contacts most of the time. I'm lazy though, so I bring glasses for those times."

"I understand completely. I had laser surgery, and it worked wonderfully," he told her, laughing when she shuddered. He stopped laughing when she motioned toward the woods.

"We need to get some supplies together and get moving," she suggested, getting up from her seat.

Ryan followed her inside.

****

Sweat slid down her back and into the waistband of her khakis. She glanced over her shoulder to where Ryan was coming up behind her. He was mumbling to himself—no doubt cursing her—and using a handkerchief to dab the perspiration from his forehead. He hadn't complained, not once, which surprised her. It had taken her an hour to find the old trail, but she *had* found it. Now they were on the right track. She hoped.

She stopped and took a swig from her water bottle. "You okay?"

"Yes, thank you," Ryan said sipping from his own

container.

"It shouldn't be much farther now." She turned and started walking, not waiting for his response.

"You really think she'll be out here?"

Casey squeezed her eyes shut for a moment. "She has to be," she whispered.

"I'm sorry, I didn't catch that?"

You weren't supposed to. "When we were little, we made a secret place in these woods. We spent an entire summer building a fort out here and never told anyone about it." It had been theirs and theirs alone. She slowed her steps when they came to a clearing.

Several trees had been cut down, and the surrounding bushes had been taken out. A cabin now sat where their fort had been. She began walking down the path, then stopped in her tracks, and Ryan bumped into her.

"Oh, God," she said, turning away from the sight in front of her.

Ryan looked over her shoulder, then took her hands in his and waited until she met his eyes. "That's her."

Casey nodded. The slip of a woman sitting on the porch, huddled in a blanket, was her little sister. She would know her anywhere.

As if sensing her thoughts, Ryan said, "You can do this, Casey."

She dashed away the pesky water leaking from her eyes and shook her head.

"You can. I know you can!" he encouraged. "Take a moment, take a breath, and be the woman who threw the principal's mug against the wall so she could stay with her sisters."

Casey searched his eyes. How did he know exactly

what to say? He was right. Casey McKay could handle this, damn it. She was the oldest; this was her job. She took a deep breath.

"Stay here, okay?" she said, and he touched her cheek. She bit her quivering lip, then turned and headed for her little sister.

Fletcher sat on the porch floor, rocking back and forth, and burrowing further into her blanket. As Casey got closer, it became apparent the blanket was dirty and stained. It was blood, she realized, when she stopped next to Fletcher. Her sister's gaze was fixed off into the distance.

"Fletch?"

Fletcher turned her head. Her long brown hair fell in a wild tangle. Her blue-green eyes were vacant and teary. "She comes back," Fletcher sneered.

Casey stood frozen while her sister continued to rock back and forth.

Fletcher sank deeper into her cotton cocoon and pointed to her chest. "Empty," she whispered. "Soul's gone."

"Fletch," Casey choked out again, afraid to touch her; afraid to move.

"Casey?" Fletcher let go of the blanket and reached for her. "I...I can feel you. You're real?" She pulled Casey down next to her.

Casey took a gulp of air. Fletcher was naked under the blanket, and her flesh was mutilated with cuts, slices, and scabs. What had happened to her little sister? Okay, she had to try to keep it light and not scare Fletcher off.

"I'm here, Fletcher, and I'm real enough to kick your ass."

"I didn't know. I thought it was the nightmare again," Fletcher said and began to shake. "I's tried and tried to make it stop, but it won't…I can't make it stop, Casey. Why can't I make it stop? I's…I don't know what's the matter with me."

"We need to get you to a hospital. You've hurt yourself, Fletch," Casey said swallowing the bile rising in her throat. Her sister, her beautiful, vibrant sister was killing herself.

Fletcher shook her head.

"Fletcher, listen to me. It's Casey, and I know best, remember? We have to get you to a hospital."

"I's don't hafta go anywhere with you. You's ain't real! You tricked me again." Fletcher brought a knife out from beneath the folds of the blanket and sliced her arm, screaming.

Casey made a grab for her but missed. "Ryan!"

He was there in an instant, wrestling Fletcher to the ground.

"Please, please," Fletcher sobbed. "Just let me be. I's can't do this no more."

Ryan got the knife away and bundled Fletcher up. "She passed out."

"Good! We have to get her to a hospital." Casey took out her cell phone with a shaking hand, giving a prayer of thanks when she got a signal. She called her sisters, who were waiting at the house, and told them to have an ambulance ready.

"Now that I know where we are, there's a straight path to the house," she said pointing in the direction they needed to go.

Ryan nodded and scooped Fletcher up in his arms.

They walked in silence, and Casey was grateful.

****

Charlie, Alexandra, and Jasper were waiting next to the paramedics when they came out of the forest. Everyone ran toward them.

"Oh, God, she's not—?" Charlie stopped in her tracks, and Alex took her hand.

"No!" Casey said.

"I think she's lost a lot of blood," Ryan said. He placed Fletcher in the arms of the paramedic.

"What happened here?" the man asked Ryan.

"I don't know. She was delusional. She's cut herself repeatedly…I've never seen anything like it."

The paramedic nodded as he put Fletcher on the gurney, and his partner began taking her vitals.

"Delusional, you say?" Jasper asked, his face ashen.

"She didn't think I was real," Casey explained, her eyes never leaving Fletcher.

"I've never seen anything like it," Ryan said again. "We'd better go if we want to be there when she wakes up."

"We'll meet you there," Alex said, and Charlie nodded.

"I'll give you a ride," Jasper offered.

"Thank you, Sheriff."

"May as well call me Jasper, boy. No point in being formal now."

Ryan nodded and turned. "Casey?"

"I'm going with Fletcher," she said and headed for the ambulance.

Chapter Five

Ryan found the sisters in the waiting room of the hospital; they looked tired and strained. He took a seat next to Charlie and Alexandra. Casey was leaving marks in the carpet with her pacing, and Jasper had stopped to talk to a nurse.

"I hate hospitals," Casey muttered.

"You're as impatient as you always were," Alexandra said, and Casey gave her a dirty look.

"I wish they would tell us what's going on." Charlie squirmed and smiled when Ryan patted her hand.

A doctor wearing green scrubs walked into the waiting area. "Who's here for Ms. McKay?"

"We are!" Charlie said and they all stood.

"We're her sisters, her family," Casey said, her tone daring the doctor to say otherwise.

"I checked your sister's medical records. Which, I might add, were an interesting read, but I didn't see any sign of high blood pressure."

"The girl don't have high blood pressure," Jasper said coming into the room. "She had a physical about six months ago. Clean bill of health."

The doctor sighed. "And you are?"

"I'm Sheriff Jasper Hart of Blue Creek. It don't get no surer than me, *boy*," Jasper said, pointing his finger in the doctor's face.

The doctor took a step back and crossed his arms over his chest. "Then you'll be interested to know I believe Ms. McKay has been drugged."

"What do you mean 'drugged'?" Casey asked.

"She doesn't have high blood pressure, but the lab work shows a prescription to treat hypertension. Not to mention a number of herbal stimulants."

"And you think my sister would take this? I don't believe it," Alexandra said and reclaimed her seat.

"The levels in her blood were considerably higher than normal, and I don't think she was taking it purposely. This is one of those times I listen to my gut."

"What are the side effects of the drug, Doctor?" Ryan asked.

"According to what one of you told the nurse, the side effects match. Insomnia, mental changes, hallucinations, depression, and strange dreams. Mixed with the herbal stimulants..." The doctor shook his head.

"Oh, my lord." Charlie sat down next to Alexandra and closed her tear-filled eyes. "Someone's trying to kill our sister."

"Kill her or destroy her," Ryan said. Someone had done this on purpose? The idea was sickening.

Casey shook her head and switched from foot to foot. "But these are just side effects, right? She'll be okay?"

"We're flushing her system out now. We've sutured all the lacerations and have her on an IV. It may take a week or two to clean her up, but yes, physically she'll be fine."

Ryan eyed the doctor. "But mentally?"

"Mentally, we'll see," the doctor said, squirming

under the weight of the sisters' stares.

"When can we see her?" Jasper asked.

"We have her in observation for the next twenty-four hours. You can come back then." The doctor turned and left.

"I can't believe this!" Casey shouted.

"Who would do such a thing?" Ryan asked. He didn't think he would ever be able to get the sight of Fletcher and that blanket out of his head.

"Yeah," Casey said and pointed to her sisters. "Who would do this?"

"How am I supposed to know?" Alexandra sat up straighter. "We're hearing this for the first time too. Goodness, Casey, you act as if we did it."

"Of course you didn't do it, Alex. Stop being a bitch," Casey said without heat.

"We're not going to figure it out right this second. Let's go home and be productive," Charlie suggested.

"Good idea, missy," Jasper said. "I'm gonna go to the station and check out her office."

"All right, let's go!" Casey started for the door. Ryan let the women go before him. What had he gotten himself into?

****

If that bitch McKay had waited one more day, the youngest girl would have been dead. It would have been perfect. But no! And who was the man? He didn't fit into the plan. No, he had to go. Things were a little off but not completely.

A snicker echoed in the small cabin. Fletcher McKay, what a joke. It had been so easy to get to her. And the locket had been an ingenious idea. Everyone knew Fletcher didn't take off that stupid thing. It had been fun watching her fall apart little by little. And the fun was just beginning.

****

Ryan shifted in bed not wanting to open his eyes yet. They had searched the house, the apartment at the B and B, and Fletcher's truck. It had been after one a.m., and they hadn't found anything. He'd suggested his leaving to the group, but all three women said he had to help them find out who was poisoning their sister. He had agreed.

Ryan rolled onto his back and opened his eyes. He almost pissed himself. He was staring into the barrel of a rather large rifle. He looked up into the coldest gray-blue eyes he had ever seen.

"You've got about two seconds to tell me what you're doing in my daughter's bed!"

"Emmit McKay! What are you thinking? What are you going to do? Shoot him?"

Ryan peeked around the giant of a man to the small woman. Her honey-brown hair was hanging to the waist of her jeans. She was lovely; an angel with big blue eyes.

"Uh." Ryan tried not to squirm.

"Pops! What are you doing?" Casey shouted, coming into the room. Her eyes widened when they landed on what was being held in the vicinity of his head.

"Your parents?" Ryan mouthed from his position on the bed. Casey nodded.

"Casey!" Mrs. McKay cried and threw her arms around her daughter. "You're home. You look wonderful, but...what's going on?"

"Case?" Mr. McKay set the rifle down and smirked

at Ryan when he breathed a sigh of relief. The man scooped his oldest daughter out of his wife's reach and held her to him. "What are you doing here? Wait...you were sleeping in Fletcher's room. Where's your sister?" he asked putting her down on the bed next to Ryan. "And who are you, boy?"

"Ryan Keller, Mr. McKay."

"He's a friend of mine. And Mom, Dad, Fletcher's in the hospital."

"What happened?" Mrs. McKay asked as Mr. McKay closed his eyes and leaned against the door. The woman positioned herself next to her husband and rubbed his back while Casey told them the entire story.

Ryan used their distraction to slip off the bed and into a pair of pants. He grabbed his discarded shirt from the chair, and Casey winked at him as he pulled it over his head.

"Why didn't someone call us?" Mr. McKay asked when Casey had finished. He gave Ryan a disgusted look, then turned to his daughter and stood up fully. "I demand an answer, young lady."

"We didn't want to worry you," Casey said. A grin spread across her face when a teenager came barreling in. His black hair stood on end, and his big blue eyes went wide as his gaze darted around the room.

"Casey, you're back. Awesome! Hey, who are you?" the young man asked Ryan.

"This is Ryan. Ryan, that's Jebb, the Bullfrog," Casey said.

Ryan shook the boy's hand.

"Cool. So the SUV down there is your ride?" Jebb asked, pointing out the window.

"Yeah, you want to take a look?" Ryan asked. Any

excuse to get out of this room.

The young man turned to his mother. "Can I, Ma?"

"Sure, honey, but don't bug Ryan to death. He's a guest here. I'm Savannah McKay, by the way. You can call me Savannah."

Ryan shook her hand. "Ryan Keller."

"That's my husband, Emmit," Savannah said, winking when Emmit grumbled and sat down on the bed.

Ryan inclined his head.

"Can we go now?" Jebb asked, shifting from one foot to another.

"Sure," Ryan said, more than happy to get away from fathers with guns.

****

Casey shook her head when Ryan left the room. No doubt her little brother would keep the PI busy with a multitude of questions, which would give her time to talk to her parents. She sighed when her mother sat between her and Pops and patted her thigh.

"So, what's Ryan Keller to you?" her mother asked with a slight smile.

"He's just helping me out. Really, I wasn't in here with him, was I?" Casey asked, uncomfortable. She refused to talk about sex with her mother.

"Good thing too; I would have shot him," Pops said.

"Pops, we all know you wouldn't have pulled the trigger."

"Maybe not," he grumbled. "But I definitely would've kicked his ass."

Her mother nudged her shoulder. "Whatever you say, Emmit."

Just then a little blur of blonde streaked past the door. What the hell? The little blur went by again and giggled. Casey eyed her parents. What was going on?

"Is there something you guys want to tell me?" She pointed toward the door and her parents winced in unison.

Then Charlie came in the room wearing jeans and a T-shirt that advertised the diner. Her hair was in a ponytail, and she looked pale. "Actually…Mama, Pops, could you give us a minute?"

"Sure, sweetheart," Ma said. They hugged Charlie, then left the room.

"There's something I, ah…need to tell you, but you have to promise not to get mad," Charlie said taking the seat their mother had vacated.

Casey narrowed her eyes. She didn't like it when someone asked for that particular promise; it generally meant she was going to get royally pissed. She nodded anyway. "Yes, I promise."

"Mackenzie, would you come here, please?" Charlie called out, and Casey stared at the door.

A tiny imp of a girl walked in. Her white-blonde hair was in pigtails. She was wearing a pink sundress with little white daisies and matching sandals. She came into the room watching Casey intently with her black eyes, then hopped up into Charlie's lap.

"Casey," Charlie said, turning so they were face to face. "I'd like to introduce you to my daughter, Mackenzie McKay."

Casey jerked back, and Charlie's eyes filled with tears.

"Why's my mama cryin'?" Mackenzie asked, then patted Charlie's cheek with a pudgy little finger.

"Y-you had a baby and didn't tell me?" Casey said around the lump in her throat.

"At first, I was scared, you know," Charlie began. "I was afraid you wouldn't come home if I asked, and I'd be crushed. Then we all talked about it and decided we'd wait. Mama and Pops wanted to tell you, but I swore them—and Jebb—to secrecy. I wanted you to come back on your own. I didn't want you to feel obligated. I'm sorry if I was wrong, Casey."

"You's Auntie Casey? Wow! Auntie Fletcher told me all abouts you. I's Mack." The child held out her hand and giggled when Casey pulled her into a hug.

"Pops must have had a heart attack." Casey laughed and hugged Mack tighter. The child smelled sweet like her mother.

"Mack, go find Grandma and Grandpop, honey," Charlie said, caressing the child's head.

"Ohskay." Mack hopped out of Casey's lap and left the room.

"I am sorry, Casey."

"I got that. I'm sorry too." And she was, more than she could express. She'd missed years of her niece's life. "She looks about three or so, is that right?"

Charlie nodded and stared at her hands. "Three and a half."

"Who's the father?"

"Save your breath, Casey. She won't tell anyone. She didn't even put his name on the birth certificate. It's the big mystery of Blue Creek: who knocked up Charlie McKay?" Alex said from the doorway, then cringed. "Sorry."

"It's all right, Alex. You're just repeating what's on everyone's mind. But you're right, it's my business, and my secret. So…" She shrugged and stood up.

Casey stood too and engulfed her sister in a hug. "My sister's a mom! Who'd have thunk it?"

"You forgive me then, for not telling you? Not letting anyone tell you?" Charlie asked, letting go of Casey and standing back.

"Yes, I'll forgive you, this time," she said. She couldn't blame Charlie, not really. When she left all those years ago she'd had every intention of speaking to Charlie, but it had been too hard. She hadn't wanted to put her sister in the middle of everything, so she had cut all ties.

"Thank you." Charlie gave Alex's hand a squeeze, then went to find her daughter.

"Any secrets you're keeping, Alex, get them out now while I'm all fuzzy-headed," Casey advised, flopping down on the bed, then jumping into sitting position when she smelled Ryan on the sheets. He smelled amazing.

"You know all my secrets, Casey."

"You're sure?"

Alex smiled.

"Hey, I noticed something else."

Alex sighed. "Yes?"

"You don't get all bitchy about being called Alex like you used to," Casey said with a half smile. She'd actually enjoyed that about Alex. "My name is *Alexandra*," her sister would insist. It was a button Casey had liked pushing. Often.

Alex gave a ladylike snort. "It's easier."

"Huh?" She made a face.

"I've found I get less resistance in the business world if I go by Alex McKay rather than Alexandra."

Casey pointed a finger at her sister. "Shouldn't you be against that?"

"What? Working the system in *my* favor?" Alex shrugged. "No, I don't think so. But to answer your question, no, I don't mind being called Alex anymore."

Casey nodded, then grinned. "I can't believe Charlie's a mom."

"Mackenzie's a beautiful child, isn't she?"

"Gorgeous. Charlie probably looked just like her when she was that age," Casey said.

"More than likely. Unfortunately, we don't have any pictures of her when she was little."

Casey pinched the bridge of her nose. "Don't remind me!" Charlie had been eight when she became a McKay, and knowing she'd been out there without them always put a knot in Casey's stomach.

"I talked to Mama," Alex said. "She said you told them about Fletcher. I know it breaks her heart." She shook her head. "If you hadn't known where to look for her—"

"Don't you think I know that? Jesus!" Casey stood and started pacing around her room. "I don't think I'll ever forget the way she looked yesterday. It fucking terrified me. Someone did this to her, and we have to find out who."

Alex gave her the once-over. "It was nice of Ryan to agree to help us."

"It was, wasn't it! He's a bit of a softy," Casey said. "Besides, he's an investigator; he finds things out for a living."

"True."

Not liking her sister's agreeable tone, Casey changed tactics. "So, where does Mack sleep?"

"Charlie had a house built at the far end of the property," Alex said and clasped her hands together.

"And she's running the diner too, right?"

"Mama turned the diner over to Charlie two years ago."

Casey's head snapped up. "You're kidding." Their mother had loved running the diner. It had been her home away from home.

"Surprised everyone. I think Mama wanted to watch Mack all day and used the diner as leverage. No one can say Savannah McKay doesn't have a few tricks up her sleeve."

"I know I wouldn't say it. Always has been tricky." Casey smiled. She turned when Ryan came in talking on his cell phone. Alexandra stood and left the room with the sly smile on her face that Casey found one part annoying, the other part amusing.

"Yes, I heard you. How do you get yourself into these things? No, no, damn it, Jake! It's not funny. You have no tact, man. Fine…yes! I said I would, didn't I? Later," he said and threw his phone on the bed. Ryan ran his fingers through his hair, then started packing his suitcase.

"Are you leaving?"

He glanced at Casey and sighed. "Jake needs me."

"Fletcher does too, or have you forgotten?" She yanked his suitcase off the bed to get his attention. He glared at her. "You don't even care that someone is threatening my sister's life."

"Casey, to be fair, I don't even know you, or her, or your family for that matter."

"You said you'd help me. Now you're going back on your word!" Casey said, taking his arm. He surprised her by giving her a gentle shove, which landed her on the bed.

"I did not give you my word. I said I would try to help, but Jake needs me. He's my brother. *I* would never turn my back on *my* brother, unlike some people I know." Ryan threw the rest of his things in his suitcase, ignoring her.

She jumped up and punched him in the belly.

"Damn it, Casey," he said rubbing his stomach. "I don't have time for this."

"You jerk! You think you're better than me, don't you, Mr. High-and-Mighty Keller! How many life-altering secrets has your brother kept from you?" she asked, taking a boxing stance.

"What are you planning to do, Casey, fight me? Please, I've never hit a woman in my life, and I don't plan on starting now. Move out of my way…please."

"Fine, you want to go? Go! Who's stopping you?"

He raised a brow and tried to get by her. She shut the door and knocked his arm away from the knob when he reached for it.

"I'm getting tired of this game. I have to go." Sighing, he set his suitcase down. Casey sucked in a breath when he picked her up by the waist, dropped her on the bed, and landed on top of her.

He was heavy, pressed against her as he was, but she didn't want him to move. She didn't want him to leave. She squirmed her legs out from under him, which put him directly between her thighs. She could feel his hardness pressing against her. Her eyes widened; he was as aroused as she was.

"Happy now?" he grunted. His hands held hers above her head. Casey lifted her hips against him, and he closed his eyes.

"I could be a lot happier," she said. He opened his sizzling green eyes. "Kiss me, Ryan." He grumbled but did what she asked. He let go of her hands to hold her head.

Casey softened beneath him and wrapped her arms around his head to bring his mouth closer. She opened her lips in an invitation Ryan didn't refuse. His tongue slid against hers, and shivers raced down her spine.

The kiss was tender at first, then their mouths demanded more. Ryan moved his hand down her ribcage to the hem of her T-shirt. He pressed his erection against her when his warm hand met her skin. She moaned when he cupped her breast. After a delicious moment, Ryan paused, removed his hand, smoothed her shirt down, and pulled away.

"What's wrong?" she asked, her voice huskier than normal. She sat up after he hopped off the bed, her body still tingling. She had been minutes away from an orgasm, and he'd stopped. Almost coming from a kiss? How embarrassing.

Ryan groaned. "I have to go, Casey." He straightened his clothes, then adjusted himself.

She snorted. "Right this minute?"

"Yes," he said, picking up his suitcase and opening the door.

"Ryan?" He didn't stop. She followed him through the house and out to his vehicle. The concrete was hot against her bare feet. When she touched his back, he flinched. "Ryan, talk to me."

"It won't work, Casey. I need to go." He turned to face her. "We both know that it wouldn't work out between us. We are two *extremely* different people. I'm sorry." He turned back around, opened the door, and stowed his suitcase.

"Wouldn't work out?" she scoffed, stepping to the side so he could get into the driver's seat. "What's to work out? I want you to stay and help find out who's after my sister. Sex would be a damn fine benefit. And that's all there is to it. Why're you making it more complicated than it has to be?"

"Is that all it would be, really? Just sex?"

"That's all it needs to be, Ryan. Sex is sex."

"Must you be so cavalier about everything?"

She could only stare at him, dumbfounded. What was his problem?

Ryan shook his head. "Obviously, you do. I'm sorry, I don't work that way. I don't sleep with just anyone."

"You know, when you came to my apartment and I said, I don't sleep with suits, you said, 'That's a shame.' So, I don't understand your reluctance now."

Ryan shook his head. "That was inappropriate, and I apologize. It was a knee-jerk reaction—"

"Yeah, something 'jerked,' all right," Casey said, and she would swear he blushed.

"I never intended to act on it."

"That's not what if felt like a few minutes ago!" She wasn't offended. She wasn't! "You know what? I don't have time for prudes. Have a nice life, Ryan." She turned, headed for the house, and resisted the urge to flick him off.

****

Ryan stared at her retreating back for a moment, then started the engine and drove away. He was relieved...honestly. Those McKays were a tad reckless for him. Was he a prude? No, he liked sex as much as the next guy, but he had his own set of morals. He hadn't lied. He didn't sleep around.

Did that mean he didn't want her? No, in fact he would love nothing more than to indulge in Casey. But he tried very hard not to give into temptation. The McKay women were a handful. They were more Jake's style. Jake! What had his brother done now? Ryan switched his focus to his brother and ignored the desire to look in the rearview mirror.

Chapter Six

Casey was the last one to get to the hospital that night. She had spent most of the day cleaning the house; it was so clean, no one would know Ryan Keller had ever been there. Stabbing the button to open the elevator doors, she mumbled, "Don't sleep with just anyone." Like she was some kind of slut.

The pig! She was glad he was gone. Casey McKay had never needed a man, and if she did it wouldn't be some suit man like Ryan Keller. Designer boots, indeed. She squeezed her eyes shut; she was being ridiculous, acting like a child denied the toy she wanted. Not that Ryan was a toy. Well...no. No, she needed to stop. It didn't matter. He didn't matter. Couldn't, wouldn't, done.

She got off the elevator at Fletcher's floor and headed down the hall. She slowed when she came upon Alex talking to the doctor. Her sister smacked his shoulder and whispered something; then the doctor turned beet red and stormed off.

"Whatcha say to the doc?" Casey asked.

Alex huffed and straightened her skirt. "I told him exactly what I thought of him." She looked in the direction the doctor had gone, then back at Casey. "It seems he didn't agree. Where's Ryan?"

She shrugged. "He left."

"Why? What did you do to him?"

"I didn't do a damn thing to him." And wasn't that a shame. "His brother needed his help, so he left."

Alexandra raised a brow. "Just like that?"

"Yes, just like that, you annoying wench," Casey said with a smirk. Arguing with her sister often improved her mood. She turned toward Fletcher's room, but Alex grabbed her arm.

"Prepare yourself. She isn't speaking to anyone. She won't even look at us. Mama left in tears, and Dad was beside himself. Charlie even brought Mack to try and cheer Fletcher up, but she wouldn't acknowledge them. She didn't look at me either, and I was sitting there for hours."

Casey sighed and gave in to her urge to hug Alexandra.

"I still cannot believe I missed you," Alex said on a laugh and pulled away.

"Course you did! I'm your only willing opponent." Casey grasped the knob and took a breath, then walked into the private room and closed the door.

Fletcher—what there was of her—lay on her side facing the wall. The monitors were beeping in a steady rhythm. Casey sat in a chair, pulled off her shoes and socks, and set her glasses on the small side table. Moving the tubes and wires gently out of her way she got under the covers with her sister. She moved to her side so they were spooned together. She placed a small kiss on her sister's head and inhaled her scent. Fletcher had never smelled like anything Casey could name, but it was spicy like the wind in the fall and sweet like a summer rain.

"I've missed you so much, Fletch. I'm sorry I

ran… I should've stayed and worked things out. I messed up." Casey sighed and snuggled closer. "I met Mack; you must have given her the nickname. She's so cute. Gonna be a handful like her Auntie Fletch." She waited a minute, not really expecting an answer. "I'll find whoever did this. I promise. I'm not going anywhere. I think I might buy Ward's old garage and open my own shop. It'll be the four of us again, you'll see. I love you, little sister," Casey said to her sister's back before closing her eyes.

****

Casey pulled her truck into an empty parking space behind Ward's garage. "Now or never," she mumbled getting out of her truck. Her boots crunched on the gravel. The building was a mess—practically condemned. Who could blame Ward for locking the door and throwing away the key?

Ward's only son had died within these walls. She and her sisters had been here that night too. Who had said it best? A web of deception and all that? Tangled webs indeed.

The building was falling apart in some places, but it wasn't nearly as bad as she had feared. The foundation still held firm. It could be fixed. She had no doubt she could handle this.

She entered the code the Realtor had given her on the phone into the lockbox and took out the key, then opened the creaking door and walked right into a spider's web. She wiped the sticky mass away from her face and crinkled her nose; the smell of oil and grease mingled with the unmistakable air of damp neglect.

The sunlight, coming in from the door, exposed thick layers of dust. Casey went to the light switch and turned it on. There was a crackle in the air, and she was glad no one was there to see her jump. She cast her gaze to the ceiling where more webs and dust resided.

The pits were still there. She could almost hear Ward telling her to watch her step. This place had been her getaway; she had decided her future career here when she was a kid. She had always loved working on cars and trucks, fixing things. It had meant the world to her when Ward had told her she had a knack for it.

She came to the stairs, and memories of that horrible night surfaced. Uncle Evan... Her throat tightened, and she swallowed.

"Get a grip," she mumbled. She straightened her shoulders and headed up the steps. She put one foot in front of the other, ignoring the groans of rotting wood and the echoes of a moment she would rather forget.

Opening the door to the small apartment, she sucked in a sharp breath. It was exactly how they had left it. Their sleeping bags were still there, or what the moths had left of them. It was morbid. The carpet was the same; she knew from the blood stains. She supposed the scents of death lingered when you kept them boxed up.

"Oh, Ward," she whispered. He had left it all here to gather dust. She had run away from facing her truths, and Ward had locked himself out. What a pair they were.

Shaking off the emotions, Casey let her practical side kick in. The apartment would be adequate for her. She would gut the place first, naturally, but it would work. She wouldn't let the ghosts deter her.

****

Casey made a few phone calls and pulled into the

parking lot behind the hardware store. She smiled. Her father's truck was in its usual place; the man never changed, not really. She wasn't complaining; she loved him for who he was.

They'd had a long talk last night when she got home from the hospital. She would have stayed all night, as she had for the past week, but a nurse had come in cursing her up and down. The woman had thought she was Fletcher's partner until Casey explained that Fletcher was her little sister. The nurse had been embarrassed but held firm. Casey had left the hospital and gone home.

Pops was sitting on the porch as if waiting for her. He said how proud he was of her for letting go of whatever it was that had kept her away and for coming back to help when her sisters needed her. She couldn't find the words to explain the truth, the why of it all, but he had seemed to understand that as well. He was just happy she was home.

Now she walked into the store and studied her father. He was damn handsome for a man about to turn fifty-one. His black hair was graying at the temples, and there were laugh lines around his eyes. In her opinion, Pops had always been the best-looking man in Blue Creek and still was.

"Hey, Pops," she called out. He looked up and smiled at her. She stepped behind the counter and ran into her brother. "Whatcha doing, Bullfrog?"

Jebb rolled his big blue eyes. "I'm helping Dad. Aren't I, Dad?"

"Dad, is it?" Pops smirked. "Yes, Casey, your brother is training to take over the store."

"Is that so? Well, you don't own the place yet...so

scram," Casey said, then made a move to catch him and he ran off. She looked back at Pops grinning, then shrugged when he raised a brow. That's where Alex got the habit. "What?"

"Whatcha scare him off for? This is important work," he reminded her, humor lighting his eyes.

"I needed to talk to you. And stop with the eyebrow thing. It's spreading. Alexandra already has it, and she's annoying enough." She smacked his shoulder and hopped up on the counter.

"Naturally, I'm curious."

"I'm buying Ward's place." She waited for a comment but got a nod. "Nothing to say?"

"Alexandra said she'd mentioned it. I figured it would only be a matter of time. You looked the place over yet?"

"Yeah, spook central. It hasn't been touched, and I don't mean hasn't been touched in a while; I mean since Uncle Evan died. Our sleeping bags are still hanging out of the closet." Casey shook her head and frowned.

"I'm sorry you had to see it again, Case."

"It is what it is, I suppose," she said and hopped down. "I'm going to need a hand fixing the place up, and I hoped you could recommend someone."

"Sure, let's take a look." He turned to his computer and started typing. "Shmittie's boys have an operation and are pretty good at what they do."

"What does the old barkeep think about that?" Shmittie owned the only bar in Blue Creek, and it wasn't a secret he wanted his boys to take over.

"He's disappointed they don't want to follow in his footsteps, but he supports their decision. They're good guys. *But* if you want the best I know just who to ask."

"Who?"

"Me," he said, and Casey laughed. "What?"

"Pops, you're not getting any younger."

His brows furrowed. "What's your point?"

"You really want do this?"

"Yes, I do. Clay can watch the store. I haven't been involved in anything of this size in a while." He shrugged. "And I'd like working with my daughter. Your mother would love to help you decorate. Or whatever it is she does. I'm assuming you plan to live in the apartment above the shop."

"Wow, I didn't realize how predictable I—Wait, is me living at the garage going to be an issue?"

"No, not at all. Charlie and Mack have their own place, and Alexandra lives at the B and B. Your mother and I are used to it being just Jebb and Fletcher," he said, moving away.

Casey wrapped her arms around his waist and rested her head on his back. He stood stock still for a moment, then turned around to get a full hug.

"You're hugging me in public, you know," he said into her bun.

"It doesn't really bother me anymore," she said, figuring it was better than saying it had never bothered her. He would think he was a bad father for not realizing it; then there would be an apology and they would both be uncomfortable.

"Good then." He tightened his arms around her once more before letting go.

"How is she today?"

"She still isn't talking, and it's breaking your mother's heart. When we find out who did this, I want them put away for the rest of their life. Jasper agrees. The old man is going stir crazy. Fletcher won't talk to him either." He shoved his hands into the pockets of his jeans. "She stares at the wall. The doctor said this is how she's dealing with all that's happened to her. But I don't know. She's always been so damn tough."

"I know, Dad," she whispered.

"They're talking about putting a tube in to feed her. She won't eat." He shook his head. "I don't know what to do. I can't help her if she won't let me. If she won't let anyone. We had hoped with you here..."

"I haven't gone during waking hours. I'll go today and see what I can do. Force works for me. Hospital beds are hell on my back." She kissed his cheek and headed out the door. She wouldn't think about the emotion in her father's eyes or how much it hurt to see him in such pain.

The diner was right next door, and Casey could use some encouragement, not to mention a good cup of coffee. Charlie made the strongest.

"Hey, Casey," Charlie said from behind the counter in her usual uniform of McKay's T-shirt and jeans.

"Hey! I could use a cup of coffee and something to eat," she said sitting at the counter. It was after lunch, so there wasn't much of a crowd.

Charlie put a cup of coffee in front of her and asked, "What's up?"

"Not much. I'm going to buy Ward's old garage."

"Figured you would, eventually. Everyone did, so don't be disappointed when no one acts surprised." She shrugged. "But I think it's great! You went inside, I suppose. Fletcher used to go and look the place over now and again. She said it was like a mausoleum."

"It is. Our sleeping bags are still hanging out of the closet, and soda cans are still on the floor. It's depressing."

"That it is. But that, big sister, is life. And who knows better than the McKays," Charlie said with a wink.

"Isn't that the truth!" Casey pulled her hair out of its sloppy bun, only to flip it back again.

"Here you go. A PB and J and some chips. Just the way you like it."

"Sweet! My favorite. Thanks." Casey took a bite. Perfect. "I'm going to the hospital after this. It's time I started pushing Fletcher's buttons. She gets mad—she fights. Always been like that."

"I thought about that too, but I couldn't do it, and Alexandra doesn't want to get smacked in the face. Did you ever notice Alexandra's a little vain?"

"*You don't say?* I never noticed." They both laughed.

****

The man had left a week ago and hadn't been back. The plan had been to finish Fletcher off at the hospital, but big sister bitch had been there every damn time. It would have been easy to get them both, but that wasn't the ideal scenario. Now, Casey was buying Ward Jessup's old rat trap. In fact, it was more like a fire hazard.

Chapter Seven

Casey walked down the all-too-familiar halls leading to her sister's room. She needed to get Fletcher to snap out of this. Luckily, Casey had an idea—she hoped. She opened the door to find her sister in the same position she had been in for the past week. The stitches would be taken out soon. Not all of the cuts had required stitches, but there had been about a hundred and sixty actual sutures.

"Good afternoon, *Jamie*," Casey began, walking into the room and closing the door.

Fletcher winced.

Casey opened the blinds. "It's a beautiful summer day out, Jamie. You should really get up and see it."

Fletcher covered her face.

"I put in a bid for Ward's old place, Jamie," she said and took a seat. "Isn't that great! I stopped by the hardware store to see Pops, and it seems the Bullfrog is gonna take over the place. Jamie, do you remember the time when we wanted to run the store? That was before I learned about cars, and before your first breaking and entering. You remember, don't you, Jamie?"

Her sister grumbled incoherently.

"I'm sorry, *Jamie*, I didn't hear you," Casey said with a Cheshire grin. "Could you please speak up, Jamie?"

"My name isn't fucking Jamie! Now leave me the

hell alone," Fletcher groused, sitting up in her bed.

"You look like Fletcher, and you cuss like her, but Fletcher would never hide from her family. So you must be Jamie."

"Casey, please?" Fletcher whispered.

"Fuck you!" Casey went to the bed to take hold of her sister's chin. "You've never backed down from a fight in your life. Not one! But now—now when you have to fight for your *own* life—you quit? I say fuck you, Jamie McKay. I want Fletcher back!" She hadn't expected Fletcher to start crying; it was such a non-Fletcher thing to do. Oh, her sister had always been a crier, but she didn't usually make a big production in front of people. They had always left the dramatics to Alexandra.

"I'm sorry, Casey, for everything." Fletcher pulled her chin from Casey's fingers and wrapped her arms around her. It was the first real hug they'd shared in years. "I love you so much," she whispered.

"You had to go and make us both look like sissies, crying all over the place, didn't you?" Casey sniffed but was too happy that her sister was talking to care. "I love you too, weirdo. And I'll forgive you if you forgive me."

Fletcher nodded. "Are you really moving back?"

"Sure am, got me a bid on the garage too," Casey said, sitting back on the bed to get a good look at her sister. Her french braid was starting to come loose in several places, making Fletch look a bit like a mad hatter. "You look like hell."

She patted her hair, then rolled her eyes. "Like I've ever cared how I look, Case."

"You've lost so much weight you look like a

scrawny kid." She smiled when Fletcher's eyes got stormy. More blue than green, which meant she was getting angry.

"You always were a bitch, Casey." Fletcher laughed. Her eyes went wide, and she covered her mouth with her hands.

"You okay?" She didn't like the look on her sister's face, like she didn't recognize the sound of her own laughter.

Fletcher's brows pinched. "I couldn't focus my thoughts most of the time, and when I could, I was angry or ambivalent. I had insomnia most nights, but when I did sleep, I had these awful nightmares about closets. And blood," she whispered rubbing her arms, "so much blood."

"Be careful," Casey said after Fletcher knocked her IV and winced.

"I started seeing things. You mainly," Fletcher began, her hands fisting in the sheets. "I couldn't tell what was real. I...I cut myself to differentiate between reality and dream. I went to the cabin to try and get a handle on the situation. I'd lose time and not know what I was doing. The only thing I remember clearly is this creepy laugh." She shook her head. "Then you came."

"A laugh?" Casey didn't want to dismiss what her sister was saying, but it sounded rather...well, insane.

Fletcher straightened the blanket. "The doctor said if I promise to eat, I can go home any time. Take me home, Casey. I'm ready to be Fletcher again. Jamie always did suck."

Casey burst out laughing, and tears filled her eyes. She might have been crying so hard she was laughing;

she wasn't sure. When Fletcher sat back and smiled, Casey realized she didn't care.

Once Casey got herself under control, Fletcher asked, "Who took my locket?"

"No one did; you left it on the porch at the B and B. That more than anything showed me how serious things had become," Casey said, touching Fletcher's cheek.

Her sister pulled away. "I've been wearing that locket every day since I was nine years old! I only take it off to clean it, Casey. I remember another time I said it was taken and no one believed me. Now history is repeating itself, and I'm saying I didn't take the damn thing off, but you still don't believe me. I was right then too!"

"Okay, Fletcher, if you didn't take it off, how did it get on Alex's porch? You weren't all there, as you well know." She stood, ignoring the pang of unease. What Fletcher was saying was the product of a drug-induced psychosis, nothing more.

"Someone was feeding me a concoction of prescription drugs and herbs to make me unstable, Casey. The idea the same person would take my necklace is not farfetched."

"You have to admit you weren't thinking clearly at the time."

"Just leave, okay. I don't need you doubting me."

Casey pointed at her. "How can you say that? How can you sit there and say that to my face? Everyone's been stepping on eggshells around you! Praying today you'd talk to them, and now you act like you don't care? Was it the drugs, Fletch, or have you really turned into a heartless bitch?" Casey was too worked up to care how harsh she was being.

"Who knows, Casey, maybe you're right. But I need to be around people I can trust, who trust me. It's obvious you don't, which, given your years of self-imposed exile, is understandable. The truth is, I don't need your shit. I've got my own problems."

"You want me to leave you alone? Fine! I'll let you wallow and brood to your heart's content, but I'm not leaving, Fletch, not this time. You, dear sister, can just deal with that!" Casey spat, slamming the door as she left the room.

Figuring she would share her frustrations with someone, Casey headed back to the diner and smiled at the full house. Charlie and Tiny were great cooks, and everyone knew it. She walked in for the second time in as many hours. Charlie was still behind the counter, but this time Alexandra was there sitting on a stool, the long skirt of her summer dress skimming the floor.

"Why didn't any of you tell me Fletcher was the genuine article bitch?" she asked, making both of her sisters turn. She took a seat next to Alex and accepted the tall glass of tea Charlie handed her.

Alex's fingers tightened around her glass. "She talked to you?"

"You could say that. What?" she asked when Charlie rattled a mason jar in her face.

"We pay for profanity here, Casey. It says so right there." Charlie pointed to the writing on the jar. "That'll be one dollar."

Casey's brows pinched. "Are you serious?"

"As a heart attack," Alex said with a smirk.

"I don't care what you do elsewhere, but in this diner if you say it, you pay it. It's that simple," Charlie said.

Casey glared at Alex. "Don't look at me," her sister said.

Sighing, she pulled out a dollar and shoved it into Charlie's jar.

"Thank you!" Charlie cheered.

Casey sipped her tea. She was about to say something snarky, but Charlie's eyes were fixed on the window behind her. She turned to see what had caught her sister's attention. It was a who, not a what. A blue-eyed blonde who seeped falseness from her pores. Casey's lip curled of its own volition.

"Oh, my goodness, if it isn't Casey McKay back from the dead?" the woman sneered at her, then sat down at the table closest to them.

"Marylou, what can I get for you this afternoon?" Charlie asked, not quite pleasantly. Casey looked at Charlie, then turned to Alex, who nodded to confirm it was indeed Marylou Thomas, the McKay girls' archnemesis.

"Oh, the usual, Charlie dear," she drawled with disdain.

"Marylou, how lovely you look this afternoon," Alex purred. "From where I'm sitting, it seems like the appointment you had with Trixy was a successful one. You can't even tell you have a weave." Alexandra's voice was so sweet, it was sickening. Casey was impressed.

Marylou giggled and fluffed her hair. "Alexandra McKay, how nice of you to notice."

"Is she really that dense?" Casey whispered across the counter to Charlie while Alexandra talked to Marylou.

Charlie winked. "Alexandra hates her guts, and the woman doesn't have a clue. But no one can tell with Alex. She's too slick. Heck, she could hate all of us, and we wouldn't even know it."

Casey snorted. Charlie prepared a plate and took it to Marylou.

"Oh hon, could you make it to go? Alexandra told me about a wonderful little boutique in the city, and I just have to check it out."

Casey sat back as Charlie tripped over herself in her rush for a box. And just as fast as she came in, Marylou was gone.

"Some people never change," Casey grumbled.

"She's putty," Alexandra said with sniff of distaste. "Now, back to the important things. Fletcher was talking? She actually talked to you? How did you accomplish that?"

"I called her Jamie until she couldn't take it anymore. She's got a mouth on her; I thought about getting a bar of soap."

Charlie pointed to the profanity jar. "Why do you think I have that?"

Casey laughed. "Now it makes sense."

"So…what happened after she cussed you out?" Alex asked.

"Yeah, why did you call her the 'B' word?"

"She said she didn't take off her locket, that someone stole it. When I didn't believe her, she told me if I didn't trust her, then I should leave her the hell alone." And now Casey was pissed off again.

Charlie pursed her lips. "She was right last time."

"Always the peacekeeper," Alex muttered, tapping her nails against the counter in a small tattoo. "Couldn't you have placated her, Casey? Let her think you believed her?"

"I was never as good at deception as you, Alexandra," Casey snipped.

"And here we have the root of the problem. You've probably set us back a couple of weeks where Fletcher's concerned." Alex's tone got Casey's back up.

"She'll talk to you, Miss Priss!" Casey said, making a face at Alex. "She just won't talk to me right away. Which is fine if she's going to be all touchy."

"Jeez, Casey, someone was trying to kill her. Why *not* steal her necklace too?"

"Whose side are you on, anyway?" Casey asked, narrowing her eyes.

"I'm on my side, and as such, I don't feel like talking anymore." And with that Charlie went through the swinging doors and into the kitchen. Where she would no doubt tattle to Tiny.

"You could never let things alone, Casey. Even when we lived in that wretched home."

Casey bounded up from her stool. "We agreed never to talk about that place, Alex." She was pissed at Fletcher, Charlie, and especially this one. Of all the nerve.

Alex sighed. "You agreed."

"You were only three when we left, what do you know?" Casey undid her bun and put it back up. She didn't want to talk about this. Ever. It had been over twenty years. Who freaking cared!

"More than one might expect. Fletcher and I went back there, you know," Alexandra said.

Casey's expression conveyed what she was feeling.

"You're thinking about hitting me, aren't you, Casey? Go ahead and try it," Alex hissed.

"Don't tempt me! I don't want to know about that place." Her anger threated to overwhelm her, so she pointed a finger in the vicinity of her sister's face. "Just keep outta my way for a few days, Alexandra McKay. For your own good!" She reached into her pocket for her cash.

"What's going on here?" Charlie asked, coming back to the counter.

"I did what Casey hates the most." Alex shrugged one shoulder. "Brought up the past."

"Shut up, *Alex*!" Casey growled.

Alex turned to Charlie. "Isn't it funny how she snarls at Fletcher for not wanting to face the facts, when she does the same thing?"

"I'm warning you—"

"Alexandra, that's enough," Charlie said.

"It must be nice in the land of make-believe you two live in."

"I'm outta here!" Casey dropped a couple bills on the counter for her tea and headed for the door.

****

Casey drove up the gravel drive without finesse. She didn't need this crap. First Fletcher flying off the handle, then Charlie taking her own side, and Alexandra putting her pert nose where it didn't belong.

"Why in the hell did they go back to that place?" she asked the empty cab. She shut off the engine and bounded out of the truck. How could they even remember it? Her own memory of the subject wasn't crystal clear anymore. She sat on the steps of the porch admiring the moon as it fought the sun for control of the sky.

She had been having a pretty good day until Fletcher hit her with theories of theft. Casey shifted to lay her head down on her arms. Could Fletch be right? Casey wasn't sure, but she didn't think so. It was crazy. Of course, being drugged wasn't in the range of normal either.

So much had happened in a couple of weeks. She rubbed her eyes. She needed to put her glasses on and take her contacts out. She had too many worries right now.

Somehow her mind went back years—a lifetime—and landed in the dirty old basement of the home for orphaned and abandoned children. She was the only one who would go down to what the other kids called "the hell pit." The basement was dark, damp, and smelled like shit; she had thrown up the first time, but she hadn't been afraid.

It was her job to set and clean the rat traps. She had hated the rodents at first, but then she realized there was a group of them living down there. Who was she to destroy the very thing she had wanted most? A family. But when the traps kept turning up empty, Miss Tina, who ran the home, got mad, and Casey had no choice but to do as she was told. If she hadn't, Miss Tina might have separated her from Alex and Fletcher, and that wasn't a chance she had been willing to take.

"Casey?"

Jerked from her thoughts, she sat up and took a breath. "Sorry, what?"

"We have a perfectly good swing, or six chairs you could sit in," her mother said.

"I know. My mind was just wondering."

Savannah sat down next to her.

"Where's Pops and the Bullfrog?"

"They're dropping Mack off at your sister's," she said, putting her arm around Casey. "Charlie told me what happened today. I'm glad Fletcher's opening up."

Casey snorted.

"She always had a temper. It's just grown along with her."

"Do you think she's right? About the locket being stolen, I mean?" Casey asked, bereft when her mother got up to sit in the swing. Casey sat on the floor in front of her, waiting.

"I do. Your father doesn't know what to believe." She laughed a little.

"You do, though? I should have known." And she should have too. But Pops was on the same page with her, and that counted.

Her mother's eyes narrowed. "What's that supposed to mean?"

Casey squirmed a bit. "Nothing, Ma. It's...well, you always believe Fletcher."

"I've never had a cause not to. I trust you as much, and you darn well know I do!" She rose to go inside. Savannah McKay would not tolerate being insulted by her daughter or anyone else.

Casey stood. "I know, Ma, I know. I'm just pissed and taking it out on you, I guess. Sorry," she said, pleased when her mother kissed her forehead.

"I will always love you and your sisters, but you can't have love without trust. I don't know what happened between the four of you, but I'm glad you're here now. Our family hasn't been complete in six years, and it was driving your father nuts."

"I can't see Pops nuts." She laughed anyway, imagining it. He wouldn't have let it show to anyone but Ma. He'd been like that since he'd married her.

"Trust me. He was driving everyone crazy. Then everything with Fletcher started up. I wasn't any help to him either. I was hurt and upset; your stereotypical overly emotional mother. That was me." She took hold of Casey's chin. "And if you or your sisters cause me to act this way again, I will not be responsible for my actions." They both laughed.

That was what being home was all about. Getting pissed off, then laughing about it later; her mother had put everything in perspective. Casey was smiling as she headed back to see Fletcher at the hospital, but the smile died a quick death when she opened the door to her sister's room. The room was empty, and the bed had been stripped. Her sister was gone.

Chapter Eight

Casey pounded on the door of Charlie's house. It was a nice-sized ranch-style home with a wraparound porch. The white vinyl siding and blue shutters were all Charlie. Toys littered the lawn, and a tire swing swung from the gigantic oak in the middle of the front yard.

"What *is* your problem?" Charlie asked as she stepped back to let Casey in. "I just got Mack to sleep, and now you're waking her up again. We need to work on your auntie skills."

"Sorry." Casey had forgotten little kids had early bedtimes. She followed Charlie through the house. It was warm and welcoming, like her sister. The colors were sunny and friendly, also like her sister.

The kitchen was a chef's dream with beautiful granite countertops and stainless steel appliances. Not one, but two ovens, a large range, and a grill on the island. Casey smiled at the industrial-size dishwasher. Charlie had always hated doing the dishes.

"What has you pounding on my door?" Charlie asked, pouring water into a kettle.

"Is Fletcher here?" She took a seat at the breakfast bar.

Charlie set the kettle on the burner, then turned. "She's not at the hospital?"

"Would I have asked you if she was here if she was at the hospital?"

"Don't get an attitude with me, Casey McKay! One child is all I can take right this minute. It took me an hour to get Mack in bed. I've told our father and brother I don't know how many times not to give Mack soda!"

Casey could only nod. "I'm sorry." She'd been doing an awful lot of apologizing lately and didn't like it one bit. "Fletcher's not at the house, and I already called Alex."

"Did you call Jasper?" Charlie asked, pulling mugs down from the cabinet.

"Why would I call him? You think she went there?"

"More than likely. Jasper would believe her about the necklace. Besides, he'd be too happy she was coming back to the real world to care one way or the other."

"I know you said they were close, but I didn't realize they were that close."

"You don't know a lot of things, Casey," Charlie said as the kettle whistled and she put tea bags in to steep. "Unfortunately, you can't snap your fingers and bring back the last six years; none of us can."

"You're pissed at me?" Charlie had rarely gotten mad at her or anyone for that matter.

Charlie sighed. "Not just you, no… Actually, yes, I am pissed at you!" she said as she got out spoons from the drawer and honey from another cabinet. "We all tread lightly making sure not to set you off, but honestly I don't really give a hoot and a half. Fletcher almost died, Casey. Someone drugged her, and she almost killed herself because of it. Standing behind her is more important than your temper."

"I don't know what to say. Do you want me to

leave?" Casey asked around the large lump in her throat. She couldn't remember her Charlie ever acting like this before.

"Oh, goodness Casey, that's not what I mean. Darn it." Charlie stomped her foot. "This is why I never say anything; I always mess it up." She rushed over and gave Casey a hug. "It's hard to remember you have feelings like the rest of us; you've always bottled them up. I forget you're not made of steel," she said and kissed Casey's forehead before she stepped back.

"Tell me about it. Who knew I was such a chick." Casey sniffled. Hormones, that's what it had to be. She didn't say anything more, just accepted the cup of tea Charlie handed her. She sighed. "You think Fletcher really went to Jasper's?"

"I noticed Tiny giving Jasper more takeout boxes than usual, so, yes, I do. It might be best if you give her a few days. Maybe she needs all of us to back off a little." Then Charlie grinned. "Give her time to stew about it, and she'll come around." She pulled Fletcher's locket out of her pocket. "We can hold it for ransom."

"You know, Charlie, what they say is true," Casey said.

"What's that?"

Casey pointed to the locket. "It's always the quiet ones."

****

Casey pulled her truck up to the garage. It was hers now; after only a week it was hers. She smiled to herself. Her childhood dream come true. She would call it McKay's Auto. Her family would own yet another local business in Blue Creek. How cool was that?

"Very cool," she said, opening the doors. She was

prepared for the smell and spiderwebs this time. She wore a baseball cap with her braided hair pulled through the back, her oldest pair of jeans, and a ratty T-shirt that announced she was "bad to the bone." Her steel-toed work boots protected her from the grit and grime beneath her feet.

Casey worked most of the afternoon on the first floor until she was dripping with sweat. She wiped her forehead with the hem of her shirt. The air hit her skin, cooling her down, and she decided to ditch the shirt entirely. Her purple sports bra was sufficient, and no one was around.

Taking off her cap, she twisted her braid up into a frumpy bun and headed for the stairs. Ripping out carpet seemed like a good idea. She grabbed her bottle of water on the way up.

The room didn't creep her out this time. She had seen it when the death had was fresh; this she could deal with. She moved the furniture to one side of the room first. Then she got down on her knees in the corner closest to the stairs and started pulling the carpet from the tack strip against the wall.

"Maybe we should call you Marty, the butch version of Martha Stewart," Alexandra suggested from the stairs.

Casey eyed her sister; they had ignored each other for a few days, as was the natural way with them. "Talking to me again, are you?" Casey asked, standing up and guzzling her water.

"I may as well; no one else is as interesting or as easy to pick a fight with."

"Wanna fight?" Casey asked. Then she smelled it: Food! Greasy food. The food of the gods. Alex produced a McKay's Diner bag from behind her back, and Casey hustled over and snatched it away. "Thanks, sis," she said proceeding to sit on the floor and pull out a big juicy burger. "Oh, yum. You eating?"

"If you don't hog it all. I suppose I am hungry." Alexandra smiled and sat next to Casey reaching for her own burger.

"Is the food a bribe of some kind?" Casey asked with her mouth full. Tiny's burgers were the best, hands down. Completely bribe-worthy.

"I see you still have your manners, and, no, more of a peace offering."

"I thought you wanted to fight?" She was almost disappointed. She wanted an argument to release some steam.

"No, I've had enough arguing. You wouldn't know what's gotten into Charlie, would you? She's being a mega bitch. She hasn't been this mean since she was in labor." Alex shuddered. "And what a bloody mess that was."

"What was it like?" Casey asked, swallowing past the lump in her throat.

Alexandra sighed. "Charlie had the easiest pregnancy known to man. I swear, she wasn't even sick—not once. Our sister is a beautiful woman, but she was positively radiant pregnant. We all had a hard time believing it at first. Dad blew a fuse when she told him. He had his rifle out faster than we could blink. It took Mama hours to calm him down."

"How'd she do that?"

"She yelled at him for a while, then took him to their room." Alexandra laughed when Casey gasped in mock horror. Their parents made love often and didn't do a very good job of hiding it. Gross!

"After that, he was obsessed with being a grandfather and making sure Charlie was in good shape. She was until she went into labor. She was a couple of weeks early, and we were all worried. She was hysterical with pain and cursed so much Fletcher was embarrassed."

"No shit?"

"I shit you not," Alex drawled with enough of a dramatic flair to make Casey snort. "As I was saying, it took almost twenty-four hours of blood, sweat, and pure hell before Mackenzie decided to make her first appearance. We all wanted to call you. Fletcher taped the whole thing so you can see for yourself."

"I might. I don't know exactly what set Charlie off, but I kinda think it was my shitty attitude the other day. She snapped at me too." Casey shook her head, then sniffed. They both got to their feet.

"Casey, do you smell that?"

"I was about to ask you the same thing. It smells like…" Her mouth went dry. "Holy shit! Something's on fire!"

They took the steps two at a time and stopped dead. There was nowhere to go. They scrambled back up the stairs and slammed the door shut. Casey grabbed Alex's hand and pulled her toward the window. She tried to open it, but years of neglect had sealed it shut.

"I'll have to break the glass," Casey said. She went to the closet and grabbed one of the sleeping bags they'd left there years ago. She covered her fist in the fabric and used it to knock the glass from the pane.

"We can knot the other sleeping bags together and make a rope," Alex suggested.

Smoke was beginning to seep through the cracks. Casey nodded. "We better hurry."

The thick fabric was worn with age and degraded by moths, so knotting it together wasn't difficult. By the time they finished the knots, smoke was billowing from beneath the door.

"We need to secure this to something," Alex said, coughing.

"The couch," Casey shouted over the pounding in her head. They pushed the couch closer to the window, lifted up one end, and stuck the leg through one of the moth-made holes. They dropped the makeshift rope out the window. It didn't need to touch the ground; it only needed to get them to a safer jumping distance.

Casey nodded to Alex. "You first."

Alex pulled the back of her skirt through her legs and tucked it into her waistband. Then she took hold of the rope and maneuvered herself out the window.

Casey kept the couch in place as it shifted against Alex's weight. The wooden planks of the door began to crack, sending her heart to her throat. She shook off her fear and focused on her task. The resistance was gone; it was her turn now. She took hold of the knotted fabric and worked herself out of the window. A piece of glass sliced into the flesh of her arm. Casey hissed. It was over in seconds.

Once her feet touched the ground, Alex grabbed her and pulled her away. They clambered behind Casey's truck as sirens pierced the smoke-filled air. The roof caved in a moment later.

The sisters looked at the burning rubble, then back at each other.

"Nothing can ever be normal when you're around,

Casey," Alex huffed. Casey laughed and hugged her sister. They came apart quickly when the pounding of running feet approached them.

"Girls? *Girls*?" Pops yelled. He waved when he spotted them, relief plain on his face. "What the hell happened?" It was the tone he used when he was upset but wanted them to think he was mad.

"Seems my new business just went up in flames." Casey couldn't help laughing. Hysteria and shock. Her dreams were going up in smoke. Literally.

"I have no idea how this could have happened," Alex said after she hugged their father. She looked at Casey with a strange expression on her face.

"What?" Casey asked.

Her sister squatted down in front of her and tore a piece away from her skirt. Alex took hold of her bloody arm and wrapped the fabric around it.

Casey hissed. "I get the feeling you like being the skirt-ripping medic." Alex gave a ladylike snort, making Casey chuckle.

They stepped farther away to give the firemen room to do their jobs. The hoses were loud as water doused what was left of the old garage. There wasn't much.

"Any clue what started it?" Pops asked.

"No," Casey said. "We were upstairs talking and smelled the smoke. We went downstairs, but the fire was spreading too fast. We used the old sleeping bags to make a rope and got the hell out of there."

"Just like you taught us, Dad," Alex said with a smile.

"Still a suck-up," Casey muttered, but she was grinning too. Their father was puffing out his chest. She couldn't be annoyed with her sister when Pops was proud of them.

"Maybe we should keep the details away from your mother," he suggested.

"Too late, Emmit McKay. We already heard," their mother said, walking right past him to hug her girls. Charlie, Fletcher, Jasper, and Todd Mae, the fire chief, followed.

Questions were asked and statements were given. It took about an hour before Casey could get away. She went to the diner wearing one of Charlie's extra T-shirts and smelling like smoke. She slumped down in a booth and waited for her little sister. Casey knew she was ready to talk.

Sure enough, Fletcher came into the diner a few minutes later and sat across from her. She looked a hell of a lot better than she had the last time. Her eyes weren't sunken in her skull anymore, she had some color, and her hair was in twin braids. This was Fletcher. A pair of overalls with an old T-shirt had always been her trademark.

She gave Casey a once-over. "Do you believe me now?"

"Believe what now? What has the fire got to do with your locket?" Casey rubbed her temples warding off the headache trying to violate her brain.

"Someone started that fire," Fletcher said, using her finger against the table to make her point.

"How the hell do you know? The wiring wasn't the best, and I knew it; I just hadn't done anything about it yet." Sheesh, she didn't need this right now.

"I'm telling you, someone started the fire, Casey. You have to believe me," Fletcher whispered.

Casey sighed.

"You think I've lost my mind, but I'm all here now," Fletcher said and tapped her temple. "There aren't any drugs making me crazy. The fire means something."

"Fletcher, it was probably the wiring. We know someone was drugging you, and we will get the bastard, I promise. But that has nothing to do with what happened today. Trust me." Casey reached out and touched her sister's hand. What could they do to help her? She had conspiracy on the brain. Casey couldn't blame her. Someone had nearly killed Fletcher and he—or she—was still out there; a little paranoia was expected.

"You don't believe me." Fletcher let out a small humorless laugh. "I can't really blame you, can I? I mean, I was the one hallucinating. And I was the one cutting my body to ribbons trying to hold onto reality." She rose, pulling her hand out of Casey's. Their family was staring at them. They'd heard the entire conversation and couldn't look away. Like an accident on the side of the road.

"Who has my locket? I'd like it back," Fletcher asked the group at large.

"I have it," Charlie said.

Casey sat back as Charlie handed Mack over to Pops and pulled the locket out of her pocket. Fletcher snatched it and walked over to their mother so she could put it on for her.

Casey's gut twisted. Her little sister was being too quiet…too calm. Fletcher kissed their parents and went toward the front of the diner.

Using her body to hold open the door, Fletcher

said, "I know none of you think I'm completely sane anymore, and that's fine. But I *am* sane. I know someone started the fire. I know it in here"—she put two fingers to her heart, then to her stomach—"and in here. You know, if any of you had been through what I have, I would still believe you. I *trust* you all that much. I *love* you all that much. I find it quite disturbing that that trust is not reciprocated. Given your blatant unease, I don't think being in your company is the best place for me." And with that, she left. It took about two seconds for their parents to follow her out the door.

Casey put her head on the table and closed her burning eyes. Emotions welled up inside her. Honestly, she was pissed at Fletcher's behavior—annoyed even— but more than that, she was pissed at herself. Her little sister was in a fragile place, and Casey had just pulled the rug out from under her. The stress of the day, mixed with the knowledge that she'd let her sister down, broke the barrier, and tears glazed her eyes. Alex slid into the booth and placed a hand on her back.

Charlie stood a foot away, soothing Mack and holding Jebb in place.

"I've got to go after her," Jebb shouted.

Charlie whispered to him, and he nodded. Whatever Charlie said had made a difference.

"I hurt her," Casey admitted to Alex. She studied her hands. How could she be so dismissive of her sister when Fletcher needed her now more than ever? Was she subconsciously holding a grudge against her? No, she had forgiven her sisters...

"We all had a hand in it, Casey. Not everything is about you," Alexandra said. They looked up when their parents came back in. "You two tell Casey that no one blames her."

"Of course not, Casey," their mother said, using the tips of her fingers to dab away her tears.

"Fletcher is hurt both emotionally and physically," Pops began. "It takes time to heal. And none of us, except your mother, brother, and Jasper, were even willing to hear her out. So, no, Casey, if anyone's to blame it's me." He held up a hand, stopping the instant argument. "I didn't want to listen to what she was telling me. For the last few days, she's been trying to get me to understand her—to believe her. And I didn't." He sat down across from Casey and took her hand.

"I did the same thing, Pops," she said, squeezing his fingers. "We can fix it. I'm positive we can. We just have to find her. Where would she go?"

Chapter Nine

Ryan was glad to be home. He pulled into the parking space in front of his condo. It had taken them two weeks to get Jake out of the mess he'd created. One of Jake's most admirable traits was also his most frustrating; his brother would go out of his way to help those who needed it, but he never looked before he leapt. It wasn't Jake's fault he was a magnet for volatile situations, but Ryan was tired of having to bail his brother out. This time, at least the blame hadn't fallen on Jake's shoulders, and Ryan was thankful.

He unlocked his front door, stepped into the air conditioning, and decided his number one priority was to freshen up. Shower, shave, and put on clean clothes. He would kill for a cup of Charlie's coffee. He winced and started unbuttoning his shirt. He had put all that behind him. Who cared if he dreamt of violet eyes, dark hair, and soft skin every night? She'd said it would only be sex. That wasn't good enough. If he got involved with a woman, he did so wholeheartedly.

He went into the bathroom and turned on the shower. Shucking his clothes, he stepped under the warm spray. It took about twenty minutes to feel clean again. He put on his boxer briefs and slacks, then scraped a razor down his jaw to get rid of the shadow that had lingered there too long.

Ryan walked bare chested into his kitchen and

started making a pot of coffee. His home wasn't exactly as cozy as Casey's parents' house had been. Ryan preferred modern furniture. Or he had until those tricky McKay women had muddled his tastes with log cabins, quaint inns, and cozy mountain views.

He hardly recognized himself. Ryan shook his head thinking about the pair of jeans on his bathroom floor. Maybe he'd burn them. It would be a fitting end to the entire business.

He retrieved a clean mug from the dishwasher, glad the maid service was still working.

"I didn't realize the PI business was so lucrative," a voice said behind him.

Ryan jumped, dropped his mug, and hit his hip against the counter. Once his heart started to beat again, he took a breath and faced the woman in front of him. He would know those blue-green devil-may-care eyes anywhere. And they scared—no worried—him.

"How the hell did you get in here, Fletcher?" he asked, his voice hoarse.

"The door," Fletcher said, smirking. "You need better locks; those are way too easy to pick."

They were expensive as hell but worthless, apparently. He narrowed his eyes. "What about the security system?" She smiled, and he was taken aback by how stunning she was. He had to force his own smile away; she had broken into his home.

"Yeah, well, that wasn't much better than the locks. You know the problem with security systems?"

"No."

She grinned. "The people who have them usually put those stickers outside to scare intruders away. The thing is, it also lets the real crooks know what kind of system they're up against. It made my job a hell of a lot easier."

"You bypassed the system?" Ryan was intrigued. He knew he'd have to call the alarm company, but her skill was impressive. That talent would be useful in his line of work and hers. Though not necessarily legal.

"I'm standing here, aren't I?" She took a seat on the floor and pointed to his bare feet. "Might want to watch that glass."

He noted the mess and turned carefully to get the broom. After he cleaned up the remnants of his mug, he got another one and offered his little friend a cup. She accepted it with a small smile playing at her lips. He sat down in front of her crossing his legs and angling them in the opposite direction. Resting his back against a cabinet, he sipped his coffee.

"It's not as good as you're used to," he said, enjoying the confusion on her face. "I've tasted Charlie's coffee."

"Ahh, I was spoiled by it. But Alex's is the best." She pointed to him. "Never tell her I said that."

"Why are you in my home, Fletcher?"

"I need your help. Here." She reached into her overalls and pulled out a thick, rolled-up wad of cash. She tossed it in his lap.

He raised one brow in question.

"Ten grand should cover your fee." She laughed when he spewed out his drink. "I'm guessing that's a good reaction?"

"For what?" He usually made this in a couple of months, if he was lucky. His other investments kept him in the life he was accustomed to.

"Your help." She shrugged. "Like I said."

"That I understood. What do you want me to do...exactly?"

She took a sip of coffee, then said, "Find out who's trying to kill me."

"I—"

"Before I forget, thank you for, you know...for before. When I'd lost my ever-loving mind."

"You think this person is still after you?"

"Yes, and it's not just me either. It's my sisters too. Someone burned down the garage Casey just bought. Casey and Alexandra were inside at the time."

Ryan jumped to his feet and lifted Fletcher up like a sack of potatoes. "Is she all right? Damn it, was Casey hurt?" He shook her and set her down on the counter, none too gently. "Is she all right?" he asked again, his heart hammering. Any more of this, and he would no doubt have a heart attack.

"Casey *and* Alexandra are fine. They fashioned a rope and went out the window," she said, giving him a funny look.

Ryan let her go and muttered an apology as he began to pace. "They went out the window?" He could see Casey doing something like that, but Alexandra?

"Sure. Pops taught us how when we were kids."

Ryan stopped pacing to stare at her. "Your father taught you to make ropes and go out of windows?" The man had held a gun to his head...anything was possible.

Fletcher nodded like he had asked a silly question.

"I guess I shouldn't be surprised," he admitted. "Why didn't Casey come with you?"

She ducked her head and stared at her combat boots. "They don't believe me."

He knew it would hurt like hell if Jake didn't

believe him about something so important. "I believe you." Could he explain it? No, but he *did* believe her. "And I'll help you as best I can. I find people and handle infidelity cases primarily, but I've worked on a couple more delicate investigations in the past. I give you my word, I'll do what I can to help you." He picked up the money and handed it back to her. "Keep it, kid. I'll do this pro bono."

"Do me a favor, no lawyer talk, okay?" she said, then looked almost bashful. "Never mind." She hopped off the counter and bent down to pick up the coffee mugs.

"Now that's one fine ass."

"What the fuck did you say?" Fletcher shot to standing position, and before Ryan knew it, he had the point of a knife against his chest. "You wanna repeat that?"

"He would, if he'd said it, but that would have been me. Name's Jake, and if you don't remove that knife from my brother's person, I'm gonna put a hole in your pretty little head," Jake said, pointing his gun at her.

Ryan looked at Fletcher apologetically, and she winked at him. "He behind me at six or seven o'clock?" she asked. His eyebrows pinched.

"Seven," he told her, shocked when she grinned and put the knife between her teeth. Then she spun around with her right leg, knocking the gun out of his brother's hands. She came back with her left leg and had Jake sprawled facedown on the kitchen floor.

Fletcher crouched by his brother's head and slipped the knife into her boot. She winked at him again, then bent down to Jake's ear. He should probably go to his brother's rescue, but after what Jake had put him through Ryan decided to let it play out. She wouldn't hurt him. Would she?

"I would like an apology, Mr. Jake. Your comment was not only demeaning, it was ridiculous," she said and got to her feet.

"Sorry," Jake said gruffly, then maneuvered himself into a sitting position. Ryan enjoyed Jake's reaction once he got a good look at Fletcher. Jake's eyes widened and then he swung around to Ryan with a scowl. "I'm disappointed in you, bro. She's jail bait."

Ryan looked at the ceiling for help, which didn't come.

"I should've cut your tongue out when I had the chance," Fletcher said, then made herself another cup of coffee and turned. "I'm legal and a client. If I were you, I'd shut the—" Her gaze darted from Jake to himself. "You're fucking twins!"

"We're twins, no fucking required." Jake chuckled. He glanced at Ryan. "Where'd you find her?"

Ryan sighed. "BFE."

"You're identical," she said, pointing between them. "Jake's hair's longer, and his persona isn't as polished as yours is, Ryan. Jake is obviously the bad twin. Don't this just beat all!"

"You are correct on all counts. Fletcher McKay, meet my big brother Jake."

Seeing Jake taken down by the tiny female was going to be a classic tale to tell. Jake—and Fletcher had nailed her description—had never had woman trouble in his rebellious life. Ryan smiled to himself.

"Like that old show, right? *Big Brother Jake*? Charlie would eat that up with a spoon." Fletcher nodded, then hiccupped.

"I'm only older by three damn minutes," Jake complained.

Ryan laughed.

Jake turned to Fletcher. "What do you need help with, kid?"

"Someone's trying to kill me and my sisters. I need Ryan to help me find out who." She jumped up to sit on top of the counter, juggling her coffee cup.

"Sisters?" Jake's smile was slow and readable. The smile faded when Fletcher snorted and Ryan coughed. "What?"

"Jake, trust me, you don't want to go there." Ryan scratched his bare chest. A bit embarrassed he hadn't put on a shirt he said, "You two excuse me for a moment." He headed toward his bedroom, his brother's heavy footfalls following him.

Ryan stood inside his walk-in closet looking for a shirt, and Jake closed the bedroom door.

"Talk time, bro. Tell your big brother what the fuck you've gotten yourself into now?" Jake said, leaning against the door frame. "And stop looking at me like that."

Ryan couldn't help it; his brother's choice of wardrobe was disgraceful. Jake wore jeans with holes in the knees and a black T-shirt that needed to be thrown away. He seriously doubted his brother even owned a suit.

Jake cleared his throat, and Ryan sighed.

"I haven't 'gotten' myself into anything, Jake. Which, by the way, is a priceless accusation coming from you. I'm simply working a case." He chose a dark green shirt and looked at his brother. "It's the case you couldn't bother showing up for. Remember Alexandra McKay? Fletcher's her sister."

"You mean that locator case from a couple of weeks ago?" Jake moved as Ryan passed him.

"Yes, that's the one." Ryan tucked in his shirt and sat on the bed. "Alexandra sent me to find her sister Casey…" He brought Jake up to speed on the case leaving out the physical chemistry between himself and a certain gypsy-like female. Brothers, even twins, didn't need to know everything. Especially when said brother was Jacob Keller.

Jake crossed his arms. "That explains it."

"Explains what?"

"All those scars on her." Jake shook his head. "Poor kid."

"I wouldn't believe it, seeing her now. She's so…I don't know, vibrant, I guess."

"It's youth. She's almost ten years younger than us. Don't you forget it!" Jake said, pointing his finger at Ryan.

"I know how old she is, Jake. I can't believe you would think I would be going after her in a physical sense."

"Fine. Just so we're clear—"

"Don't let her age fool you, she's tricky. She broke in here."

Jake's eyebrows bunched. "Past the security system?"

"Yes." Ryan opened the door and headed for the kitchen. Jake mumbled something behind him, but Ryan ignored it.

"Did you two vote on what to do?" Fletcher asked when they came back into the room.

"Vote?" they said in unison.

Ryan took a seat at the kitchen table while Jake, after getting a cup of coffee, decided on the counter. Fletcher refilled Ryan's mug and handed it to him.

"You know..." She shrugged and took the seat across from Ryan. "A vote...on whether or not to take the case. You are partners, right?"

"Yeah, we're partners, but Ryan doesn't need me for this. He can handle it."

"You mean you don't want to get involved." Ryan sighed, then snorted into his coffee; so much for protecting "the kid." After everything he had done for his brother in the past week alone, Jake wasn't going to offer his help. He wasn't surprised; Jake did his own thing. Always had.

"You're not going to help us out?" Fletcher glanced from one to the other. "Never mind, we don't need you. Ryan and I can handle it."

"You can handle anything, is that it, kid?" Jake asked nonchalantly. "Those sure as hell aren't bug bites on your arms."

Fletcher sputtered.

Ryan took her hand across the table. "Fletcher, you and I can, and will, do this. I think you're ready. My brother has conveniently forgotten you could have killed him earlier. Don't worry about him." Ryan relaxed when Fletcher nodded and let go of her hand.

"What are you trying to prove?" Jake asked, hopping off the counter and standing next to Ryan.

"Who said I'm trying to prove anything? Fletcher needs my help, and I'm going to help her." What was Jake's problem? Was he being protective? "If you're going to add your assistance, great! If you're not, then

I'm sure you have something else already planned."

"Yeah, I do. Have something else planned, that is." Jake scratched his stubbled jaw and turned to leave. "Call if you need me, bro. I'll be around."

Ryan stared at his brother's retreating back, then turned to Fletcher and sighed. "Where should we start?"

Fletcher skooched forward in her chair. "Let's get back to Blue Creek. To the scene of the crime."

Chapter Ten

Why was he in the woods again? Ryan mopped the sweat from the back of his neck with his pocket square. He and Fletcher had driven back to Blue Creek late this morning and gotten in around three. They hadn't even stopped for lunch—coffee and supplies, but no lunch. The woman was a tiny dictator.

They had left her truck in Jasper's garage. The sheriff seemed worried, but Ryan hadn't had a chance to ask on it. They had left his vehicle at the edge of the woods on the opposite side of Blue Creek. It was a longer hike than he had taken with Casey, and his head was starting to spin.

He stopped when Fletcher turned around to study him. Ryan wasn't an outdoorsman. Casey, at least, hadn't mentioned anything about that fact, but Fletcher wasn't as understanding.

"A body would think a man who looks like you could handle this type of thing," she said now.

"Sorry," he said annoyed. "I was never a damn Boy Scout!"

"Didn't you play sports?"

"Yes, in college. That was almost ten years ago!" Ryan pointed out, reminding her he was not as young as she. He was in shape, damn it. He just wasn't a hike-to-the-middle-of-the-forest type of man. Being a PI required using his mind and quick logic, not hiking miles on end. He didn't like working behind a desk either, but this was getting ridiculous.

"You don't need to get in a snit about it. Jeez, if I would've known you didn't like to hike, we could have just driven out here."

Ryan stopped and lowered his water bottle. "I'm sorry...we could have driven out here?"

"Of course, we could have, there's plenty of space. I thought you'd enjoy the fresh air," she said with a laugh. "Your face is priceless right now—all red with mad. Have a temper, do we?"

Ryan composed himself while Fletcher smirked.

"We can drive up next time." She started walking again.

Ryan stared at her back for a moment, then, muttering a few choice phrases, followed her.

The cabin came into view about ten minutes later; it looked like heaven to Ryan. He hadn't been inside the last time he was here; the thought hadn't even occurred to him. Now, he was anticipating sitting down.

Fletcher hit the light switch when they entered. Taking off her pack, she motioned to the couch with her chin. "Take a load off, or, if you'd rather, there's a small shower in the back room."

Ryan looked to where she pointed. "You have electricity and plumbing all the way out here?" he asked, sitting on a plush chair after taking off his own pack. Heaven. He ignored the fact that he could smell himself.

"We aren't as far from civilization as you think," she said with a snort. "The power is solar. It's easy enough to get systems in place when you know what you're doing." She got up and moved to the small kitchenette.

Ryan turned in the chair to keep an eye on her. "And you do." It wasn't a question, but she confirmed it anyway.

"Honestly, the plumbing was trickier. I had a well and a septic tank put in." Fletcher moved to the fridge and got out two bottles of water. She threw one to Ryan; he caught it and guzzled it down.

"Thanks." He took a moment to look around the small, cozy cabin. The floors were finished in a cherry oak, and the furniture was tan to complement it. There were two other rooms not including the kitchen or the front room. Ryan got up to investigate.

"You built this place by yourself?"

"Not entirely. Some things are best left to the professionals. You're the first *invited* guest I've ever had here."

"Casey knew it was here, though." He turned toward her. She appeared tiny and fragile. What a joke.

Fletcher shrugged. "We built a fort here when we were kids. A few years after she left, I built this place. We all need that place, you know? Where we feel safe...at peace." She rubbed her arms and turned away from him.

"I know what you mean." He had had a thinking place at his grandparents' home. It's where he dreamed of the future. He regarded Fletcher's back; who was she behind the mask she wore...

"Go ahead. Take a shower. I'll make us some food, and then we can get started."

"You mean you'll start talking?" She hadn't told him anything of any real importance yet, and they both knew it. She nodded, and he headed for the shower. The sooner they began, the better.

Ryan took his time in the compact stall and allowed the hot spray to loosen his muscles. Once he was feeling more himself, he turned off the water. He shaved and put on clean clothes. When they had stopped for supplies, Fletcher had insisted he buy more jeans and T-shirts. The jeans were stiff and the shirt's fabric was flimsy, but he figured when in Rome.

Stepping out of the bathroom, his mouth watered at the delicious aroma in the air.

"What smells wonderful?" he asked, stepping up behind Fletcher in the small kitchen. He peeked over her head and into the simmering pot.

"Chili. I know it's summer, but I make great chili and I had some in the freezer." She swatted his hand away when he tried to sneak a taste, then shoved him out of the room. "I'm going to take a shower. By the time I'm done, it'll be ready to eat. Can I trust you to behave?"

"Yes, ma'am," he promised and sat his butt down. She was stalling, and they both knew it, but a few more minutes wouldn't hurt. She nodded and turned toward the bathroom.

"There's beer in the fridge if you want," she called out before she shut the door.

Ryan got a beer and ignored his growling stomach. He walked around the room looking in cabinets and at pictures. There was an entertainment center set inside the wall. It seemed strange out in the middle of nowhere. There was a fireplace and bookshelves. The titles surprised him, but he remembered Casey saying Fletcher had a high IQ. If she understood half of these texts, then he would have to agree.

The water shut off, and he sipped his beer. It was almost time to hear the full story. He turned around when the front door swung open. And there she was, the object of his recent fantasies, wearing jean shorts, a ripped T-shirt, and a lethal expression.

****

Casey stood with both the door and her mouth hanging open. She had been out running and decided to stop, as she had once or twice in the past couple days, to see if Fletcher had come back. "What the hell are you doing here?" Casey sputtered at Ryan. She never expected to see him again, much less find him sitting here on her sister's couch with his hair slicked back looking sexy. Before he could answer, a noise came from the other room.

"Ryan, could you please bring me my pack?" came the muffled voice from behind the door.

"You bastard! You brought someone here?" Casey accused. There was a feminine huff and a cloud of steam when the door opened. Casey took a boxer's stance. Then she was staring at her little sister, who was wearing only a towel and her tattoos. Her eyes flashed to Ryan, and her breathing became labored. Her sister? He was here with her little sister?

"We have company, Fletcher," Ryan said, walking around Casey to get to the pack. He sipped his beer and handed the bundle to the younger McKay.

"I see that," Fletcher said, taking the bag from him and turning back into the bathroom. The door closed with a distinct click.

"You're screwing my baby sister!" Casey said from between clenched teeth. She launched herself at him. She'd kill him!

Ryan met her halfway, catching both her hands. They landed on the couch with him on top of her. Hadn't they been here before? In this same position? Casey ignored her thoughts and ranted at him. She called him all the horrible names she could think of and again accused him of sleeping with her sister.

"No, Jesus, Casey! Would you listen to reason? Watch it!" he warned when her knee missed its target, hitting his thigh instead. She was surprised when he lowered his head and kissed her. She smiled under his lips before she bit him.

He leapt off her. "Damn it, Casey. Why'd you do that?" He went to the kitchen and grabbed a paper towel to dab his lip.

Casey shoved her hair, which had fallen out of its bun, away from her face. "You're having sex with my baby sister and you kiss me. What did you expect? A threesome?"

"I'm not sleeping with Fletcher. She's practically a child, for Christ's sake!" Ryan shouted.

"If you're not sleeping with her, then what are you doing here?" Fletcher had been naked under that towel. Casey wasn't stupid. She knew her sister had just taken a shower but so had Ryan. She tried to mentally feed the anger. If she didn't, she was afraid the hurt would show. Not that she cared who he slept with. As long as it wasn't her sister—any of them.

"He's helping me. He believes me," Fletcher said, coming back into the room. She wore jeans and a T-shirt. Her hair was in a braided bun at the top of her head. She walked in the kitchen to stir whatever was in the pot. Fletcher mouthed, "Sorry," to Ryan, who shrugged.

Casey controlled her urge to growl. "Good for him, you selfish bitch! Do you know what kind of hell you've caused everyone these past few days? Do you even care?" Casey was done blaming herself for hurting Fletcher's fragile feelings, or that's what she kept telling herself. She swept her hair back into a sloppy bun and shoved past Ryan to corner her sister by the stove.

"You have no right to call me selfish! I was gone for a couple days; you were gone *years*." Fletcher turned to face Casey. "And hell? How would you feel if everyone thought you were crazy? If the people you love and trust didn't trust you? Well, Casey, I'll tell you what, without trust, there is no love. So shut your mouth and get out of my face." She tried to get by, but Casey had a knack for making herself immovable.

She took hold of Fletcher's shoulders. "How can you doubt I love you? How can you doubt your family's love?"

"The same way you doubted it for six years!" Fletcher hissed.

Her words hit home, and Casey let her go, but Ryan caught her again.

"Fletcher, we need all the help we can get. You haven't even told me everything yet. I know you love your family—I wouldn't be here if you didn't—and they love you too; that's why I got involved in the first place."

"Oh, shut up, Ryan. This isn't any of your business," Casey said. Okay, she was being a bitch, but she was starting to feel things she didn't like. She met the intensity of his eyes and had to look away. He saw too much.

"It *is* his business. I made it his business. He believes me," Fletcher said and he let her go. "Ryan's going to help me find the person who's trying to kill us."

Casey sighed. "Someone was trying to kill *you*, Fletch. Not us."

"There is someone. Why can't you believe me?" Fletcher turned and went to one of the bookshelves. She removed a few books and pulled out a small box. She set the box on the coffee table and took a seat on the floor. She lifted the lid and pulled out a small stack of papers. "You want proof? Then here you go."

Casey and Ryan both sat down on the couch. Casey rolled her eyes when he made great strides to put distance between them. Ryan took the papers from Fletcher before Casey could get to them. His expression changed, and his face was a bit whiter when he looked at Fletcher. That couldn't be good.

"You didn't show these to the sheriff, did you?" Ryan asked. He shoved the papers into Casey's hands, then got up to throw away his empty bottle and get another beer.

Had he slept with Fletcher? No, he wouldn't have. Ryan had too many damn principles. She looked away from him, ignoring Fletcher's stare. Casey felt like the lowest of the low for not believing her sister when a basic stranger did. And that particular feeling only increased after reading her sister's "proof."

All of the warnings looked the same. Each told Fletcher to back off whatever she was looking into. Then they became taunting, fueling what would have been the height of Fletcher's madness. And then they were threatening. The last one sent a chill running up

Casey's spine.

> *Four little bitches sitting in a tree;*
> *one went mad, then there were three.*
> *Three little bitches awaiting their turn;*
> *two will watch while one will burn.*
> *Two little bitches left in the game;*
> *one covered in blood, the other in shame.*

Casey crammed the papers back in their box. "When did you get this, Fletcher?"

"Two days before the fire at the garage." Fletcher got up and rubbed her arms. She passed Ryan, who was leaning against the kitchen counter, and grabbed a beer from the fridge. Casey followed suit and also took a bottle. Fletcher turned off the stove, filled a bowl with chili, and handed it to Ryan.

"Why didn't you tell anyone before?" Casey's brows pinched. She ignored the agreeable noises Ryan made while he ate. "Answer me, Fletcher!"

"I wanted you to believe me! Trust me!" Fletcher walked toward the bedroom, motioning to the coffee table with her beer. "You trusted that…Not me."

Fletcher shut the door before she could respond. "Do you believe this shit?" Casey asked Ryan. She opened her beer and took a long sip while she studied him.

He finished scraping the bowl, put it in the sink, and turned to Casey. "I believe her."

"Funny that. You don't even know her." She couldn't hide the resentment in her tone. He shrugged and went back to the couch to go through the papers again. She closed her eyes a moment to control her temper and knelt in front of the coffee table. She wanted another look at the notes too.

"You're wrong. I do know her," Ryan said after a moment.

Casey looked up. "What?"

"You made sure I knew her, remember? What I don't understand is how you don't believe her or didn't until you saw these," Ryan said.

"She hasn't been the most stable of people recently. As you well know. She claimed her locket was stolen for starters—"

"Someone was trying to send her over the edge of sanity. God, Casey, someone wants you all to suffer. You read the last note. Doesn't it have some meaning to you?" Was he angry with her? That got her back up.

"I'm neither stupid nor blind, and I can certainly read. Fletcher was the first, going mad, as it were. Then the fire; the second to burn. But they couldn't have known Alex would show up—that wasn't part of the plan." Casey stood up and started pacing. "But we got to Fletcher in time, and Alex and I got out of the fire."

" 'One covered in blood, the other in shame,' " he read aloud. "Where are Alexandra and Charlie?"

"Oh, shit! You don't think—?" Casey whispered, standing and snatching the notes out of his hand. "God, Ryan, you don't think…?"

Ryan stood with a slow nod.

"Fletcher!" Casey hollered.

Fletcher opened the door. The knife gleamed in her hand before she slipped it in her boot. "Believe me now?" she asked, and Casey nodded. All three headed for the door.

Chapter Eleven

Ryan's grip tightened on the door as Casey sped around curves in the road. Why had he let her drive his baby? he asked himself for the twentieth time. Once again, he smelled of sweat, and his feet squished in his sneakers. He had grabbed his shoes and hurried after the two women; there hadn't been time to put on socks.

It had taken less than half the time they had hiked to get to where he had parked. He would have chosen the path back to the McKay house, but Casey said this way was faster. He hadn't thought so, but he hadn't argued.

Fletcher sat in back putting together some sort of weapon. He glanced over his shoulder. It was a rifle and a complicated-looking one at that. Ryan hadn't used a rifle since before his grandfather died. The old man had liked to hunt, for food, not sport, and he'd taken both his grandsons with him.

Hunting hadn't been Ryan's personal favorite. He owned a gun—he had to in his line of work—but he rarely carried it with him. He was a decent shot; however, he doubted he was half as good as either of the women in his company.

"Can't this thing go any faster, Case?" Fletcher asked while she loaded the rifle.

"Yeah," Casey said, flooring it. Ryan's knuckles went white.

They had called Charlie, and she was at home serving their parents dinner. Ryan didn't understand why someone would want to prepare and serve a meal when they'd been doing so all day. He'd voiced his opinion, and Casey told him that if Tiny was working, he was the one who did most of the actual cooking.

Fletcher had called Jasper after they tried to call Alexandra but got the answering service. They screeched to a halt in front of the B and B. Fletcher and Casey ran for the house the moment they were out of the vehicle, and Ryan was right on their heels.

They all stopped when a scream came from the apartment behind them. Turning on a dime, they ran as one toward the sound. A gunshot pierced the silence.

"We're too late," Casey said, hurrying up the steps behind Fletcher.

"No." Fletcher paused at the door and drew her weapon. With the utmost care, she turned the knob.

The apartment was dark for less than a minute before Ryan hit the lights. Everyone stopped. Ryan looked down and swallowed the bile rising in his throat.

Fletcher laughed. "I shoulda known not to worry."

Alex glanced up with a bit of a smile.

"God, Alex, what the hell happened?" Casey asked. She patted Ryan on the back, but he remained frozen in place.

Alexandra stood and kicked at the man's body next to her. "He's ruining my carpet," she said, shaking her head with a sigh.

"Ruining your carpet?" Ryan sputtered while he stared at the body. The man was about his size, plus fifty pounds or so. He looked up to find the sisters in a group hug.

"Yes, rude of him, don't you think? He tries to kill me, then has the nerve to die," Alex said, stepping away from Casey and Fletcher. Ryan could only stare at her.

"You know this guy, Alex?" Casey asked. She and Fletcher both stood above the body.

"Don't touch anything," Ryan reminded them.

Fletcher snorted, and Casey rolled her eyes.

Alex bent down closer and shook her head. "Never seen him before. What about you, Fletcher?"

"I don't recognize him."

Jasper came in the room and holstered his gun. "I swear, you girls can't keep doing this kind of thing." He huffed. The women stepped back while he motioned for the paramedic to check for a pulse.

"He's dead, Jasper," Fletcher said.

"We do things official 'round here, missy, lest you're forgetting."

Fletcher shrugged, but her cheeks pinkened.

"Call the coroner, boys! Got us a dead one here," Jasper hollered down the stairs after the paramedic told him what they already knew.

Ryan stepped back when Jasper shooed him out of the way to stand in front of Alex.

Jasper rocked back on his heels. "Well, girl, what's it gonna be this time?"

"It was self-defense," Alex began, pointing at the body. "He broke into the apartment and was destroying my things—Granny Vaughn's things—and then he attacked me."

"Sounds like self-defense to me," Fletcher said.

"I second that," Casey agreed.

"I have to agr—"

"Did I ask you, PI?" Jasper shook his head.

Ryan closed his mouth. He had never been at a crime scene conducted in this manner. Was this the way of things in small towns? He doubted it. He figured it had more to do with Jasper's relationship with the McKays. Alex made a sound between a sigh and a growl, which took him from his thoughts.

"Look at me, Jasper," Alex said, using her hands to encompass her person. "Have I ever appeared more like someone tried to kill me than I do at this moment?" Her hair was coming out of its perfect twist, her dress was ripped, and there was a bruise forming on her left cheekbone.

"Can't say as I have." Jasper took her hands so he could get a better look at her arms and swore a blue streak.

"It doesn't hurt," Alex said.

"It will," Casey and Fletcher said in unison.

"Your dad's gonna have heart failure for sure this time." Jasper sighed and pointed to the door. "You all know the damn drill; let's get it over with."

Ryan took hold of Casey's arm before she could pass him. She stared at where his hand was holding her and cocked her head to the side. "What does he mean 'this time'?" He wasn't reassured when she patted his hand and smiled. He followed her out the door, hoping to get some answers.

A half hour later, they were seated in the screened-in porch at the main house of the B and B. The lab technicians and coroner had kicked them out of the apartment. The rest of the McKay family had shown up. Jebb reluctantly took Mack inside to babysit, while everyone else waited to hear Alex's version of events. Ryan didn't want to miss anything, so he took a seat next to Jasper.

Charlie served coffee, then sat next to Savannah. All eyes were on Jasper, but his never left Alex.

The sheriff pointed to her while sipping his coffee. "Go on, let's hear it."

Alex sighed. "My two guests had turned in for the evening, and I was putting away the dishes from supper—"

"Wait! You cook for your guests?" Casey asked.

Ryan couldn't help smiling while the others in the room either tried to hide their laughter or, in Charlie's case, let out a few giggles.

Alex sat back in her seat. "No, Casey, I don't. You know very well I have no culinary prowess."

"Oh, I remember." Casey snorted and saluted Alex with her mug.

Ryan looked over at Charlie. "Do you prepare the meals for the B and B as well?"

"I did until I took over the diner," Charlie said.

"Alexandra hired a girl from the Internet," Savannah explained.

"The Internet," Jasper mumbled with a shake of his head.

"Kim is a chef," Alexandra explained.

"Tiny and I have been trying to steal her," Charlie admitted.

"She's that—"

"Can we get back to the matter at hand!" Jasper said, cutting Ryan off.

Apologies were muttered by the group.

"As I was saying, after my guests turned in, I put away the dishes, then came out here to sit for a while. That was when I saw the light go on in the apartment.

First, I thought it might be Fletcher," Alex said, glaring at Fletcher. "Then I heard things crashing, and thought maybe it was Casey, instead of Fletcher. She has the destructive temper."

"Oh, really," Casey began, but Emmit coughed and she sat back in her seat.

Jasper snickered. "Go on."

"I opened the door and stepped inside, but before I could assess the situation, the lights went out. The man grabbed me and tried to restrain me, but I fought back. He got in a couple of punches, then pulled out his weapon," she explained. "We struggled for the gun, and it went off. I guess you could say he drew the short straw; he's dead and I'm not... Then they showed up," Alex said, pointing to Ryan, Casey, and Fletcher.

"And why were you three coming here anyway?" Jasper asked, sitting back and sipping his coffee.

Ryan looked between Casey and Fletcher. Before he could explain things, Jasper growled.

"I saw that look between the three of you!" Jasper shouted. "You better tell me what's going on, dagnabbit!"

Casey pulled the notes from her pocket and handed them to Jasper. "Fletcher has something to tell you, dontcha, Fletch?"

"Uh, yeah..." Fletcher said. She got up and sat on the arm of Jasper's chair.

"Do I look like Santa Claus?" Jasper mumbled.

Ryan turned his chuckle into a cough when the sheriff glared at him. He tried to gauge the room's reaction while Fletcher told her side of things. She started from the beginning, using the notes as a timeline. The room was silent when she finished.

"What are the chances that the same night you show your sister and the PI the notes, someone acts on their plan and comes after Alex?" Jasper asked.

"I don't think he was coming after me, Jasper," Alex said.

"Then what the hell was he doing?" Emmit asked.

Alex folded her hands in her skirt. "I think I surprised him."

"Some surprise," Casey said, and Fletcher snickered.

"Sorry," they said in unison after their father warned them to knock it off.

Jasper straightened in his seat. "Either way, it's quite the coincidence."

"You don't believe in coincidences, Jasper," Fletcher said.

"Damn straight!"

They all took a moment to think about the implications, and something occurred to Ryan. "You came back today, Fletcher," he said.

Casey nodded. "He's right. You haven't been back since the day of the fire."

"They wanted all their pieces in place before they made their next move," Fletcher said.

"Or just you," Ryan said.

"I can handle myself," Fletcher said, causing Emmit and Jasper to stand and start shouting. They spoke over one another to remind Fletcher just how well she had handled things.

"Will you two please settle down?" Savannah stood up and went to Fletcher. She hugged her and whispered into her ear.

"What was that?" Emmit asked.

"Yeah," Jasper seconded and took his seat.

"What?" Savannah said.

Jasper hooted. "Don't play innocent with me, Savannah McKay. I know that's a big ol' bag of bologna!"

Ryan smiled at the mischief that danced in Savannah's eyes before she changed tactics. "If we're done, Jasper," she said, "I'd like to get my daughter to the hospital to be checked out."

Jasper sighed. "Go on then."

Emmit pointed to Fletcher. "We'll talk later, young lady," he said, then followed his wife and daughter out, hugging the other two girls as he went.

"I hate it when you do this kind of shit, Fletcher. I'm taking the kids and going home," Charlie said with a flushed face. She opened the sliding door and hollered for Jebb to bring Mack and meet her outside.

Jasper leaned toward Ryan. "I can't remember the last time I heard Charlie cuss."

Ryan shrugged. He didn't know Charlie well enough to have an opinion. The woman in question left the screened porch in a huff.

"Who broke Charlie?" Fletcher wanted to know.

"Broke Charlie?" Ryan repeated. What did that mean?

"Who, indeed?" Jasper mumbled.

"No one broke her," Casey said, rolling her eyes. "Even though I've wondered the same damn thing. Apparently, Charlie has a bitchy side she's kept in check all these years."

They all looked to the parking lot where Jebb was helping Charlie put Mack in the back of her vintage SUV.

Fletcher scratched her nose. "Who knew?"

"It's always the quiet ones," Jasper said, getting a snort from Casey. "Well...not always."

Ryan turned to Jasper. Something was still bothering him. "What did you mean by the 'this time' comment?"

"May as well tell the boy," Jasper said. "He could ask anyone in town tomorrow anyway."

Ryan didn't understand why neither of the McKay girls spoke, but he knew he'd get an answer when the sheriff made a big production of sighing. Jasper, no doubt, would fill in the blanks.

"Almost fifteen years ago, someone else was after the McKays..."

"Jesus," Ryan said once Jasper had finished. He stood. "What the hell is wrong with you people?"

Jasper chuckled. "Been wondering the same damn thing myself, for years."

"There isn't anything wrong with us, Keller. We had to do what we had to do to protect our family," Casey said.

Ryan couldn't name outright the look that passed between the sisters; it was loaded with a shared memory. Hurt? Betrayal? He wasn't sure, but something was there. "What have I gotten myself into?" Ryan said more to himself than anyone else. He looked across the lawn as the coroner removed the body bag from the apartment and put it into the black van.

"A mess is what it is," Jasper said. "Always a mess with these ones." He shook his finger in Fletcher's face. "Just like your daddy withholding information from an investigation. Causing a ruckus. And you a damn deputy."

"Ah, now Jasper," Fletcher began, but the sheriff stood, took hold of her arm, and pulled her toward the door.

"We're going to the station to see what we can do," Jasper said. "The paperwork alone will be a nightmare. We'll see you two later."

"Bye." Fletcher waved as she was hustled out the door.

****

Casey waited until Fletcher and Jasper left to turn to Ryan. "Where are you staying?" *Not that you give a damn, Casey McKay.* She didn't! His brown hair was disheveled, and a beard was starting to shadow his jaw. She met his eyes.

"I was going to stay at the cabin," he said with a shrug. He turned toward the window when headlights passed.

"I've been going out there for the last few days hoping Fletch would be back, and I noticed there's a path large enough for a vehicle, so you should be able to drive right up. I can take you there if you don't remember the way."

He turned back around. "Thank you, but I can find it. No need for you to go to the trouble."

"Fine!" she said through clenched teeth. He could get lost for all she cared. She shook her head and turned, swinging around when he touched her.

"Casey," he whispered and lowered his head.

Their lips met without hesitation, but their eyes held. She closed hers first. Ryan wrapped his arms around her bringing her body close to him. Casey took hold of his belt loops and stood on tiptoe to get closer. She slipped her tongue out and licked his lower lip seeking entrance. He didn't allow it. Instead, he pushed inside her mouth, changing the angle to deepen the kiss. She let out a small moan, then gently sucked on his tongue.

"If you don't remove yourself from my daughter's person, I will shoot you, son," Emmit said, and they jumped apart.

"Daddy! I thought you'd gone."

Pops stared at her. "I figured as much. I came back for my hat," he said, pointing to a baseball cap on the table.

"I'm twenty-six. I can kiss a man if I want to," Casey said. She was embarrassed, but not as much as Ryan, who was getting redder by the minute. The man could kiss too. She wanted to touch her lips to make sure they were still there but thought better of it.

"Course you can, Case, when I'm not around," he said, putting on his hat. "Now, boy, I'm sure you need to start heading toward wherever it is you're heading."

"Yeah," Ryan said, and he held out his hand to Casey. "Keys."

She smiled and handed them to him. "Are you sure you can get to the cabin safely?" Casey asked, ignoring her father's sharp intake of breath.

"Cabin?" Emmit crossed his arms over his chest and bunched his thick black brows together.

"He's staying in Fletcher's cabin." She didn't like it, but at least she wasn't the only one.

"What? You're kissing one and sleeping with the other one?"

"I am not sleeping with any of your daughters, Mr. McKay. And I have no intention of doing so."

"Son, the road to hell was paved with good

intentions. Remember that," her father said, but his lips tilted up before he left the house.

She eyed him. "Sticking to your guns, Keller?" He was the one who had initiated the kiss, after all. Not that she was complaining; she liked kissing him.

"I'm going to try, Casey," he said and walked away.

"We'll just see about that," Casey whispered to his receding back.

Chapter Twelve

His nose twitched, waking him. Ryan rubbed the grit out of his eyes and opened them. He'd found his way back to the cabin without incident last night. He'd shed his clothes and fallen into a deep sleep.

His fingertips found the prickly beard forming on his chin, and he sat up. Ryan checked his watch; it was little after five in the morning. He sniffed the air. Was that coffee he smelled? Fresh, hot coffee?

He went to the bathroom and brushed his teeth. He looked around the floor and picked up the jeans he'd worn yesterday. They were dirty, but so was his body.

Ryan followed the aroma into the next room. He found not one sister but four. Alexandra's gaze swept over his attire, and she wrinkled her nose. Well, you couldn't please everyone.

"Good morning," Charlie said, handing him a cup of coffee.

He sipped and sighed; she had fixed it just the way he liked it. Ryan took a moment to enjoy the hot liquid as it made its way to his stomach. Now he was ready to face the dawn and the sisters. "Morning, ladies. You're all up early."

And looking fresh and rested. Alexandra was wearing a khaki skirt with a dark blue camp shirt, while her sisters were in either jeans or jean shorts with T-shirts of various colors. He'd forgotten his shirt, he realized, after he noticed the women staring at his bare chest. Ryan went back and put on a black T-shirt.

"Better?" he asked when he came back into the room.

"Thanks," Charlie said, winking at him.

He turned to Alex. "How are you feeling, Alexandra?" She had done a good job with her makeup. There was only a hint of a bruise.

"No worse for wear, thank you."

"Okay, Ryan, it's time to fill in the blanks," Fletcher said from her perch on the counter. She took a gulp of coffee and looked around the room at her sisters.

"Where should we begin?" Alex asked.

"Try the beginning," he said and took a seat next to Alex. "That would be helpful." Another look passed between the sisters, but he let it slide. He focused his attention on Casey, who lifted herself onto the counter across from him.

"Be careful what you wish for, Keller. In the beginning, there were three orphans," Casey said, and he smiled. "Already knew that, did yah, private dick?"

"Casey," Charlie said.

"I did research, yes," he said. "I couldn't find your adoption records, though. Apparently, they've been misplaced."

Casey rolled her eyes. "Why doesn't that surprise me."

Fletcher snorted, then shrugged when her sisters all turned to stare at her. Ryan was about to ask on it when Casey spoke up.

"I was five, Alex was three, and Fletcher was two. We lived in a home for abandoned and orphaned children. That's how the three of us came together. Emmit McKay and his wife Gracie wanted to adopt a couple of kids."

"Dad, of course, fell in love with us, and we became a family," Alex said, her eyes meeting her sisters.

"A few years later we were introduced to Charlie," Casey said.

"And the McKay girls were formed," Ryan said.

"You forgot the part where Gracie died," Alex said.

Casey narrowed her eyes. "Did I?"

"Best to be accurate," Charlie said.

"How did she die?" Ryan asked, trying to diffuse a situation he didn't understand.

"Car accident," Fletcher said.

"That's one of the reasons it was a bit of a struggle to adopt Charlie. Dad was a widower," Alex explained.

Casey stiffened. "You know damn well that wasn't why—"

"I said 'one of—' "

"Cool it!" Charlie said and gave Ryan a small smile. "The point is, I was adopted, and the five of us were a family."

"Pops called us his little task force," Fletcher told him.

Ryan smiled. "I can see that."

"Much to the dislike of some of the people in town," Casey said. Ryan was surprised by the bite in her voice; he knew she loved Blue Creek.

"They called us the McKay heathens," Charlie explained.

Fletcher snorted. "Don't let the melodrama fool

you, Ryan. We lived up to the name."

"And then some," Casey said, chuckling, and just like that the tension was gone. The sisters relaxed.

"A couple of years after I was adopted, Savannah Walker came to Blue Creek to be the new principal of the elementary and middle school," Charlie said.

"And all hell broke loose," Fletcher added.

Ryan smiled when the sisters all laughed.

"Basically, her coming into Pops's life reawakened the hatred in a man who wanted Pops dead. He'd tried to kill Pops years before when he was in the FBI."

"Your father was an agent?" The man did have a tendency to threaten bodily harm...

"Sharpshooter," Fletcher said with pride.

"The short and sweet version," Casey began as she hopped down to refill her mug, "is what Jasper told you last night."

Ryan nodded. "You were there when your uncle..."

"Yes, that's when he gave Fletcher and I the letter," Alex told him. He knew what letter. Its contents held the reason why Casey had left. He didn't ask about it. They'd tell him if he needed to know.

"We hid it. But that's later." Fletcher shrugged when Casey accidentally hit her legs.

"Ma falls in love with Pops—"

"She fell in love with us first."

"Do you want to tell this, Fletcher?" Casey asked, and Ryan couldn't fight off his grin any longer.

"You're doing a fine job." Fletcher smiled sweetly, making Charlie giggle.

"She loves us and Pops. They have sex—"

"Tact, Casey, please," Alexandra said. "Who wants

to hear about that?"

"Sorry." Casey continued filling in the blanks for Ryan. "Our parents got married and then had the Bullfrog. Years later, I found the letter and left town."

Ryan nodded, praying he had been able to absorb everything. Charlie took his mug and refilled it before he could move. "Thanks. To start, whoever is doing this wanted you back in Blue Creek, Casey. Then they waited until Fletcher returned before making their next move. Perhaps, so you could suffer together."

"Duh!" Charlie huffed. "They want all their ducks in a row. Two birds with one stone kinda thing."

"Exactly! It's easier to get to all of you if you're here. The question is, who is this person? Who has a grudge against you? All of you?"

Fletcher snorted. "Who doesn't?"

If he didn't know better, he would say she enjoyed that fact.

"We've made plenty of enemies over the years just being us. Outsiders in our own sort of way. Some people still don't accept us. Dad was born here; so was his family. The McKays were part of the founding fathers of Blue Creek," Alex informed him.

"Does anyone stand out?"

Charlie shrugged a shoulder. "A bunch of folks do, but really they're harmless."

"I would have said the Thomas family, but that falls flat now that the prince of darkness is dead," Casey said.

"Who?" Ryan asked.

The sisters laughed and said together, "Ian Thomas."

"Besides, Marylou has some misguided hero

worship for Alex. Sooo…" Casey pointed to Charlie. "What about Mack's father?"

"He's no longer an issue," Charlie said, making Alex choke on her coffee. She didn't make eye contact with her sisters but continued to straighten the kitchen.

"Mack's your daughter?" Ryan had seen the child but wasn't sure what the story was. It was interesting. An absent father—identity unknown.

"She's mine."

"If he's 'no longer an issue,' then why not tell us who he is?"

Charlie crossed her arms over her chest. "Because, Alexandra, it's my secret to bear, and that's all you need to know."

Ryan was surprised when everyone left it at that. If they were going to let it drop, then so was he. "What about your parents?" Coffee cup in hand, he got up and started moving around; he thought better on his feet.

"No, if anyone were after our parents they would have gone straight for them. Most of the people here remember what happened years ago. They wouldn't risk it," Casey said.

"But someone *is* risking it, and in a big way. Hell, they could have killed me anytime, but they wanted to toy with me and you guys. Whoever it is, they're smart and they know us. What we're like, what our schedules are like, and they knew about my cabin. I know they were here," Fletcher said, putting her finger on the table.

"Everyone knows us and our schedules. And anyone could have followed you here, Fletcher. We don't have a clue," Charlie said and tapped her watch. "I need to go open the diner."

"I have to go too. Kim will be at the B and B any minute."

"That's your chef, right?" Ryan asked.

"Yes. You'll have to have a meal while you're here; she's an excellent chef," Alex said before she followed Charlie out saying her good-byes.

Casey stretched her arms over her head. "I guess I should go too. I'm meeting the construction crew at the garage, or what's left of the garage anyway."

"It's just you and me, kid." Ryan smiled at Fletcher who puffed out a breath after the door closed behind Casey.

"What is it with the two of you anyway?" Her blue-green eyes went wide when he laughed.

"There's nothing between Casey and me," Ryan said, but even he doubted the veracity of those words.

She shrugged. "If you want to delude yourself, that's your business, but I know my sister and she always gets what she wants." She jumped off the counter and patted his cheek. "Usually, by force. It's a nasty habit." She sat down on the couch and sipped her coffee.

"Why aren't you worried? Why aren't any of you worried?" he asked changing the subject. Fletcher looked almost relaxed, and the others were going on about their lives.

"If you let a crazy person control your life, then they win. Besides, it's your job to worry for us." She smiled when he sat down on the chair next to her.

"Your parents are worried, and Jasper's worried," he pointed out.

"Jasper's always worried about something, and our folks know we'll handle it. They don't like it, but they know." She jumped up.

Ryan shook his head. "Are you always this full of energy or is it the caffeine?"

"Bit of both. You go take a shower. Then we'll go see what Jasper's got on our dead guy."

"I like the way you think," he said and headed for the bathroom.

****

The sheriff's office was a compact building containing three small offices, two secretarial desks, and two jail cells in the back. The small box-like room that smelled like stale booze and vomit was what Ryan assumed to be the drunk tank. Fletcher's office was smaller than he had expected, but it suited her. She had a window, a file cabinet, two chairs, and a desk littered with notes and folders.

Ryan sat in one of the chairs and went through the police report on last night's events. The John Doe had been identified as Sean Johnson, a man with a long rap sheet. He'd served time for assault with a deadly weapon, robbery, and fraud, to name a few. A thug for hire from the West Coast. What was Mr. Johnson doing in the mountains of North Carolina? A hired hand? If so, then who was footing the bill?

It hit Ryan then: no one had assumed this was over. Not one of them, himself included, had thought for one minute that this was *the* guy. Because it was too personal? The person they wanted was too close? Probably; that was the direction his gut was leaning.

Fletcher was talking to Jasper in the larger office down the hall. She said he'd read her the riot act for not informing him of the notes she'd received. Ryan had a feeling that was putting it lightly. The man was hurt because Fletcher hadn't come to him. And from the yelling coming from behind his door, the sheriff didn't care who knew it.

Not that Ryan could blame him. He stiffened when another deep voice was added to the argument. He knew that voice. Emmit McKay, father with a gun. Apparently, the small sheriff's office let the community know its business.

He turned in his seat when the door banged open. Fletcher came out tugging on both braids and rolling her eyes.

"We ain't done with you, little girl," Jasper said coming into the main hall, Emmit right behind him. Fletcher stopped cold, then spun around.

"Little girl? That's rich. Jesus, Jasper! I'm not some little sissy girl, and we both know it. And Pops, I know you have a store to run," she said, turning back around.

"Young lady, we're not done here!" Emmit hollered. Ryan didn't look away fast enough. "What is *he* doing here?"

"He's helping me, Pops. What in the hell is wrong with everyone?" Fletcher asked, throwing her hands up in the air. There was a snicker, and Ryan peered around the McKays to see the secretary trying to regain her composure.

"Jasper, you're letting this boy in on an official police investigation?"

Ryan was getting sick and tired of being called *boy*. He stood up. "I'll have you know I happen to be a licensed investigator, Mr. McKay, and I have an outstanding record assisting the police. *I* was hired by your daughter to help with the investigation. Unlike yourself, I am supposed to be here. You can try to patronize me by calling me *boy*, but I am an educated and experienced *man*. I find your comments and actions toward me not only belittling but also disrespectful." He took a breath and caught Fletcher's grin. It gave him a boost. "I would appreciate it if you would keep your contempt of me to yourself. You may call me Ryan or Mr. Keller, not 'boy' or 'son' or any other nonsense. It's beneath the both of us." Ryan sat back down and picked up his papers.

Fletcher came in and shut the door, cutting off any comments that may or may not have been made. She hovered next to him for a moment.

"What?"

"You just put Pops in his place," she said with an awe to her tone that made him quite uncomfortable. She went to her chair and put her boot-clad feet on the desk.

"And no one talks to your father like that?" The churning in his gut told him they didn't.

"Mama, but that's about it. You know you did two things just now?"

"Signed my own death warrant?" Ryan was only half joking.

She laughed. "Pops wouldn't hurt you. I'll tell you honestly the first thing you did was add to his dislike of you."

Ryan groaned.

"But second, and more important, you earned his respect. Pops likes people who stick up for themselves, and you just stood up to him. Yep, you got his respect and his attention. He's usually not so pissy with people he doesn't know." She put her hands behind her head and smiled.

Ryan was relieved. "I helped myself out?"

"In a manner of speaking."

"Good. Now, what did they say to you?" He sympathized when she paled a bit.

"The usual." Fletcher sighed and put her feet down. "I have a tendency to keep things to myself. Jasper gets upset with me when I do that. Keeping those letters secret was dangerous, but in my defense, I wasn't thinking too clearly at the time."

"Do we know how you were drugged? Did anyone find out how you ingested it?" Ryan asked, sitting back in his chair.

"You see my coffee pot anywhere?"

Ryan looked around the room. "No."

"Ah ha!"

His brows pinched. "Someone tampered with your coffee?"

"The powdered creamer. Jasper thought of it. Beyond clever, if you ask me. Whoever the guy is, he's got balls of steel coming into the station, into my office, and poisoning me."

"No one saw anything?" He never used instant creamer, and this was a good reason not to start. He had to agree it took balls or loose screws to attempt something like that.

"There are only two deputies on the nightshift, and they're usually patrolling town, keeping an eye on things. The place is locked up tight when they aren't here. Of course, the locks are crap, which I've been telling Jasper for years."

"Broke in here before, did you?" He hadn't been serious, then she smiled. "You didn't?"

"I did. I was eight and wanted to take the unguided

tour."

"Did you get caught?"

"I did…once. I got grounded for a month too. Pops was beyond pissed and talked about sending me to finishing school." She shuddered.

Ryan laughed. "Finishing school? That doesn't sound too bad."

"They make you wear dresses in finishing school. I haven't worn a dress since I was a baby; even then, it wasn't by choice."

"You're kidding?" He looked at the young woman in front of him. She was truly lovely. Didn't she know?

"Nope, even wore a tux to my parents' wedding." She smiled when he laughed.

Chapter Thirteen

Casey wiped the sweat from her neck with her towel. The crew was dispersing for lunch. They had accomplished a lot more in six hours than she had estimated they'd do in a day. The lot was almost cleared, and if they kept at this pace they would probably be finished by quitting time. There was only a small wall left; the rest had been reduced to ash.

She thanked her lucky stars she had purchased an insurance policy on the garage before the ink was dry on the closing documents. If she hadn't, she'd be screwed right about now. The insurance agent said he would try to get the papers filed posthaste. He had come through in one week, which had to be some sort of record.

Casey stood back and took stock of the rubble. Starting fresh wasn't so bad. Sure, she'd planned on keeping most of the old equipment, but such was life. She glanced at her watch; lunch was a good idea. A tall glass of iced tea sounded damn good about now.

"Hey, Case!"

Casey turned at Fletcher's voice. It seemed everything was back to normal, whatever normal was. They'd talked this morning before Ryan had gotten up. They'd all apologized to Fletcher for not taking her at her word. Casey had done more apologizing in the last few weeks than she had in her life.

She squinted against the sun. "Whatcha doing, Fletch?"

"Not much. I wanted to see how it was going over here." She looked around, then back to Casey. "Looks gone."

"For the most part. We're taking lunch. Interested?"

"Charlie and Tiny are cooking and you have to ask?" Fletcher said while Casey walked the distance between. They started toward the diner on foot. It was only a few blocks.

Casey stretched her arms over her head. "Where's the private dick?"

"You mean *your* private dick?" Fletcher asked, tongue to cheek. Casey knocked her to the side, and Fletcher bounded back with a chuckle.

"Shut up! He isn't my anything."

"Funny, he said the same thing."

"He would." Casey rolled her eyes. "Where's the pig anyway?" Ryan didn't want anything to do with her, or so he said, but it didn't mean he didn't lust after her. Casey wasn't the type to doubt her ability to attract men. It was men in general she doubted.

"He went to the library."

"Why?" The Blue Creek library was small and musty. "Is Millie still the librarian?" Ms. Millie Mitchell had to be about eighty now. She was a tiny speck of a woman with white hair and squeaky shoes.

Fletcher smiled. "Yep, she's still peddling those damn true-crime books too. You gotta love that woman." They were both laughing when they opened the door to the diner. The place was crowded with regulars and the construction crew. They took the only remaining booth in back.

"What's Ryan looking for?" Casey asked after Fletcher came back from getting them drinks.

"He's going through old newspapers and that kinda thing. He said something about digging for information. Like we didn't tell him what he needed to know." Fletcher laughed then. "He told Pops off earlier."

"Ryan?" Casey sipped her tea. She couldn't see him telling anyone off. He was too damn polite.

"Yep, it was the funniest thing. He told Pops to stop patronizing him. He said, I'm an educated man, not a boy, or something. Put Pops in his place, saying he was an investigator with a good reputation and Pops was basically putting his nose where it didn't belong."

"What did Pops say?" Casey wanted to know. Her father wasn't the type to sit around and take that kind of talk.

"I shut the office door before he could say anything. But he respects people who stick up for themselves. He doesn't particularly care for the guy, but he can respect him."

"That sounds about right." Casey smiled and moved over when Charlie sat down next to her.

"Hey, girls. I went ahead and ordered for you, so it shouldn't take long. How's the clean up going?"

"It's going," Casey told her. Charlie smiled and jumped back up to get their order. She set their plates on the table and went to help someone else.

"She's the craziest one out of the four of us," Fletcher said around a french fry.

"Wouldn't catch me running this joint, that's for damn sure." They clinked their tea glasses in agreement.

"You got a thing for Ryan?" Fletcher asked, after she'd finished her lunch.

"Maybe." Casey put her napkin on her empty plate. "You saw him without a shirt. How could I not want him?"

"I reckon that's true enough. You making the move?"

She narrowed her eyes. "Why?"

"Not for the reason you're thinking. Hells bells, I'm not interested in him. I just wanted to know so I could prepare."

"Prepare for what?" Casey sat back in the booth and stretched.

"The fallout."

"What's that supposed to mean?"

"It means I like Ryan, in a brother-sister way, and I need to know if I'm gonna have to pick up the pieces."

"You think I'll hurt him?" Oh, didn't that just beat all.

"Not purposely, but yeah. He's the forever kinda guy, Casey."

"What in the hell are you talking about?" She kept her voice low because even the napkins had ears in this town.

"He wants the whole fairy-tale bullshit. You can tell."

"And I don't?"

Fletcher sighed. "Casey…"

"Maybe I do," Casey said. "I've never thought about it, and there's no reason to think about it now. It's just sex between two consenting adults. Why the hell am I discussing this with you? You're probably a virgin."

Fletcher sipped from her straw; a deep wave of crimson swept up her face.

"You are!" She looked at Fletcher, really looked at her. Her sister was…was saving herself? "I don't think even Alex is still a virgin, Fletch," Casey whispered.

"Will you keep your damn voice down?" Fletcher hissed.

"No, I'm not. Though, I don't flaunt that fact," Alexandra said, taking a seat next to Fletcher. "Fletcher"—Alex gave her a once-over—"you're an odd shade of fuchsia."

Fletcher sputtered.

Alex caught Casey's eye. "And why are we discussing my sexual exploits?" she asked as she sipped from Fletcher's tea glass.

"Did you know Fletch is a virgin?" Casey shifted when Alex dispelled the tea she had been attempting to swallow. A slow smile spread on Casey's face while Alex dabbed at her mouth with a napkin.

"Why, Fletcher McKay, I do declare," Alex said in her best Scarlett imitation.

Casey snorted when Fletcher tried to push Alex out of the booth. "Where are you trying to go, Fletch?"

"It's all right, sweetie," Alex soothed. "I think it's nice that you're saving yourself. You're not the type for casual sex."

"Shut the fuck up, Alexandra." Fletcher sneered. Casey couldn't stop her guffaws when Fletcher ducked under the booth to escape; she practically tripped over herself to leave the diner.

"What did you two say to her now?" Charlie asked, coming over to the table with a pot of coffee in one hand.

Alex leaned across the table toward her. "Did you know Fletcher's a virgin?"

"Yeah," Charlie whispered, taking a seat next to Casey and setting the pot down. A small smile played on her lips. "I think she's afraid of it."

"Why?" Casey and Alex asked in unison.

Charlie shrugged, then bit her lip. "Not afraid of the act itself, but the emotions involved. Her senior year of college there was this boy."

"A boy? I knew nothing about this," Alexandra said.

Charlie ignored her. "I can't remember his name, but Fletcher really liked him. Fletcher's a beautiful woman, but she doesn't do anything to bring attention to that fact. Her idol is an older, widowed woman. There's no sexuality there."

"Charlie, I love you, but could you cut to the chase here? The crew looks to be heading back," Casey said, pointing to the group of guys rising from their seats.

"Oh, fine. She liked the guy, and it hurt her pretty bad when he called her sexless. Fletcher doesn't handle emotional pain well, as we all know. She's afraid of getting hurt. She likes herself the way she is, but she doesn't think she's cut out to be in a sexual relationship with a man." Charlie took a deep breath. "Was that fast enough for you?"

"I—"

"You know, Charlie, I think you're in the wrong business."

"And why is that, Alexandra?"

"Because you can psychoanalyze people in seconds. Therapy isn't cheap, you know."

"You're right," Charlie said with a smile. "I should

have opened a bar."

"I think you both need to go get psychoanalyzed," Casey said, then got out of the booth to catch up with the crew.

****

Ryan was tired by the time he finally opened the door to the cabin. It was dark and looked like it was going to rain. He'd been in the library until it closed. He smiled as he opened the fridge and reached for a beer. The librarian, Millie, had told him more than any newspaper had. Hell, when it came to Blue Creek, the Internet had nothing on the woman.

He'd found answers to most of his questions. Millie had been exceedingly forthcoming, so he'd taken notes and recorded their conversation. She had told him some crazy tales about the "McKay heathens." Sipping his beer, he chuckled remembering.

Ryan toed off his shoes, put his beer on the table, lay back on the couch, and rubbed his tired eyes. His white tailored shirt was wrinkled, he had a bad case of five o'clock shadow, and he was starting to feel comfortable in the jeans he had on. These facts led him to one truth...he was exhausted.

He had gone back to the station to find Fletcher and had been told she was working out. Apparently, there was a full gym in the basement. The male deputy said Fletcher had insisted Jasper build it after the sheriff's physical had come back with a less than desirable rating.

Fletcher had been down there pounding away at a punching bag. Ryan was glad he wasn't the bag. He'd asked what was wrong. "Shouldn't have done that, Keller," he reminded himself for the umpteenth time.

Never ask a woman what's wrong because they might answer you. He closed his eyes.

"I'm a virgin," she had said, hitting the bag harder with each enunciated syllable.

He had stood there staring at her like an idiot. What should he have said? What the hell could he have said? He had just nodded, making no sudden moves as he backed away, and got the hell out of there.

Now he stared at his beer. What would Jake have said? No doubt Jake would have been vulgar. Better his way. He jumped when the door opened.

"Scare you?" Casey asked, shutting the door.

"I thought you might be Fletcher." He sat up, slipped his feet back into his shoes, and followed her into the kitchen. She was wearing tight jeans with a hole at the knee and a purple T-shirt that made her eyes look endless. The shirt fitted snugly against her breasts, and her hair was in its normal bun. He looked away before he could get any ideas.

"And that would scare you?" Casey asked. She took a beer from the fridge, opened it, and took a long sip.

"Tonight, yes, it would. She told me she's a virgin." Ryan hadn't expected Casey to fall over laughing, but she did.

She wiped her eyes. "I can't believe she told you!"

"She was in boxing gloves at the time, so I left," he said, smiling. He sat down on the floor across from her and leaned against the fridge.

"That was smart. I wouldn't worry about her coming out here; she said to tell you, you can have the place to yourself for the time being."

"That was nice of her."

Casey laughed. "Yeah."

"So how was your day?" he asked, then wished he hadn't because it made them sound like a couple, which they were not. But there was something about her that drew him, something beneath the surface.

"Good. The construction crew Pops found doesn't mess around; we finished clearing the site today. Then I had dinner with the folks. I brought you some food too," she said. Ryan stood and helped her to her feet. He backed up when she took the containers out of the plastic bag.

He was starving, so he grabbed a fork from the drawer and dug right in. "Thanks," Ryan said after he took a few bites. He glanced up to find her staring, but he looked away. There was something in her gaze he didn't want to think about.

"No problem." She moved around him to sit on the counter.

"Did you always want to be a mechanic?" he asked, putting some distance between them.

She nodded. "Since the first time Pops let us hang out with our uncle at Ward's garage."

"The uncle who died?" Something flashed across her face, something like pain, and he wished he hadn't asked.

"Yeah," she said, then changed the subject. "Did you get enough background on us?"

"I was researching the town more than anything else. But, yes, I did get a little more background on you all." He sipped his drink. "I was curious about something."

"Shoot," she said, but she seemed weary. He would try to remember not to bring up the uncle.

"You were in the system from the time you were an infant until your father adopted you."

She shifted. "Yeah, so."

"I was under the impression babies were, and are, in high demand."

"*Healthy* babies are," she said and sighed. "Both Charlie and I were given up at infancy, and we were both sickly, even as toddlers. I, like a lot of kids, fell through the cracks in the system, moved from one group home to another. Alex came to the home when she was two. It was just us for a year before Fletcher came; then we were together about six months before we were adopted. Charlie's the only one of us who lived with a couple of foster families."

He stood straighter. "Really?" He knew Charlie had been older when she was adopted, but he hadn't heard the history behind it.

"Yeah," she said and looked down at her fingers. "She doesn't talk about it much, and it's her business, so I don't pry. She was in one place for three years."

"But they didn't adopt her? That must have been hard."

Casey shook her head. "The woman she was with had filed for adoption with the court, but she got sick and couldn't take care of Charlie anymore. Again, Charlie doesn't talk about it."

There was something in her tone, not jealousy...but something. "Why does it upset you?"

"It doesn't upset me. I'm happy she wasn't completely alone all those years; the homes she was fostered in were good places."

He motioned with his fork. "But?"

She rolled her eyes. "*But*...she's our sister, and I

wish she had been with us."

"I understand." And he did. "Even though he drives me to the edge of reason, I don't know what I'd do without my brother."

She snorted as she sipped her beer. "Ah, the infamous Jacob Keller."

"Yes, that's the one." He closed the container and put his fork in the sink. He turned to her; he knew so much about her life, it was only fair for him to share something from his. "Jake and I were orphaned when we were eight."

"What?" She stared at him. "You never mentioned that."

He shrugged. "It's not something Jake or I discuss."

"What happened?"

"Our parents went out to celebrate their tenth wedding anniversary, and there was an accident. Their car was hit by a drunk driver. Dad died on impact, and Mom was in a coma for two days before…"

"Oh, Ryan," she said, reaching out to squeeze his arm. "I'm so sorry."

"Jake and I were lucky; our grandparents took us in and raised us. Sometimes I think it's odd Jake and I aren't closer than we are, but we were close with them. I spent a lot of time with our grandfather, talking about nothing and everything, while Jake spent those times in the kitchen with our grandmother. Then we would trade off, making sure we got equal time with both. They were wonderful people."

"You've mentioned them more than once," Casey said with a small smile. "I knew they were important to you."

Ryan nodded. They sat in comfortable silence, watching each other when the other wasn't looking, and then the window exploded.

Chapter Fourteen

Ryan covered her with his body. Casey was impressed by how quickly he sprang into action. In a matter of seconds, he had her off the counter and on the floor, where she now shoved at him to move.

"Will you please hold still?" Ryan hissed.

"We need to go check it out."

He nodded, rolled off her, then helped her up. They moved toward the window together. There was a rock on the floor surrounded by shattered glass. They both looked out the window.

"My fucking baby!" Ryan shouted as he ran outside. Casey hit the floodlights and followed him out.

She stopped in her tracks. His SUV was destroyed. All the windows had been smashed, the tires slashed, and the interior sliced to ribbons. Why hadn't they heard anything? "Doesn't that thing have an alarm?" she asked.

"Yes, but the damn thing kept going off, so I shut *it* off. Shit!" Ryan ranted while he surveyed the damage.

Casey dialed 9-1-1 and inspected her own truck. Nothing. Why leave her vehicle intact and vandalize Ryan's? She told the emergency dispatch to send the sheriff and Fletcher out here, then ended her call.

Ryan pulled a slip of paper out from underneath the glass fragments on the front seat. "Oh, shit."

"What is it?" she asked, coming to stand behind

him. He ignored her.

"Shit!"

"Find a new word, Keller. That one's been retired for the night," Casey said, trying to peek over his shoulder. "Fletcher and Jasper are on their way. What is it? What does it say?" She moved around him for a better view. It was a picture of Ryan, but he looked like a biker. There was a note on the back. The writing was the same as in the letters Fletcher had received.

Take care of the things most precious
to you, Mr. Keller!

"What the hell does that mean?" Casey asked.

"Whoever's after you wants me gone," Ryan mumbled. "The picture…"

She smirked. "Yeah, who would have thought you had a wild side?"

"It's not me; it's my brother," Ryan explained.

She squinted at the phot, then stepped back. "Strong genes! He's older than you, right?"

"Yes, by three minutes. Jake and I are twins."

"Twins," she hissed. "Let me guess—he's the devil-may-care type?" She gurgled a scream when Ryan grinned and shrugged. Didn't it just figure, she had met the wrong guy! She'd bet Jake didn't have any hang-ups about casual sex. Then the words on the picture hit home. She covered her mouth with her hand. "Oh, God, Ryan." The story he had told her about his parents spun in her head. She searched his eyes. "I'm so sorry. We dragged you into this and now…you need to leave." Casey started back toward the house. The nutjob was going after Ryan and his brother. He'd lost so much in his life, and now someone was threatening to take his only family—because of his involvement with her. She had put him in danger. She couldn't live with that!

"Casey? What are you doing?" Ryan eyed her from the doorway. She was mumbling to herself and dragging out his suitcase. He got out a clear plastic bag from the kitchen and slipped the note and picture inside. He turned when Fletcher and the sheriff jogged in.

"Where's the note, bo—uh—Ryan?" Jasper asked, walking up to Ryan. He took the bag and read the contents, angling it so Fletcher could read it too.

"Ryan, isn't that Jake?" Fletcher asked.

"You knew he was a twin?" Casey asked, coming to the doorway. Ryan sighed as she glared between Fletcher and himself.

"We had a little run in when I brought Ryan back," Fletcher said. "He's more balls to the wall—"

Ryan coughed, and Fletcher stiffened her spine.

"Hells bells, Casey, you're acting like you're jealous or something, which is just fucking stupid. Get a hold of yourself! I don't need your crap, and it's scaring Jasper," Fletcher said and stomped outside.

"Not scaring me a bit there, Casey. You're acting a mite strange though. Whatcha do to her?" Jasper asked, turning to Ryan.

"Not a damn thing! Look, I need to call my brother and then the insurance company." Ryan glanced at Casey, then took his new cell phone into the other room. By the time he'd finished talking with the insurance agent and yelling at Jake, everyone had gone. Except Casey. No, she was staring those icicles at him again. What the hell had he done?

"Where did Fletcher and Jasper go?" Ryan asked. The window was boarded up, and the scent of fresh coffee permeated the air.

"They left. You were in there for almost an hour. I gave Jasper my statement. You can give him yours in the morning before you leave," Casey said.

"And I'm going…where, exactly?" he asked and went into the kitchen. His temper was up as it usually was after talking—no, shouting—with Jake. His brother lived for this kind of thing and could take care of himself, thank you very much.

"You're leaving," she told him.

"Really? Where is it I'm to go?" he asked, caging her in. He was edgy and didn't understand what her issue was. The look in her eyes when she turned in his arms had him hardening against his zipper. Every time he was alone with her, all he could think about was fueling this chemistry between them. No matter how hard he tried, he couldn't resist her.

"I'm not gonna be responsible for some nutjob going after your brother. The brother you neglected to mention was your twin! You tell me other really personal shit but not that."

"You're not responsible for me or my brother, Casey."

He was gazing at her lips again. They were glossy and pink. She punched him. "Don't get all"—she waved her hand in the air—"all prissy with me."

"Prissy?" Ryan stopped rubbing his stomach and stared at her. "*Prissy?*"

"Yes, exactly! Like Alexandra gets when she doesn't get her way." Casey moved past him and went into the den. He swung her around by her T-shirt, and she landed on the couch.

"Let me get this straight. You think I'm prissy?"

"Yes, and you're always shoving me around."

"Shoving you around? I'm not only prissy, but I'm abusive too?"

"Did I say that? No! I said you're always shoving me around. There's a difference, Keller." She made to get up, so Ryan sat on her. "Lord have mercy, you're heavy." She shoved at his back and then giggled.

"Are you laughing at me?" He turned and pinned her, so they were lying chest to breast. He couldn't help but smile.

"Y-yes." Then she started laughing harder when he tickled her. "Stop! I'm gonna pee my damn pants."

"Really?" He was relentless in his pursuit.

"Ryan, I'm gonna pee all over you," she warned. He jumped off her, and she ran to the bathroom, opening her jeans as she went.

Ryan shook his head while he waited on the other side of the bathroom door. She really had needed to go. The toilet flushed and he stepped back, smiling when the faucet turned on; at least she washed her hands. When was the last time he'd laughed like this? To be able to laugh after the night they'd had—that was something, wasn't it?

She stuck her tongue out at him when she opened the door. "I should have peed on you," she said, brushing past him. He snatched her against him and chuckled into her hair.

"I was never the golden shower kind of man. Sorry to disappoint you." She laughed, and he hugged her tighter, kissing the top of her head. Then his lips moved down to the nape of her neck.

She stopped laughing.

Ryan moved his hands up from around her waist to

the hem of her shirt. Goose bumps appeared on her tight stomach the moment his palms made contact with bare flesh. It only took seconds for his fingers to find the front clasp of her bra. She grabbed his hands, and he stopped.

"Casey?"

She knew what he was asking because she nodded and turned around. She took a step away and walked toward the darkened bedroom. He followed, catching her shirt when she took it off and flung it backward. He dropped it next to where her bra landed.

The light was on in the bathroom, and the skylights let in the full moon's glow. He watched her back as she let her hair cascade down in black curls. She was a goddess.

Casey was trying to get control of her breathing. Her skin was too soft. Too tender. The door closed, and she exhaled. She couldn't see his eyes, but she knew they were on her—devouring her. Her hand shook as she reached for the button of her jeans. She slipped out of her shoes, glad she hadn't worn socks, and slid her jeans and panties down her legs. She stepped out of the pile of clothes around her ankles, took a slow, deep breath, and turned to him. She lost that breath.

Ryan stood naked in front of her. He hadn't just watched her undress but had joined her by taking off his own clothes. His chest was bare, except for the dark hair that trailed from below his belly button to the thatch surrounding his impressive erection. Impressive? All the moisture in her mouth seemed to go straight to the juncture of her thighs.

He was muscular; she'd known his chest and arms were, but so were his thighs and calves. She looked at his feet. In this case, that myth was oh, so true. Finally, she gazed into his eyes and stepped closer. She took his offered hand in hers.

He brought her body to his. Casey closed her eyes enjoying the feel of his skin against hers. She rubbed her body against him, then lifted up until her lips were a breath away from his. She leaned in to taste him, and Ryan's lips met hers.

Casey slipped her hands into his hair while his slid to her bottom. He picked her up, and she wrapped her legs around his waist. He walked them to the bed; his erection glided back and forth, nestling between her thighs. Their lips didn't part even when Ryan sat down on the edge of the mattress.

He ended the kiss and rolled so he was lying on top of her. Casey moved her head to the side as Ryan spread her hair across the pillow and bent to kiss both her eyelids. He worked his way down to her neck, and she trembled.

Ryan cupped her breasts, pressing her hard nipples into his hands. Casey moaned. He dipped his head and placed a feather light kiss to each bud, and she shivered. His warm tongue came out leaving a moist trail that chilled when he blew softly.

"Ryan," she whispered. "Please…" She closed her eyes against the sting that threatened—she'd never made *love* before. He bit softly at her earlobe, and her body hummed.

"Are you ready, sweetheart?"

"You don't need anything; I'm on the pill," she said. She didn't want latex between them—she didn't want anything between them. He nodded and shifted so she could open her legs wider for him. Casey loved the way his hips fit between her thighs. Her eyes didn't leave his when he raised himself up on his elbows and sought entrance.

Casey bit her lip as he entered her. She relished the feel of him inside her, filling her. She held onto his shoulders and pushed up making both of them moan.

"How do you feel?" he asked, moving his hips. He kissed her, then pulled back for an answer.

"Honestly?" Perfect. "I feel pretty damn good." She smiled and moved her hips with the rhythm he'd set. Drawing his head down, she kissed him to demonstrate what she couldn't express with words.

Ryan pushed completely into her, stretching her to a point that was too amazing to be painful. Every stroke sent tiny sparks through her veins and quickened her pulse. The sweat prickling her skin mated with his to slicken their bodies. His arms haloed her head, and he bent to kiss her neck.

Pressure built slowly at first, then was just out of reach. Ryan seemed to know because he moved a bit faster, a bit harder. He stopped for a second and moved so their eyes were locked. Ryan brought his hand to where their bodies were joined, and his fingers slid against her most sensitive spot, sending chills throughout her. He pressed hard back and forth with both his fingers and his hips until she moved eagerly against them.

Ryan bent down to kiss her softly, then pulled back and plunged into her fully again. Casey's entire body seized on one precarious cord, until Ryan's lips were on hers and she went over the edge.

Casey relished each delicious pulse of her orgasm as she quaked around him. Her own guttural moan echoed in the room. She squeezed her thighs tighter around Ryan's waist and invited him to join her in the ecstasy.

She was still trying to recover when Ryan began hammering into her. He held himself still inside her, and she dug her nails into his shoulders. His head bent back, and he growled with his release. He sprawled on top of her, and his heart beat against her chest. She wrapped her arms around him.

Once she had herself under control, Casey opened her eyes. Ryan's breath quivered from between his lips. They didn't move from the bed for what felt like hours. Kissing softly and touching each other seemed more appropriate.

After a while Ryan slid off her, sending shivers across her flesh. He lay on his side and brought her next to him so they were spooned together. He reached down and pulled the tangled sheet up and over them.

She stared at the bedroom door while his breath caressed her neck. Neither of them had said anything. And what would she say? She squeezed her eyes shut. Would she admit this was her first experience sharing this kind of intimacy with someone? Sex she understood, but this was…

Was this what scared Fletcher? This closeness you can feel with another person? Feeling like something inside you is no longer the same. No longer yours? Casey couldn't blame her little sister for her fear.

She lifted his arm away and got off the bed. "I still want you to leave." She made a grab for her jeans. He sat up, his eyes burning holes in her back. She fastened buttons and stuck her panties in her pocket.

"Casey?" he said, but she ignored him and left the

room, shoes in hand. He followed her as she slipped on her bra and pulled on her shirt. "Casey? What's going on? I'm asking because I sure as hell don't understand what's happening."

She put her feet into her shoes and stood looking for her keys. He grabbed the blanket from the couch and wrapped it around his hips.

"I still want you to leave. Tomorrow would be best." She found her keys on the counter by the fridge and walked past him. She wouldn't meet his eyes. She had the door open before he spoke.

He followed her out to the yard. "Why?"

"There's still glass out here, Ryan, remember? Watch your feet." She opened her truck and hopped inside. He took hold of the door before she could close it. She stared at his chest and tried to swallow whatever it was that seemed to be choking her.

"Damn it, Casey, answer me! Why? I think I deserve that much. You owe me that much."

That brought her eyes to his. "I don't owe you a damn thing!" Yes, get mad! Mad was better than whatever it was she was feeling. She tugged on the door.

"Are you telling me our making love meant nothing to you?" Ryan asked, his tone accusing.

"We had *sex*. And sex is just sex no matter how you try to decorate it." She lied with the precision of a pro. He stepped back, and she slammed the door shut, started the engine, and roared away. She glanced in the rearview mirror before she could stop herself. Ryan was standing in the middle of the woods basically naked, watching her leave. She looked away and turned on her CD player. She breathed deeply and let Three Doors

Down take her "away from the sun again."

****

The figure in the woods turned around with a wicked smile. Finally, things were going their way. It would have been nice if big sister bitch had died in the fire along with her ice for veins. But they'd been scared, hadn't they?

It was a shame about Sean though. Stupid fool. At least he'd accomplished burning down the garage, even though no one died. He'd been warned not to let his guard down; the McKays were tricky bitches. The figure sighed. Good help was so hard to find.

But Keller was leaving, and that was good. It had been so much fun destroying the private investigator's SUV, and it worked beautifully. People would do anything when they cared.

The plan had been changed a bit due to negligence, but things were looking up again. What came next would be worth the wait. "Four little bitches sitting in a tree…"

Chapter Fifteen

Ryan held onto the armrest as the tow-truck driver maneuvered his way through the woods. He had called his twenty-four-hour roadside-assistance service around six this morning; he hadn't been able to sleep, so he figured he may as well start his day. It had taken the young man they sent quite a while to reach the cabin, but who was he to complain.

He asked the driver to drop him off in town so he could wait for his rental car. His vehicle would be towed to the dealership; there was a body shop on site, and they would work with his insurance company. It didn't hurt that he'd gone to college with the shop's owner, who would give him a deal on anything he needed to pay out of pocket.

"You can stop at the diner," Ryan instructed the young man.

The driver put the truck in park, and Ryan thanked him for the ride as he removed his belongings from behind the seat. He shut the door and waved goodbye, then stared as his precious broken vehicle faded into the distance.

With a sigh, he walked into the diner; it was nearly ten and the breakfast crowd seemed to have thinned out. The bell chimed over his head, and he nodded at the few patrons in the back booths. Charlie hustled out of the kitchen, her wild curls, restrained in a ponytail, bobbing with every step.

"I wasn't expecting to see you this morning, Ryan." She motioned for him to sit, then poured him a cup of coffee.

He was wearing his regular slacks and a tailored shirt, the cuffs rolled up to his forearms. At the moment, he was more comfortable in his clothes than in his skin; memories of what he had shared with Casey wouldn't leave him alone.

Charlie pointed to his suitcase. "Going somewhere?"

He took a sip and let the coffee settle in his stomach. He needed the extra boost, and a reprieve from his thoughts. He could almost feel—

Charlie cleared her throat.

He shook himself. "Home. I'm going home."

Her brows rose. "The threat scared you, did it?"

"It's not that, Charlie." He rubbed his smooth jaw and sighed. No, he knew Jake would take care of himself. What was getting to him was the woman he had made love to last night.

The most intense experience of his life had been reduced to a one-night stand. Hadn't she said all she wanted was sex and nothing more? Why had he expected it to affect her as it had him? Casey was capable of caring; that wasn't the issue. It was letting *him* in that she couldn't, or wouldn't, do. He was a fool for thinking otherwise and for opening himself up to her.

"Casey?" Charlie asked.

Ryan inclined his head.

"Did you two"—she waved her hands in the air—"you know?"

"A gentleman doesn't tell." He left it at that, glad she did the same.

"Does Fletcher know you're leaving?"

"No!" Damn it! Ryan ran his hands through his hair. He had promised Fletcher he'd help her; he had given her his word. Unfortunately, that meant something to him. Ryan's gaze swung up when the kitchen door banged open. The man Casey had referred to as Tiny stood holding the door so Alexandra and Fletcher could make their presence known. How much had they heard?

"Figured they could hear better from this side of the door," Tiny said, shaking his head.

"Turncoat!" Fletcher hissed.

The big man took the towel from his shoulder, twirled it, and swatted Fletcher with it. He motioned toward Alexandra, who moved with some speed to the other side of the counter. Tiny grinned and nodded at Ryan before he went back to the kitchen.

Charlie topped off his coffee, then poured cups for her sisters and one for herself.

"Do you always listen in on people's conversations?" he asked, looking at the three of them.

Alexandra took the seat next to him. "In this town?" She glanced over her shoulder at the other patrons, then leaned into Ryan and whispered, "You better believe it."

"What did Casey say to you?" Fletcher asked. She walked around the counter, cup in hand, and moved his suitcase so she could take the seat on his other side. They had him boxed in.

"She told me to leave."

"Was this before or after you slept with her?"

164

"Alexandra!" Charlie hissed but leaned closer to hear his answer.

"Both, if you must know. Why am I telling you this?" He looked at them individually, then rubbed his eyes.

Fletcher snorted. "Peer pressure's a bitch, ain't it."

"That's one dollar," Charlie said and held up the blue Pay for Profanity jar.

"They didn't hear me, Charlie," she complained, motioning to the customers eating their breakfast.

"I did," Charlie said.

Fletcher huffed out a breath and dug a dollar bill out of her pocket.

Charlie smiled. "Now, was that so hard?"

Ryan laughed.

Alex rolled her eyes. "Can we please get back to the subject at hand? Ryan's leaving."

Ryan winced. "I—"

"We reminded him of his promise to help me, so now he's honor bound to stay." Fletcher grinned. "Right?"

"I'm staying," he said, but it didn't sit well with him.

"You can stay at the B and B," Alex suggested. "The events of the other night have spread like wildfire, and I've had a few cancellations."

"And we won't tell Casey," Charlie said.

"Really?" Ryan said. "And how may I ask will you do that? I'll have to be in town to look around and ask questions."

"Tell us what you need, who you need to talk to, and we'll bring them to you," Alex suggested.

Ryan shook his head. "It's not that simple." He

didn't work well behind a desk; he liked being out in the thick of things. You never knew what small piece of information would break a case. Besides, his work was primarily about finding people and cases of infidelity. He was a damn fine investigator, but this was new territory for him.

"Sure it is," Charlie said and patted his arm. "You have to have an open mind."

Ryan wasn't encouraged. "And when she finds out? We all know she will. What happens then? She left once, this time might not be any different. Are you all willing to risk that?"

The sisters looked at each other.

"When she finds out, we'll deal with it," Alex said. "I'd rather have her in a snit than dead. And, unfortunately, we *are* dealing with someone who wants us dead."

"Fine." Ryan looked directly at Charlie. "What about your daughter? Have you thought about that?"

"I always think about my daughter," she snapped and drew curious stares. She leaned in and whispered, "We've talked about it, and she's safe."

"Think about it, Charlie," Ryan began. "I want each of you take a moment and let this sink in. I've read every newspaper clipping about the man who was after your father. He didn't mind harming anyone who got in the way, including all of you. Your daughter could be used against you...and your sisters."

"He's right, Charlie," Fletcher said. "Anyone we care about could be used against us."

Charlie fidgeted. "She's with Mama now. I'll need to get someone to help Tiny here."

"I can spare Kim for a while," Alex offered. "I'll

call her now and see if she can do it."

"Let me go talk to Tiny." Charlie headed for the kitchen.

Ryan and Fletcher sipped their coffee while Alexandra spoke on the phone. He sighed when Charlie came back out front with Tiny behind her.

"Okay, I'm going to pick up Mack, get some things, and leave town," Charlie said.

"Where are you gonna go?" Fletcher asked.

"You can stay at my place," Ryan offered.

Fletcher snorted. "Not with that lousy security system, she's not."

Ryan glared at her. "My security system is perfectly—"

"Whoever is doing this knows about you too," Charlie reminded them and shook her head. "I know where to go, and I'll call you when I get there."

Alexandra hung up the phone. "Kim said she'd do it. She has a few things she needs to take care of; then she'll be on her way. And she said she'd cover the nightshift if you needed her to."

Charlie bit her lip. "I hadn't even thought of the other shifts."

"Don't worry about it now, shug. We'll take care of it," Tiny said.

"I'll stay with Tiny until Kim gets here," Fletcher offered.

"We'll be fine, Charlie. You go take care of that angel girl. Besides, I'm sure your mama will help out if we need her," Tiny said, giving Charlie's shoulder a squeeze.

"See, Charlie, it will all be fine. Now, you go take our girl to safety," Alex said.

No one spoke while Charlie grabbed her things and left.

Once the door closed, Alexandra turned to Ryan. "We should leave before Casey comes in and finds us out."

"I'm waiting for my rental," Ryan said.

"Just call and have them drop it by the B and B," Alex suggested.

"Good idea," Ryan said and lifted his cup to gulp down his coffee.

"Let me make you some breakfast. Everyone knows a body thinks better on a full stomach," Tiny said, then crossed his massive arms over his chest. "Don't give me that look, Alexandra McKay. You could use some food too."

Ryan looked between Tiny and Alexandra. His stomach was thankful when she gave a dramatic sigh and sat back down.

Tiny's gold tooth flashed before he headed through the swinging door. "I'll make it to go."

****

Casey helped her father unload the supplies from her truck. Pops had his contractor's license and had already gone over today's schedule with her that morning at breakfast. While she had been working with the crew to clear the lot, her father had been drawing up plans and obtaining the proper permits. She had been both pleased and impressed with his work. Everything was exactly how she had pictured it.

They worked all morning and dispersed at lunch. They'd made a lot of progress too. She sat on the ground and shielded her eyes as her father approached her with a picnic basket.

"Your mother requested I serve our daughter a lunch she prepared today!"

He took a seat next to her and opened the basket. He pulled out a small cloth to set the food on and handed her a plastic container of fried chicken. There were some carrot sticks, apple slices, and a thermos of iced tea. He reached for the antibacterial gel, squeezed some in one hand, and tossed the bottle to Casey.

"I know this wasn't your contribution." She laughed rubbing her hands together.

"True," he said with a smile. "Your mother has a thing about eating with clean hands."

They discussed the garage while they ate. She had always enjoyed her father's company. Once they'd finished, she sat back while he packed up the empty containers.

"I'd almost forgotten how good Ma's fried chicken is. I'm so full I might puke."

"Thanks for the visual, Case," he said, then waited a beat. "Jasper said he saw the PI's SUV being towed out of town this morning."

Casey winced. "I asked Ryan to leave," she said, then brought her knees up to rest her chin on. "Actually, I *told* him to leave."

"Why's that?"

"I had sex with him." She'd always been honest with her father. She could tell him anything. His body tensed, and his lips pinched. Maybe she should keep it to herself from now on. "Too much information? Sorry." She was about to get up when he shook his head.

"You can tell me anything, Casey. You know that. I would never judge you." He let that sink in. "But if that's the case, then why ask him to leave? I know about the threat, but if there was something between the two of you—"

"We're two different people, you know? I'm not a slut, Pops."

He choked on his tea. "I never assumed you were."

"I figured as much, but I wanted to make it clear. I slept with him, and I hardly know him." Didn't she though? Ryan was honest, loyal, and caring. And he told her about his parents... But then again, he was a suit and kind of prissy for a man. But when he touched her? When he kissed her? She shook the thoughts out of her head.

"Attraction doesn't always have to do with the knowing someone so much as the desiring them."

"What would you have done? You know, told him to leave after or..." She waved her hand in the air.

"I don't know, Casey. But if he cared, why would he leave without a fight?"

She groaned, then bit her lip. "I...I think I may have hurt him." She looked at her father, needing him to tell her she hadn't.

"How so?"

"Ryan isn't the kind of guy to sleep with just anyone; he's 'the forever kind,' as my sister put it."

Pops removed his baseball cap, scratched his head, then pulled the brim back down. "And that's a bad thing?"

"It is when there's nothing in common between two people," she said and dug a pebble out of the tread of her boot. "He even said in the beginning that it wouldn't work. He tried to be noble, but shit happens. He even told you he didn't plan on sleeping with me, remember?"

"How could I forget?" Pops mumbled. "Are you saying you took advantage of him?"

"I don't know, Pops. I mean, we both wanted to, but I think he thought it meant something more. No, I know he did." And it *had* meant something. Something Casey wasn't equipped for. Something that kept trying to choke her.

"The question is, did it mean something to you?" he asked, looking over when the crew headed toward them. He stood and helped Casey to her feet.

"I sent him away, didn't I?" she said and went to meet the others. They both knew it wasn't a real answer.

Chapter Sixteen

It was beginning to rain, but that couldn't become an issue. The setup was ready—any minute now. The waiting was hard, but worse was the chance someone else would come along. People in Blue Creek were eager to help, to be neighborly.

There really was a lot to be said for small town living, and, of course, small town gossip. Some concerned so-and-so sees something unusual, like Charlie McKay leaving the diner early, and tells someone else because something *must* be going on. If one didn't already know what was in the works, it wouldn't take long to be bogged down with neighborly curiosity. Had something happened? Had something spooked Charlie?

Ha, something indeed. Without meaning to, the McKays had provided an opportunity that could not be passed up. An inspired change of plan that would bring them to their knees.

A vehicle was approaching—a vintage SUV. Charlie McKay. Excellent.

Charlie rolled down her window. Such a good neighbor. "Hey, do you need a hand?"

"Yeah." Hook. "I think the battery died." Line.

"I have some jumper cables in back, but we have to be quiet because Mack's asleep," she whispered, motioning to the back seat.

"Thank you! I appreciate the help."

"No problem; that's what friends are for!" And sinker.

****

Ryan stretched and rose from the bed. He was in one of the guestrooms at the B and B; it was a cheerful room with butter-yellow walls and green ivy stenciling. He straightened the bed, then checked his watch; it was almost six p.m.

That's what he got for staying up all night. He made his way to the adjoining bathroom and started the shower. He took off his clothes and caught sight of himself in the mirror. He looked like hell. Shaking his head, he pulled the curtain closed and ducked under the spray.

About twenty minutes later, he stepped out of the bathroom, dressed and refreshed. Laundry was a priority, but first a cup of coffee to get him started. He wandered down to the kitchen, jumping when he found he wasn't alone.

"Sorry, I didn't know there were any guests left this evening. I'm Kimberly, the chef," the blonde said. She was a pretty woman with big blue eyes.

"It's Ryan, and I'm just passing through." Better she didn't think he was staying, in case she ran into Casey. "Got any coffee brewed?"

She went to the counter. "Always!"

"I can get it."

"Please, it's my job. Besides, I love serving handsome men. Gives me a rush," she joked. She handed him the cup and grabbed her purse.

"I hope you're not leaving on my account?"

"Don't be silly! I'm closing the diner in town

tonight, and I'm running behind," she said, making a production of checking her watch. "There's chicken on the stove and tea in the fridge. Guests usually eat in the dining room, but if you prefer, you're welcome to eat here in the kitchen."

"Thank you," he said, guessing that was what she'd been waiting for.

She saluted him and dashed out the door.

Ryan fixed himself a plate and sat down at the kitchen table. The food was excellent, and he went back for seconds. He had just wiped his mouth when Alexandra breezed in.

"It lives! Enjoy your nap, sleepyhead?" she asked. She fixed a cup of coffee, then sat down across from him.

"I didn't think I'd sleep so long. I met your chef," he said and nodded to his clean plate. "She's got my vote."

Alexandra smiled. "Isn't she fabulous? Now you know why Charlie's been trying to steal her from me."

"Speaking of your sister...has she called yet?"

"Not yet, but she told Mama she was going to take her time and try and make the trip fun for Mack. She said she'd call first thing in the morning. Apparently, it takes a long time to get there. Wherever *there* is." Alexandra's tone was annoyed, but Ryan knew she was worried.

"I'm sure she's fine."

"I hear that brother of yours is actually your twin."

Ryan shrugged and tried to ignore the once-over she gave him.

"Are you in love with my sister? If you are, you're not as intelligent as I had you pegged to be."

Ryan choked on his coffee and took the napkin Alex handed him. "Are sisters always so nosy?"

"Yes. Are you in love with Casey?"

"I have feelings for her, yes."

She faced the window and whispered, "You're a fool then, Ryan."

"I'm well aware, thank you," he admitted rubbing his forehead. He needed to talk to somebody. He had called Jake before he'd taken his nap, but all his brother had said was "Get over it, bro. Lust is lust." But it was deeper than the physical. "Have you ever been in love?"

"I'm not foolish."

"Noted." He turned quickly when a noise came from the pantry. Fletcher stepped out with a sheepish shrug.

"Fletcher McKay!" Alexandra hissed. "What have I told you about hiding in the passageways?"

Fletcher grunted, fixed herself a cup of coffee, and winked at Ryan.

"Wait, did you just say—"

"This place has hidden rooms and secret passageways. The gentleman who built the house was a bit paranoid," Alexandra explained.

"I see," he said, though he didn't. He was becoming much better acquainted with the idea of not understanding the McKay women. He looked at Fletcher, who was staring at him with eyes more stormy green than blue. "What?"

"I heard whatcha said. You wanna talk about it?" she asked.

Ryan sat back in his chair. "What is it you want me to say?"

"Sometimes it's easier to understand your feelings

when you open up about them."

"And how would you know?"

"I know things, Alexandra." Fletcher smirked and turned to Ryan. "Go ahead, speak freely."

Ryan eyed the women for a moment, then sighed. In for a penny… "When I'm with Casey, I feel like I'm a part of something important. She gets under my skin most of the time, and she's infuriating, but I still feel good about it. I seem to enjoy watching her throw a temper tantrum."

They burst out laughing, and he smiled.

"You've got it bad," Alex said.

"It isn't just the sex?" Fletcher asked.

Ryan squirmed. "Casey thinks it is, but that's not what happened last night." Had it only been last night?

"No?" Alexandra asked.

He shook his head. "It was…more than I've ever shared with anyone. Sorry, I sound pathetic."

Fletcher patted his hand. "You stood up to Pops, and no one stands up to Pops. You're keeping your promise to me, and that's honorable. Most men are afraid of the word 'emotions,' let alone admitting they have any. I myself have nothing but respect for you."

"Fletcher's right, Ryan. You may be foolish, but having feelings doesn't make you less of a man. And you're not pathetic! Casey has a hard time with emotions, and she doesn't like depending on anyone. Let's not even talk about her trust issues."

"She told me to leave. She said last night didn't mean anything to her." It had been like a hit to the solar plexus.

"And you still have feelings for her?" Alex asked.

"It's not something you can turn off."

Alex raised a brow. "Of course, you can!"

He shook his head. "There was a moment last night when I was tickling her when she let her guard down. I swear I could see who she really is." Not the hard shell she projected but the breathtaking pearl inside. She had been within reach. Attainable. Beautiful. His.

"Did you know Casey was ticklish?" Alexandra asked Fletcher, ignoring the latter half of his comment.

"Nope. You?"

"You're kidding, right?" The sisters smiled at each other.

Headlights flashed across the window as a truck pulled into one of the rear parking spaces, and they all jumped.

"It's Casey. Go upstairs, Ryan, before she sees you," Alexandra advised. He didn't wait for her to say it again.

****

Casey walked up the steps, shaking out her hair. The damn rain had put a hold on work. She had hung out with Pops and the Bullfrog at the hardware store for the rest of the day. Her mother had shown up and filled them in on the Charlie and Mack situation.

Casey was in a bad mood, and she knew she had no one to blame but herself. She shouldn't have sent Ryan away. Even knowing things between them probably wouldn't work out, she had liked having him here. Liked him in her corner. Hell, she even wanted to talk to him about the goings on of the day, and she was by no means a conversationalist.

She opened the side door. She was losing her mind! She thought she smelled Ryan's aftershave. It wasn't a woodsy scent like Pops always wore; no, it was a powdery masculine smell. She loved the way he smelled.

"We're in the kitchen," Fletcher called out. Casey took off her boots and headed in that direction.

"Got any beer in this place?" she asked, annoyed when Alexandra shook her head. "Figures." She grabbed a mug and had coffee instead. It would probably keep her up, not that she would be able to sleep anyway. She sat down and pointed to the unaccompanied mug on the table. "Someone else here?"

"One of the guests just went upstairs," Alex said. "Let me fix that for you." Alex motioned to Casey's hair. Without a word, Casey sat while her sister went to work on a french braid.

"Thanks," Casey said smiling. Not that she would ever admit it, but one of the things she'd missed most was having her sisters play with her hair.

"You're welcome," Alex said, taking her seat. "How's everything at the garage?"

"It was going fine until the rain started and didn't have the courtesy to stop. I went with Pops to the store. Ma told me Charlie left town." She paused and pursed her lips. "Would have been nice of one of you to tell me, but at least someone thought to. Whose bright idea was it anyway?"

"Ryan's," Fletcher said and winced.

"He stopped by the diner before he left," Alex said. "We talked, and he said that Mack could be used against us. We agreed, and Charlie decided it was best to leave."

"Oh," Casey muttered. She was glad he was gone. That little jump in her system was hormone related, nothing more.

"Whatcha do to him anyway?" Fletcher asked as she fiddled with one of her braids.

"Whadyah mean *do*?" Casey didn't like the way they were staring at her.

"She's asking why Ryan left," Alex said, getting up to pour out her coffee and replace it with iced tea.

Casey sighed. "I asked him to leave." She toyed with the handle of her coffee cup. It had been easy to talk to Pops about this. And wasn't that strange. She'd always been able to talk to her sisters before; maybe she wasn't ready to open up completely. Who knew what else could come out if she did?

"That's it? You asked him to leave and he did?"

"You don't see him here, do you, Alex? Damn it," she grumbled and got up to pace. "We had sex last night, okay. He's the forever kind; remember you even said so, Fletch. He's the forever kind, and I'm not."

"You know, Casey, this all goes back to the home—to those rats."

"Will you shut the fuck up about the rats, Alexandra! Not everything is about the damn rats."

"You know what, Casey, I'm about two seconds shy of kicking you out. Now sit down and shut up. For once in your life you're going to listen to what *I* have to say, whether you like it or not!" Alex hissed.

Casey shut up and sat down.

Alexandra patted her bun and pointed to Fletcher, whose mouth was hanging open. "Not a word from you either!"

Fletcher held up her hands in mock surrender.

Alexandra took a breath. "Fletcher and I went back to the home a while ago. We'd wanted to see it—it's abandoned now. Fletcher picked the lock, and we had the grand tour down memory lane," she said, then sipped her tea. "We ran into a woman who's lived across the street for thirty years, and she told us the home was closed the same year we were adopted."

"What does this have to do with anything?" Casey didn't want to hear this. What was the point?

"Fletcher and I went to public records and found it was closed not two months after we left. We dug deeper and found the social worker who worked the case. We asked her what had happened, and she told us one of the children was taken to the hospital after getting bitten by rats. Miss Tina—you remember her—had found your replacement, but this kid wasn't you. Do you remember the little girl who slept in the cot next to us?"

Casey rubbed her face. "Yeah, I remember. Her name was Lee."

"Exactly. The social worker was assigned to the case and was horrified by what she'd found. Want to know what it was?"

Bile rose in Casey's throat, but she swallowed it. All the other kids had been terrified of the rats; she had been too at first, but she'd kept her mouth shut. She remembered little Lee; the girl was a whiner, always complaining about something. Casey had suspected the girl was a tattletale because Lee always got the best stuff. But goodness, she was in no way—

"They hired professionals to deal with the problem, but the exterminators couldn't find the source of the infestation. The social worker said they were already bringing charges against Miss Tina for endangerment, but then they talked to the kids. They told her about you always having to go down there, and the social worker got suspicious. They searched Miss Tina's private home, and she found the missing piece."

Casey looked up from where she'd been staring a hole into the table. She met Alex's gaze.

"Miss Tina's home was full of caged rats. She bred them and put them in the basement herself. The social worker said she asked why she did it, and Miss Tina told her it was how she kept everyone in line. It was how she controlled us. The woman wasn't mentally stable, Casey." Alex reached across the table and took both of Casey's hands.

"But why? Why would she do that?" Casey whispered. It didn't make sense.

"We didn't understand either, Casey, so I dug deeper," Fletcher said and sniffed. "I met this woman head doctor, and I told her about the rats. We discussed several different scenarios, and one rang true for me. Rats are associated with filth, disgust, even death. They also tend to instill fear in people. By using rats, Miss Tina could control us. She sent you to the basement because you weren't scared, and she needed you to be afraid to keep the upper hand."

"But…" Casey prompted.

"She couldn't control you with fear, so she played on your humanity. She brought in the baby rats to ensure you would get attached to them; who could be hardened against a teeny, tiny little thing? You stopped seeing them as everyone else did. To you, they were harmless creatures trying to survive—like we were. Miss Tina threatened punishment unless you set the traps; she made you kill the very creatures you identified with and wanted to protect. Subconsciously, you were killing not only yourself, but us as well.

That's why you're always quick to take the blame, and why you're so untrusting; deep down you still feel guilty for betraying the rats. She couldn't control you, Casey, but she sure as hell fucked with your head…your heart. That's how she got you, and you're letting the bitch win."

"Do you hear yourself? This is crazy! You're trying to tell me I feel guilty for killing rats. They were rats, for Christ's sake," Casey shouted pulling away from Alex and pinching the bridge of her nose.

"You bonded with them. Unwanted and unloved creatures. Why am I the only one who can understand this shit?" Fletcher said, shaking her head. "Think about it, Casey. Why aren't you worthy of the forever kind of love? Why did it take you years to accept that Pops loves you? Then Mama? You could accept us and our love because we're like you. Like those damn rats— unwanted, unclean, and unlovable. But here's the fucking news flash, Casey. You aren't like them. You *are* wanted, and you *are* loved! So get out of the fucking basement, and face reality!" Fletcher stomped out of the house and slammed the door.

"She *is* highly intelligent, you know?" Alexandra said after a moment.

Casey was still staring after Fletcher, but she smiled when she turned back to Alex. It was a small smile. "Kind of hard to remember when every other word is the f-bomb, though." Casey let out a shaky breath and sat back down. Alex pulled a bottle of whiskey from the cupboard. "I thought you said you didn't have—"

"I don't have any beer. You didn't ask the right question." Alex opened the bottle and poured two small glasses of the amber liquid. She handed one to Casey and took a seat.

"Thanks."

"Here's to the rats of the world," Alexandra toasted, clinking glasses with Casey.

The whiskey sent a fireball through Casey's bloodstream, but it felt good. In a matter of minutes, her life had been psychoanalyzed by her kid sister. Was what she said true? Did she feel deep down she was unworthy of love? Had everything in her life, her very personality, led back to that dirty basement? She looked at Alex. "I love you, Alexandra," she said on a sigh.

"I know, Casey. I love you too. And God knows Fletcher loves you. She wouldn't expose her genius if she didn't." They both laughed, then took another shot of whiskey.

"Burns like hell." Casey capped the bottle and sat back. "What happened to Miss Tina? You said she was charged with endangerment. Was that it?"

"No. After they found the rats, they brought her up on multiple charges. She died three years later in a mental institution. She was a sick woman, Casey. Fletcher's right; you have to stop letting her win."

"It's all kind of spinning in my head, to tell you the truth. I had nightmares for years, still do sometimes. About the basement, I mean; I was never afraid of Miss Tina, not really."

"You weren't?"

"No, not in a physical sense. She never hurt any of us. Hell, she wasn't even all that mean."

"It was psychological."

"Yeah, I was afraid she'd take you and Fletcher away." And she'd be alone.

"You've never said."

"I've always felt like our lives started when Pops adopted us, but I guess you just don't know what shapes you as a person." She looked at her sister. "I'm scared now, Alex." The words felt funny coming out of her mouth, but there they were.

"We're all scared, Casey. It's nothing to be ashamed of. We have some unhinged person after us, and that's scary. Charlie's afraid of too many things to name. I can't even begin to imagine what exactly scares Fletcher, because who in the world understands Fletcher. You're afraid of being weak, and though you may not admit it, you're scared of being alone."

"And what is Alexandra McKay's afraid of?" Casey wanted to know now that she felt bare.

"Let's see. What am I afraid of?"

****

Casey wrestled with her sister's admission the entire way home. Her sister was afraid of herself. "Must you always be so damn cryptic, Alexandra?" she muttered as she let herself in the house.

Her parents were sitting at the kitchen table talking. They stopped when she walked in.

"What are you two doing up?" It was late for them. They were usually in bed by now. She didn't want to know if it was actually to sleep.

"Hoping Charlie will call."

"I thought you said she'd call in the morning if she got there too late." Casey's stomach turned over. Hadn't they said that?

"I can still worry," her mother said, and Pops nodded.

Casey sat down and rested her head on her arms.

"I'm glad you two are up. I want to talk to you about something."

"What is it, Casey?" her father asked.

"Basements and rats, Pops. Basements and rats."

Chapter Seventeen

Casey woke to the buzzing of her alarm. She threw out her arm feeling around with her fingers until she landed on the snooze button. Ten minutes later, she groaned when the incessant noise started again. She turned it off and tried to open her eyes.

"Damn it," she huffed. She'd left her contacts in. It wouldn't be a problem if she used the brand you could sleep in, but she didn't. Good going! She forced her dry eyes open and went to the bathroom. After emptying her bladder and washing her hands, she reached for the re-wetting drops and flooded her eyes with the stuff.

"It's a good thing they didn't roll back in my head." She snickered and peeled the lens out of each eye, then put them in their individual spaces. She brushed her teeth and turned the shower on full blast. Once steam was filling the room, she got in and started to sing the first few bars of "9 to 5" while she lathered her face. Who couldn't relate to Dolly Parton?

She didn't linger long in the comforting heat of the spray but finished post haste and patted herself dry. She slipped on her robe and, once she'd located her glasses, combed her hair.

She smiled in the mirror when she remembered her parents' outrage last night. She'd never told anyone about the basement. Well, no one other than Charlie; Alex and Fletcher had been there. Pops had nearly woken Jebb up with his yelling.

"Why the hell didn't you ever tell me? Damn it, Casey, I could have done something about it," he shouted, pacing around like a caged bull.

Ma had understood. After all these years, it still surprised Casey that her mother understood her and her sisters. It had taken a while for her to accept she loved Savannah Walker; she'd given the woman a hell of a time, not that Ma let her forget it.

She laughed to herself as she made her way to her bedroom. She went to her closet to get her usual uniform of T-shirt and jeans. The sky was hazy this morning, and she hoped it didn't rain again.

Today, she would put the past behind her and start fresh. Or that was the plan, at least. She wished starting over with Ryan were an option. "If wishes were raindrops and all that," she muttered and made her way downstairs where her sisters and parents were.

Fletcher had stayed wherever it was she stayed when she wasn't here. Jasper's perhaps, or maybe the cabin now that Ryan was gone? Casey winced. The sheets needed to be cleaned on Fletcher's bed. Maybe she could hint to her sister that she should do some laundry. Casey knew she should do it herself, but she couldn't go back there. Not right now, anyway.

She went through the swinging kitchen door and was startled when a cup of coffee was shoved in her face. Taking the cup out of Alexandra's hand, she made her way to the table. Fletcher was sitting in the window seat reading the paper. Casey took a seat across from her father, who was also reading a portion of the paper. Alexandra was whispering to their mother. Probably making sure she looked good, Casey suspected. Her sister was the prissiest person she knew. Well, prissiest female; Ryan was up there on the list of prissy men. Not that she was thinking about him.

"Where's the Bullfrog?" she asked the room at large.

"He's still sleeping," Pops said, not looking up from the paper.

"It's seven o'clock. Why the hell is he sleeping? We were up at six every day, like it or not," she complained, and Fletcher snorted.

"Growing boys need their rest," her mother said. "Besides school starts in a few weeks, so…"

"She lost at Clue last week and they made a deal that if he won, he could sleep in late for the rest of the summer," Pops said, laughing when Ma slapped him with a towel.

"He beat you at Clue?" Casey asked. Her mother had an uncanny knack for the game, and she rarely lost.

"Yes, and I'm pretty sure he had help." She pointed her spatula at the window seat.

"Whatcha looking at me like that for? I wasn't even here last week," Fletcher pointed out, folding the paper and getting some coffee. She checked her watch, then looked at Casey.

"Charlie call yet? I'll take that as a no," she said when no one answered her. "Damn it, I don't like this." She got up from the table to look out the window.

"Who does? We agreed not to start searching until ten. If she hasn't called by then, we go get Jasper," Alexandra said, spinning her charm bracelet around her wrist.

"Did she say where she was staying? Did she leave a note?"

"No, Casey, she didn't. I already checked her house to see if she left anything, she didn't. Now we wait," her mother said, taking a seat.

"Isn't that just peachy." Casey huffed, then turned to her father. "Pops, are you coming to the site today?"

"Yep, at least 'til ten."

Casey nodded and sipped her coffee. It would be life as usual until ten.

****

Ryan sifted through the papers on Alexandra's desk. She said he could use it as a base of operations while she was out. He called a few of his contacts and was able to get a list of patients in the area who had been prescribed the medication they'd found in Fletcher's blood work. One name stood out...Thomas.

He remembered Charlie talking about Marylou Thomas's father having a heart attack. The "prince of darkness," as Casey called him, had been dead for a couple of years, but his name was still on the list. Ryan's gut told him not to ignore it.

He had called Jasper in an effort to share information. The sheriff had been impressed, which pleased Ryan on some level. He'd asked for any information on the Thomases, and Jasper had faxed him what he could.

Presently, he was sorting through Jasper's personal files. The canny old goat had a file on every one of his citizens. The information covered everything: when and where they were born, where they attended school, who they married, the names of their children, and so on. Jasper had also added his personal feelings about said persons. From what Ryan had read, there was no love lost for the Thomas family. Some things were very interesting, like the fact that the deceased Mr. Thomas was an adulterer. Ryan shook his head and sipped his now-cold coffee. He returned the mug to its coaster, and something caught his eye.

Almost a year ago, there was a break-in at the Thomas estate. He was about to call Jasper for the police report when Fletcher burst in and slammed the door shut.

"Whatcha got?" she asked, slumping in a chair. She was wearing a T-shirt and shorts. Ryan's stomach twisted at the scars on her arms and legs—there were a lot of them.

"Don't look at me like that." She pulled her legs under her and stared out the window.

"Sorry. Do they burn or anything?"

"Not since I got the stitches taken out."

"That's good then. Do you remember the Thomas home being broken into?" he asked, changing the subject so she would relax.

She cocked her head to the side and snorted. "How could I forget? Marylou had a conniption fit, going on with 'how dare someone break into our home,' and her mother had to be sedated. Then that ungrateful little priss-pot Marylou didn't want me coming in her house. Jasper set her straight right quick."

He leaned forward. "Do you remember what was taken?" He could read the report, but she was sitting right here with first-hand knowledge.

"Yeah, it was strange. The Thomases are loaded and like to show it off with fancy knick-knacks and crap."

"Antiques?"

"Gaudy ones, but yeah. Nothing of any actual

value was missing. The burglar was interested in Mr. Thomas's desk and bedroom. Which was funny being the man had been dead for a while. Even stranger was the fact that the Thomases hadn't packed away any of the man's things."

"Perhaps they wanted to preserve his memory."

"Ha! Those people are about as sentimental as a sack of crap set on fire and left on your doorstep."

Ryan turned his chuckle into a cough. "I see."

"Anyway, there were a few files missing—personal shit—and the perp had cleaned out his medicine cabinet. Mrs. Thomas said the contents were probably worth a fortune because Mr. Thomas had tons of drugs; he never used them but refilled them so the docs wouldn't find out he wasn't following their orders. Never liked that man," she said, then sat up straighter. "Wait, what are you insinuating?"

Ryan held up his list of prescriptions and handed it to Fletcher. "This is the list of medications Mr. Thomas was prescribed. Anything seem familiar to you?" He sat back while she scanned the page.

"Holy shit," she whispered, looking up at him. "I'm not even going to ask how you got confidential patient information."

He shrugged. "I know people."

She smirked. "Mr. Thomas was taking—or not taking—the same prescription used on me. This means…"

Ryan held up a hand. "It would have meant. Unless you guys found the person or persons responsible for the break-in at the Thomas home, we don't know who it was. This is too much of a coincidence to ignore." He stood up to pace. It was like being thrown a bone and having it just out of reach. "Whoever is doing this wanted to incriminate the Thomases."

"That's smart. Everyone knows they hate us and we hate them. They like Alexandra, though; she's on all the committees." She set down the paper and rubbed her temples.

"What started the feud?" They were on the right track; he could feel it. Every little bit of information was important.

"The McKays and the Thomases both helped build Blue Creek. They didn't like each other but were civil. Then Pops's family lost most everything during the Depression, and the Thomases showed their true colors—bunch of pretentious pricks." Fletcher shook her head. "Grandpa McKay was able to get the family finances back in the black, but there's no love lost between the families. Then again, some of the more recent animosity has to do with Pops's first wife. If you want to know about her, ask someone else."

"Touchy subject?" Ryan remembered the argument the sisters had when Casey didn't mention Gracie McKay's death.

"To put it mildly."

"I can respect that," he said, then got back to business. "The hostility between your families is a mutual thing, even now."

"Growing up, Marylou was a little darling and we were the McKay heathens—bunch of no good orphans, some said. She was a bully, but she was no match for us. Now we're older and it's mostly the same, except she's an airhead."

"Does everyone in town know about your families?"

"You can't sneeze without someone knowing about it in Blue Creek," Fletcher said with a nod. "The Thomases would be the perfect family to pin all this on. No one would question their involvement or bother to look anywhere else."

"Exactly!"

"Ryan, you're damn good at this!"

"Thank you," he said. All of a sudden Smashing Pumpkins' "Bullet with Butterfly Wings" started playing.

Fletcher fumbled with her pockets. "Shit, what time is it?"

"Ten after ten," he said, standing.

"Hey, Case," she answered. "Shit, okay. I'm on my way now. Don't get bitchy, I lost track of time. Yeah, I know. I'll call Jasper… She did? That's good then. I'll see you in a few."

"Charlie didn't call?" It wasn't a question. The tears glazing her sea stormy eyes gave it away. Charlie hadn't even considered leaving until he opened his big mouth. "I'm sorry, Fletcher."

"What for? You didn't do anything." She shook her head and started for the door. "Your specialty's finding people, Ryan, so find them." And with that she left.

She was right. This is what he was good at! He needed to talk to the family; he needed to be there, in the thick of things. And he wanted to be there for Casey to offer his support. Ryan shook his head. What he *needed* to do was focus.

If there was no family to talk to, what was his usual next step? Normally, he'd look around the missing person's home. Personal belongings often spoke for people. Charlie's house! He picked up the keys to the rental car the insurance company had brought by yesterday. They had come while he was sleeping, and Alexandra had signed for him.

He rummaged through the spare keys he'd seen in the desk drawer earlier. Bless Alexandra's organized soul. Ryan picked up the key with the keychain that had Charlie's name on it; he was glad he wouldn't have to resort to breaking and entering.

****

Ryan pulled into Charlie's driveway and hung up with Alexandra, who he'd called for directions. She was at her parents' house, and Jasper had just arrived. He shut off the car and walked up the front steps.

Ryan surveyed the area before he unlocked the door and walked inside. "Damn," he muttered, tripping over a toy and closing the door behind him.

It was strange going through the house of someone you knew. He was invading Charlie's privacy, and Ryan didn't care for the feeling. With a sigh, he began to go through her home, which was lived in and cozy. Inviting, like the woman herself.

He found nothing in the three bedrooms, two bathrooms, or den. His search of her closet, desk, and pantry were fruitless. The kitchen was amazing and empty.

He shoved his hands in the pockets of his slacks. There was nothing here; not one damn clue. He turned to leave when a photo caught his eye.

The picture was of the sisters standing with a distinguished-looking older gentleman, and in the background stood a farmhouse. It was a nice picture. He smiled, tapping Casey's young face. She'd been a force to be reckoned with even then; you could see it in her eyes.

The edge of the breakfast bar was an odd place to put a picture. In fact, it was out of place. He turned the frame over and removed the photo. On the back, as he had hoped, was writing.

Granddaddy Vaughn's Virginia Farmhouse

The date was under the writing. And in small print in the bottom corner was the address. Ryan ran his finger across it, and the ink smeared; it would only do that if it were fresh. Smart, Charlie. Real smart!

He input the address into his phone's GPS, then dialed Fletcher's number.

"Fletcher, it's me. I found a clue at Charlie's— your grandfather's farmhouse in Virginia. I'm heading there now. I'll let you know what I find. Call if you need me," he said, finishing his message and locking Charlie's house back up.

Ryan wouldn't think about how he would have rather left the message with Casey, so she'd know he was still here helping her. Those thoughts were personal, and he had to keep his feelings out of the way. Emotions could make you slower on the uptake, and he needed to be at the top of his game. The only thing that was important right now was finding Charlie and Mack; anything else would have to wait.

Chapter Eighteen

Her feet pounded against the forest floor, and sweat slid down her neck pooling between her breasts. Casey didn't care. Thorny vines pricked her legs; she ignored it. Her glasses kept fogging up, but she paid no mind. She just ran.

She had worked until nine thirty, then came back home to wait with her family. By the time Fletcher arrived, it was apparent something had happened to Charlie and Mack. They'd been a sight to see when Jasper showed up.

Alexandra had left the room to take a call.

Taking a business call when your sister and niece are missing? It had pissed Casey off. "Maybe you should go, Alex. It seems you have more important things to do," she had told her sister. Casey rubbed her swelling eye and dropped her hand. Her legs pumped harder.

She hadn't seen the punch coming, but she sure as hell felt it. She was lucky nothing was broken. She hadn't broken any of Fletcher's bones when she had hit her sister back either. Years ago, Tiny had taught them how to protect themselves—to block a punch and deliver one.

Pops had stopped them before they could do any real damage. He'd grabbed her around the waist, carried her into the downstairs shower, dropped her in the stall, and turned the water on ice cold.

"You cool off, right now!" he had said and sat on the toilet watching her.

Jasper had seized Fletcher; Jebb had had to help him because Fletcher was slippery like a snake. Casey didn't know where they'd stuck her little sister, and she didn't rightly care.

She had sat in the cold stream of the shower until she started to shake. Pops turned off the water and handed her a towel. His taut movements told her just how pissed he was.

"I don't know what the hell's wrong with you, but you need to adjust your attitude right now! Your sister and niece are missing. Damn it! We need to be a family and work together, not fight each other. What you said to Alex was inexcusable—just plain cruel. You know your sister would sell her soul to the devil to find Charlie and Mack. And if for some reason you *don't* know it, I'm telling you now." He'd left without letting her speak. He came back a few minutes later with her jogging clothes, running shoes, and a bottle of water.

He'd put them on the sink and left, but not before he said, "You can't cool off? Go sweat it out. But don't come back until you can control your temper."

So here she was, sweating it out. She was still pissed she'd gotten the brunt of his anger when she hadn't thrown the first punch. She hated it when Pops was disappointed in her. He was too—she'd seen it on his face—but worse, he was hurt. He needed her, and she'd let him down by being a bitch.

She slowed her pace, turned on her heel, and started back. In a way, she *had* thrown the first punch, only hers had been verbal. Alex might seem like an ice queen, but Casey knew her sister loved their family as much as she herself did.

Hell, Alexandra had killed a man to survive. The memory nearly stopped her in her tracks. If killing rats could fuck up a mind, what did killing a person—a living, breathing human being—do to you? And Alex had killed, self-defense or not. What had Alex admitted her fear was? She was afraid of herself. Could one be related to the other? Fletcher would probably know. The little bitch! Why couldn't she punch like a girl rather than a two-hundred-pound boxer? She had probably kept up her training with Tiny all these years. Casey almost laughed.

It had been a few weeks since Fletcher's bout with insanity. Casey had a sneaking suspicion her little sister was even stronger now. Both physically and mentally. She wouldn't be letting her guard down anytime soon. None of them would. Had Charlie?

Shaking off the feeling of doom, she sent up a prayer as she came into the clearing. Her mother was sitting on the porch swing staring into space. Pops came out with a glass of iced tea in his hand. Casey slowed to a crawl. Pops set the glass down and picked Ma up and into his lap.

Casey stopped dead when they kissed. She'd seen them kiss before—who hadn't—but this was different. She didn't want to interrupt their private moment, and she started backing up. Her heart was near to bursting; her parents still loved each other as much as they had when they first joined forces, if not more. It was beautiful.

She was almost back in the woods when she tripped on her little sister.

"Damn it, Fletcher! I'm getting sick and tired of this," she hissed, getting up and swatting away the grass clippings that clung to her sweaty legs.

Fletcher shrugged. "*You* should watch where *you're* going."

Casey eyed her. She'd changed clothes, now wearing jeans and an old green T-shirt. Her hair was in a bun at the top of her head instead of her usual braids. But it was the swollen split-lip that stood out; she looked like a collagen mishap.

"What are you doing out here?"

"Hiding."

"Why?" Casey looked around. If they were going to talk, she was going to rest. She sat down in the grass and sipped her water.

Fletcher sat down next to her and picked at the dandelions. "Jebb thinks he's Pops trying to lecture me, and Jasper's acting like an old woman hovering about. I don't know what their problem is; it's not like they've never seen a fight before." She kept picking at the grass.

"True. What did they make you do?" They were both adults, but that didn't mean Pops couldn't punish them.

"You mean after they hosed me down?" Fletcher made the mistake of grinning, which split her lip again. She dabbed at it with the hem of her T-shirt.

"Pops stuck me in a cold shower, then told me to sweat it out." Casey looked down at her hands. Her knuckles had a couple of scrapes, but they weren't swelling.

"Figured as much. Jasper and Pops are twisted." She stuck her hands under Casey's nose.

199

Casey started laughing.

"It ain't that damn funny," Fletcher said and sat on her hands.

Casey snickered. "How'd they do that?"

"They each held an arm while Jebb sat on me. Then Alex didn't want to be left out so she painted my damn nails. She then got rid of the crap you take it off with. I'm stuck with this." She brought her hands back into view and looked at her nails. "Had to be bright pink."

Casey bit her lip, she didn't want to start laughing again. She just wished she'd seen it. Only one time in her memory had Fletcher ever had her nails painted. They'd been playing one on one at the school's basketball court. Fletch had lost. It had been hilarious then too. "I think I have some nail polish remover in my bathroom." They both knew it was an apology.

"Well?" Fletcher said jumping to her feet. "What are you waiting for?"

Casey got up and put her arm around her sister. "This brings new meaning to cruel and unusual punishment," she said, nodding to her sister's fuchsia nails.

"No shit."

They headed back to the house. Casey was relieved when only her mother was on the porch. She and Fletcher walked up the steps together.

"Have you two made up now? Because if you're quite finished, your sister and niece are still missing. We have enough to worry about without the two of you trying to kill each other."

"We're sorry, Mama," they said in unison and sat down on the cushions on the floor.

"I know you are, girls," she said with a sigh. "I'm sorry I snapped at you, but fighting isn't going to help us find Charlie and Mack. And, Casey, what you said to Alexandra was hateful. You'll go apologize to her."

"Yes, ma'am," Casey said, standing again. Savannah caught her hand and pulled her down to the swing.

"I know you love Charlie and Mack very much, but you have to trust we all love them as well. Understand?" Her voice had taken the low "I'm mad, but I want you to understand I love you" quality, and the ever-ready lump formed in Casey's throat. Her mother smoothed her hair and kissed her cheek.

"I understand, Mama." She stood up and headed for the door. She needed to take a shower and figure out what to say to Alex. Then they needed to figure out what to do about Charlie and Mack.

About half an hour later, she stepped out of the bathroom wearing a bra and panties. She put her contacts back in so she didn't have to bother with her glasses. When she got to her bedroom, Casey stopped short. Alex was lounging on her bed. She had decided what to say in the shower.

"Sorry about what I said. I didn't mean it." It was short, sweet, and to the point.

"I know," Alexandra said.

"Did Fletcher find the nail polish remover?" she asked, going to her closet.

"Yes, to everyone's enjoyment." Alex smiled. "She's promised retribution though. I think she's planning to paint Jebb's nails in his sleep. Which would be a disaster; she wouldn't know what in the world she was doing."

"Sounds like something she'd do. Any word on Charlie? Has she called?"

"No. And I don't think she's going to be calling anytime soon." Alexandra got off the bed and went to the door.

Casey followed her with her eyes. "You think someone has her? That this is all related?" Casey did, but she wanted a verbal agreement.

"First Fletcher gets poisoned…or were the notes first? Whichever. Then the fire and the dead guy. The threat to Ryan, and now Charlie's not calling and we don't know where she is. Coincidence? I think not."

"Me neither. What should we do?" Ryan specialized in finding people. Could she swallow her pride and ask him to come back? They could hire someone else. She trusted Ryan though and—Casey turned away from Alex to catch her breath. She trusted him! She had trusted him with Fletcher, and she would trust him to find Charlie.

"We wait." That brought Casey back from where her thoughts had gone. "Whoever is doing this is going to want us running around. We need to stay calm and wait. They'll send us something telling us they have Charlie and Mack. At that point, we make a plan and go from there."

"Sounds good. I'm not that patient, but in theory it sounds good."

Alex nodded and left the room.

"Charlie, wherever you are we'll get you out, I promise." There was no response from the great beyond, but she hadn't really expected one.

****

Charlie had finally stopped ranting and raving; of

course, that probably had more to do with the gag than anything else. Mackenzie was having a great time with this long game of make-believe. It was an adventure, and Charlie wouldn't contradict the story either; she didn't want her daughter to be frightened.

By now those McKay bitches should realize Charlie and Mack were missing. Would they be scared, thinking of all the horrible things that could happen to their loved ones? Caring was a weakness, and one way or the other it always came with a price. This time it was the McKay's turn to pay.

"Four little bitches sitting in a tree…"

Chapter Nineteen

It was late afternoon by the time Ryan pulled into the lane leading to the old farmhouse. The sky was dark from the storms passing through, only adding to his unease. All the back roads had looked the same to him, so he had stopped at a gas station to make sure he was going the right way.

He pulled into the driveway and waited a few minutes before cutting off the engine. He retrieved his gun from the glove compartment and got out of the car. He closed the door with as much finesse as possible and put the 9 mm in his slacks, so it rested against the small of his back.

The farmhouse was a good size, two stories. He knew it had belonged to J. T. Vaughn, their grandfather. Vaughn had been the father of Emmit McKay's first wife. The sisters didn't like talking about her, even amongst themselves, which piqued his curiosity. He had done a bit of research on the matter, but that was neither here nor there at this point.

He edged around the overgrown lawn and headed for the house. He had yet to see any signs of life. There was a shed at the rear of the property, and Ryan decided to try there first.

The grass was thick and damp from the rain. An ominous screech filled the air when he lifted the latch. The scent of oil and rust hit his nostrils as he shone his pocket light into the darkness. Empty.

And, really, what had he expected to find? A note saying exactly where Charlie and her daughter were? A big black X marking the spot? Bodies? He shook his head and shut off the light. He took his time lowering the latch, then headed for the main house.

Ryan's phone vibrated in his pocket, but he ignored it. There wasn't any movement coming from the place. He walked up the porch stairs and lifted the deteriorating welcome mat. Alexandra had said there should be a key, and she was right.

If Charlie had made it out here, she would have taken the key inside with her, right? Pushing the thought aside, he unlocked the door, wincing when it creaked open. So much for surprise.

"Hello," he called out. He didn't think anyone was here *to* surprise. Walking through a spider web confirmed that notion.

He walked around the house. No one had been here in a while; if his foot prints in the dust weren't evidence enough, then the fact his were the *only* tracks should do it. All the furniture was blanketed with faded sheets, and none of it had been touched.

Ryan went up and down the rickety steps, which reminded him of something from a horror movie, and searched each room twice. There was no doubt in his mind that this was where Charlie had been heading, but she never made it.

He sat down on the dirty steps in the front hall. Had Charlie and Mack been followed? Had they even made it out of town? Ryan pulled out his phone seeing the missed call. It had been Fletcher; there wasn't a message, which meant no news about Charlie.

He ran a hand through his hair. The consensus was Charlie and Mack had been taken. How would they have been taken? When? There was no sign of a struggle at Charlie's home. If they'd been captured, would they have taken Charlie's vehicle or left it behind? He pulled out his phone and searched for the number he needed.

"Trent," the gruff voice answered on the third ring.

"Marty? It's Ryan. I need a favor."

"Hey, boyo, I heard about what happened to your brother. Always said his white knight antics would get him in trouble." Marty laughed. "What do you need?"

Ryan smiled. Marty Trent was a homicide detective in DC, but he had connections the FBI and CIA would fall all over themselves for. He was also the self-appointed uncle to the Keller twins. Ryan explained what he needed, giving his uncle the short version.

"Hold on a sec, and I'll check it out," Marty said, the receiver clicking when it hit the desk.

A spider crawled up the wall while Ryan waited. Finding the vehicle would be a double-edged sword. Good, because they'd have something to go on; bad, because that meant the worst had happened. Charlie and her daughter would more than likely be in the hands of a killer. Would they kill Mackenzie too? He rubbed his forehead.

"Got it here. One blue SUV registered to Charlie––no middle name—McKay. It was found abandoned about two hours ago. Looking at the map, it seems to be ten, maybe fifteen miles out of the small town you were talking about."

Ryan was almost to his car. As soon as the words

"got it" had hit his ears, his feet had hit the floor. He'd locked the house back up and put the key back under the mat.

"Thanks. I'll take care of it from here." He opened his car door and started the engine. "I owe you one, Uncle Marty."

"You just keep yourself safe, boyo, and we'll call it even."

Next, Ryan found Jasper's number on his phone and dialed.

"Sheriff Hart."

"Jasper, it's Ryan. Charlie didn't make it out here. I figured she had to have been followed. I called a friend, and he told me her vehicle was found about an hour ago several miles outside of Blue Creek. It was abandoned."

"Good work. I'm at the station now. Casey and Fletcher are with me," the old man whispered. He knew they were keeping Ryan's involvement a secret. "I'll check it out."

"Call me and let me know what you find. I'm heading back to Blue Creek now."

"All right, Hank, thanks for the tip. Yep, I'll see you later."

Ryan looked at the phone to see his call had ended. "Hank? Canny old goat." He shook his head. He put his cell on the seat next to him and returned his gun to the glove compartment.

On the drive back, he could only hope Jasper had better luck than he'd had.

****

Casey sat in the back of Jasper's official SUV as they drove to check out a lead on her sister's abandoned vehicle. The three sisters had agreed not to say anything to their parents until they were clear on a few things. Alexandra had gone to the diner to check on Kim; they would meet up later.

She wasn't sure when the rain had started, but there was no ignoring it now. The humidity was suffocating, and the downpour wasn't making it any easier to breathe. Jasper had the air conditioning on, but she needed to taste the thickness of summer. Casey touched the button on the panel of the door to lower the window, but it wouldn't budge. What did she expect? She was, after all, in the back seat of a police car.

Casey took in a slow breath and tried to relax. Charlie and Mack had been taken. Her sister and niece…gone. She couldn't understand why this was happening. Why would anyone go to these extremes? She turned to the window; the familiar trees were dancing in the wind against a darkening sky.

Jasper and Fletcher were lost in conversation. She was glad they didn't want her input, because she didn't have anything to add. All she had were facts.

Someone had been drugging Fletcher and sending her threats. That same someone had tried to burn down the garage with Alex and herself trapped inside. Then what? The warning to Ryan? Had that come before or after Alex was almost killed? After. Jesus! And now this nutjob had Charlie and Mack. Casey shook her head and sat up when Jasper put the SUV in park. It hadn't taken them long.

"Here we are, girls. Let's go see what they got." Jasper hopped out of the driver's side and opened the door for Casey.

The three of them walked toward the station. The

building was much larger than Jasper's office and looked more intimidating—bleak. Casey couldn't imagine working in a place this leached of life.

The inside resembled a shopping mall the day after Thanksgiving, with people running around everywhere. Casey hated malls, so the comparison was apt. A plump older man sat behind a great wall of a desk. He would look as though he were holding court if not for his uniform or the jelly stain on his tie. His hair was white, and his eyes were an unfriendly brown. He reminded her of the man behind the curtain on *The Wizard of Oz*.

Jasper showed his ID to the wizard wannabe. Jasper Hart had always made his official sheriff's uniform look almost elegant. Casey knew for a fact the old man polished his badge twice a day. She got a spurt of admiration for Jasper. She was proud he was the sheriff of her town, though she'd never tell him; he had a big enough ego as it was.

"I know who you are, Jasper. Been fishing with yah the first Sunday of every month for twenty damn years!" the officer said loud enough that one would assume he couldn't hear his own voice.

"I know that, Larry boy, but none of these other folks do," Jasper said scratching his temple below his hat.

Larry's eyes shot to Fletcher with a condemning look, and Casey stepped up to say something. Okay, maybe the two of them seemed like riffraff, both wearing jeans and sneakers.

Casey hadn't changed from her tank top, and Fletcher still had on a T-shirt. Not to mention her little sister looked like a teenager.

And, okay, she could understand between her black

eye and Fletcher's split lip they looked like delinquents or something, but rude was rude and Casey didn't like it. She had just opened her mouth to express her displeasure when Fletcher stepped on her foot. Casey glanced at her sister, who shook her head.

"Hello, Officer Hines, how are you?" Fletcher asked sweet as sugar.

"Deputy McKay," Larry said tersely and pointed toward the staircase. "Officer Reed reported the abandoned vehicle. Go up them steps and to the left, first door. Can't miss it, missy." With that, he turned around to answer the phone.

Casey followed behind Jasper and whispered to Fletcher. "What was all that about?"

Fletcher shrugged.

"Larry just don't like her is all," Jasper answered as they walked up the stairs.

"Why?" Casey wanted to know. Again, Fletcher shrugged. Casey snatched her sister's arm and asked once more.

"Hells bells! I don't know, Case. He just doesn't," Fletcher replied, snatching back her arm and knocking on the door. Casey caught the quick glance that passed between Jasper and her sister. She mentally squashed the anger boiling up. She was getting sick and tired of secrets, even small ones.

They entered the room when a voice from behind the door asked them in. The office was a good size and methodically organized. Casey's eyes widened and she had to do a double take of the man behind the desk. He was huge, no, gigantic; she could definitely see him as a defensive lineman for the Oakland Raiders. He even had the coloring. Black hair and silver eyes. Yep, not the type of guy to mess with. Her back instantly straightened.

His shoulders were twice the size of her own and probably three times bigger than Fletcher's. He wore a suit instead of a uniform, which screamed detective. And the name plate on his desk said Detective Noah Reed, so why had Larry called him an officer? Why worry about it, Casey? This wasn't her scene, so she'd keep her mouth shut. For now anyway.

"Jasper, what a surprise," Detective Reed said with obvious affection. His smile and good will seemed to fade when he turned to Fletcher. "McKay. What the hell happened to you? Fighting with thugs again? And who is this?"

Casey shivered when his silver eyes focused on her. It was odd; people didn't scare her, as a rule, but this guy gave her a damn chill. She couldn't be losing her edge, could she? Nah.

"She's my sister, and we weren't fighting any thugs, just each other. Casey McKay, meet Detective Reed," Fletcher said between clenched teeth.

Casey narrowed her eyes and stuck out her hand. If Fletcher didn't like this guy, then neither did she. Reed rose and engulfed her hand with his. It was a brief, hard shake, yet gentle. Casey didn't know whether to be thankful or annoyed. He sat back down and glared at Fletcher. Oh yeah, annoyed fit the bill! Casey took a seat in one of the four empty chairs. Jasper sat next to her, while Fletcher stood still.

"What brings you here?" he asked, resting his arms across his massive chest.

"Noah, my boy, seems the vehicle you found earlier belongs to these girls' sister Charlie," Jasper explained. If she didn't know better, Casey would think Jasper was getting a kick out of the active dislike between Fletcher and the detective.

"Is that so?"

"You should know all this being as how Jasper called you earlier," Fletcher said and crossed her arms over her chest as well.

Noah leaned back in his chair and looked briefly at Jasper. "Ah, yes. Larry said something about that. You, Deputy, can understand I'm a very busy man with more to think about than what the sheriff here is interested in. I have a murder investigation consuming my time."

Casey jumped to her feet and held back a grin when Fletcher swiped everything off of the detective's desk. Like ashes after an explosion, the papers floated to the floor. It was hypnotic. Seeing Fletcher worked up was always a treat—as long as her anger was focused on someone else.

"There now, your damn plate is clear. This is my fucking sister and niece we're talking about, Reed. If you don't get off your ass and help, it may *their* murders you're investigating," Fletcher spit out. Her sister's frame vibrated with what Casey could only conclude as rage.

"Fletcher, that's no way to act toward an officer," Jasper said wearily and pulled Fletcher back. "Especially a superior officer."

"Fuck diplomacy, Jasper! Someone has Charlie and Mack, so he can take his superiority and shove it up his ass for all I care!" Fletcher snarled. She flicked Reed off and said, "Sit on it and rotate, *Detective*." She whirled around and slammed out of the office.

Casey knew to leave Fletcher alone after she'd had

an episode. Her sister did have a temper, and she didn't take shit from anyone. Casey respected that completely, but this was a little dramatic, even for her.

"Jasper, you need to put that girl on a leash," Noah said. He squatted down and began picking up his things.

"Who the hell do you think you are, talking about my sister that way?" Casey shouted.

Noah ignored her. "Jasper, do you really think Charlie and her daughter are in danger?"

"Unfortunately, I do. Had an inside source tell me the abandoned SUV you found was hers and that don't bode well. We need some help here, Noah—your help. Pushing Fletcher's buttons isn't what she or we need at the moment. And you know better than to get her riled up!" Jasper said, rising from his seat and maneuvering Casey at the same time.

Noah stared at his door, then stood with a nod and replaced his papers. "I'd like to know who your source was. We'd just made the ID when you called Larry. It was simultaneous."

"Won't name a source without a subpoena, Noah, my boy, and you know it. Just the same, Larry said you found the vehicle, and I'd like to know what condition you found it in." Jasper shifted his feet and took off his hat to scratch his head.

"That's the thing, Jasper...it wasn't in any suspicious condition. The vehicle had been cleaned out, and I'm talking a detailed clean. There wasn't so much as a crumb on the floor. I know Charlie's neat but not like that."

"Wait just a minute. You know my sister?" Casey was instantly on alert. She'd never met this man before.

Hadn't even heard of him.

"I know your family, Ms. McKay. I've lived in Blue Creek for the past few years." He reclaimed his seat and motioned for them to do the same.

"*Really?*" It pissed Casey off because she hadn't been here to know this man lived in her town. It was obvious she didn't know a lot of things. She sat down hard and almost jumped when Jasper patted her knee.

"I'm quite good friends with your parents, actually."

"He bought J. T.'s old place, Casey," Jasper said, shifting in his seat.

"On a cop's salary?" she asked with disbelief. Her grandfather's home was more of an estate than a house. She let her suspicions supersede the pang in her chest at the mention of her grandfather. What she wouldn't give for the Judge's help on this matter.

"Casey…"

"No, it's an understandable question, Jasper, and one I feel I don't have to answer. Your father doesn't question me, Ms. McKay, which should tell you something. I know all three of your sisters, and I know all about you."

"Well, good for you," Casey said.

"If we could get back to the matter at hand," Jasper suggested.

"The SUV was cleaned out, and the license plates were removed. There wasn't any obvious sign to tell us who it belonged to. That's why I'm curious as to your source, Jasper. We had to go by the VIN number—it was partially removed, by the way."

"I don't doubt my damn source," Jasper said.

"If you say so. There's no evidence of foul play,

Jasper, and I'm not in missing persons. I'm a homicide detective, and this isn't my case."

"I know, Noah! But you found the vehicle, and you're a citizen of Blue Creek; you know the McKays, so you know what's been going on," Jasper insisted.

"No, I don't know what's going on. In fact, I remember specifically asking you to enlighten me."

"Well, *boy*, I'm telling you now," Jasper said, and Casey couldn't help but snicker.

Chapter Twenty

It was late by the time Jasper and Fletcher dropped Casey off at her parents' house. She wanted to take a quick shower and grab a bite to eat before she headed to the B and B. She shook her head as she unlocked the front door. Through the entire ride home, she'd felt twelve again. Jasper had laid into Fletcher just like Pops used to when they'd gotten in a fight at school. But, unlike when they were young, Fletcher hadn't argued. Much, anyway.

She followed the noise coming from the kitchen. Her parents and little brother were sitting at the table about to eat.

"Perfect timing. I'm starving," she said in way of a greeting. She washed her hands and poured a glass of sweet tea.

"Any news?" her mother asked.

"Nothing solid," Casey said. She fixed herself a plate of meatloaf and mashed potatoes, then took a seat. "What do you know about this Noah Reed, Pops?"

He paused. Emmit McKay was not the type of man to give pause about anything he was sure of. "Noah is a good man, Casey, and none of your concern."

"Emmit," her mother hissed. Shadows played across her father's face. He sighed and put his fork down.

"Noah is real cool, Case," Jebb said around a

mouthful of mashed potatoes.

Casey took a bite of her dinner and studied her little brother. His hair was standing up in the front, but his blue eyes were huge. She swallowed and pointed at him with her fork. "You know him?"

"Yeah, who doesn't know Detective Reed?" Jebb's eyes circled the table, and he rubbed his forehead. "You know what I think, Mama?"

"No, Jebb." Their mother sighed. "What do you think?"

"I think this family has way too many secrets for its own good. We should be honest with each other, right? But we're all chock full of 'em—the secrets, I mean. Like why can't we tell Casey about Noah? What's the big deal?" He filled his mouth with another fork full of food.

"I think you're right, Bullfrog. I think you're absolutely right. This family has too many fucking secrets, and I for one am sick of it."

"A, you watch your mouth at this table, and B, that's mighty hypocritical of you, isn't it, young lady?" Pops asked. The legs of his chair scraped against the floor when he stood. "Who here is the best at keeping secrets? Like the one about why you left; you never gave me a real reason, did you? But you know what? I'd like a damn explanation!"

Casey flinched. "I—"

"Did she ever tell you what happened, Savannah? She sure as hell didn't tell me. Not one of my daughters said a damn word. Our family was falling apart, and I couldn't do anything to stop it. You want answers? Well, so do I," Pops hollered. He stomped out of the house and slammed the door.

Jebb gulped. "I'm sorry, Mama."

"Oh, baby, it's not your fault," Savannah soothed, then stared at Casey. "It's your sister's fault. In fact, they're all to blame."

"Mama?" Casey's voice shook, and the lump in her throat wasn't something her tea could dislodge. She was ashamed for the hurt she put in her parents' eyes.

"I'm sorry, Casey, but it's the truth. Your father's right, and Jebb is too. There are too many secrets in this family, and they started the day you left. If we can't trust each other enough as a family—no, love each other enough, to be honest—then what hope do we have of finding Charlie and Mackenzie?" She stood and started putting the unfinished dinner back in its containers. "And your father and I know her SUV was found abandoned. Noah was kind enough to call and offer his help. Funny, how someone who isn't a part of this family was willing to share information our own daughters wouldn't tell us."

"Mama, we didn't want you to worry," Casey said, nauseated. She willed away the tears that threatened.

"Don't you think not knowing is worse? Because, let me tell you, in this situation all you can grasp on to are the facts and hope for the best. I've sat here and taken everything I've been dished out, but I'm at the end of my rope, Casey. As your sister would say, I am sick of this shit!"

Jebb's silverware clattered on his plate. "Mama!"

"Go on upstairs, sweetheart," their mother said, pointing him out of the room. Once he was gone, she took a breath and waited for Casey to meet her eyes. They both turned to Pops when he came back into the house.

"Right now, Charlie and Mack's lives depend on us," Savannah said. "Their *lives*, Casey. This is not the time for secrets. If you three don't respect us enough to tell us the truth, then don't belittle us by being here." With that she turned, kissed Pops on the cheek, and left the room.

Casey was unable to move. She struggled to grasp what had happened. What the hell *had* just happened? She turned to her father. "Pops?" She swallowed. Was that her voice?

"Your mother's having a hard time with this. Hell, we all are, Casey. We're counting on you girls. It's been years since you've been here, and many things have changed. The people in this town…the people in this house." He shook his head and sat down next to her.

"I've changed too, Pops. I'm a fucking adult. I can handle this situation." Anger always worked. Get angry and the pain, the hurt, eased a little.

"You seem to have always been an adult, Casey. Hell, you were twenty at five; but that's not the point. This isn't yours to carry alone; it involves all of us. No one expects or wants you to take the whole thing on by yourself. That's what family is for."

"I know that. Don't you think I know that? I was the one who didn't have a family for—"

"That was *your* choice, Casey. Your damn choice! Not mine, not Savannah's, and sure as hell not your sisters'." He stood. "This conversation is getting redundant, and I need to go make some calls. I'm behind your mother one hundred percent; if you girls can't be honest, then don't bother being here."

She stared at her father's back as he left the room.

Rubbing her temples, she tried to make sense of the last several minutes. Nope, nothing. She glanced at her watch; she needed to take a shower and go to the B and B. She should probably pack a bag while she was at it. It seemed Fletcher wasn't the only one capable of losing her mind.

****

Casey walked up to the back porch of the B and B with a sigh. She could see her sisters through the window talking, and when she got to the door she could hear them. Deciding she may be interested in what they were saying in her absence, she stopped and leaned in closer.

"What is it, Fletcher? You're staring at me," Alexandra said.

"Nothing," Fletcher said. "Given what we know, I believe whoever is behind this has been planning it for a while. It has to be someone from Blue Creek. Someone we know and someone Charlie knows, who she wasn't threatened by."

"I agree. Whoever it is not only knows us but is close to us as well. Especially to you. We still haven't figured out how someone drugged your creamer."

"Don't I know it!"

"Know what?" Casey asked coming inside. She dropped her bag and plopped down in the seat next to Fletcher.

"What's with the bag?" Fletcher asked.

"I was told not to come back home until I spill my guts."

"Whatcha do now?"

Casey glared at her little sister. Why was it that she always *did* something? "I didn't do a damn thing.

220

We"—she made a circle with her finger indicating the others—"have left Pops and Ma out of the loop. And it's not appreciated." At the innocent looks on her sisters' faces, she explained. "It seems your friend Detective Reed called the parents after we left the station. They were pretty pissed they had to get their information from someone other than their daughters."

"Noah called them?" Alex asked.

"Know him, do you?" Casey asked, noting the sly look in Alex's blue eyes.

"Of course. Noah owns Granddaddy's old home. He renovated and redecorated. The place is fabulous. Like the man himself."

"Did you have sex with him?" Fletcher hissed. Her cheeks reddened, and Casey smirked.

"Wouldn't you like to know!"

"God, Alexandra, who haven't you slept with?"

Alex looked her up and down. "And what is that supposed to mean, Casey?"

"I really don't care if you slept with the whole fucking planet. I just want to know if you slept with Noah Reed?" Fletcher said. She clenched her fist on top of the table.

Alex raised a brow. "If you don't care, then why ask?"

"Never mind," Fletcher said, pushing away from the table and leaving the kitchen.

Casey sat up when the back door slammed shut. What was Fletcher's problem, and just who the hell was this Noah Reed character? "Did you sleep with him?" Casey wanted to know. She held her grin when Alex turned to her with fire in her eyes.

"If you must have an answer, then no, I didn't."

"Why the hell didn't you say so in the first place?" Casey rubbed her temples.

"Why should I have? I don't see how it matters."

"Who is this guy anyway? And don't give me that look, Alexandra McKay. I know you know." Casey had a feeling Alex knew a lot more than she was telling. She seemed to always have an answer, and if Casey didn't find that talent so admirable it would be annoying.

"Yes, I'm acquainted with Noah," Alex sighed. "He's a good man, Casey, despite what Fletcher thinks. He's in his early thirties, is a respected member of the community, has great taste, is heterosexual, and has never been married. Is that enough?"

"No, what is he to Pops, and why does Fletcher hate him if he's so damn perfect?"

"First of all, I never said he was perfect; he has flaws like the rest of us. Dad met him first because he sold Granddaddy's house to him. Then they got to talking, and they have a lot in common. Noah's father was in the FBI and knew Dad; they had even been on a few assignments together. Dad trusts Noah; we all do. That is, except Fletcher. Why she doesn't like him is beyond me, Casey. Apparently, it was hate at first sight for the both of them."

"I told you, you knew," Casey said with a twist of her lips. Maybe he wasn't so bad.

Alex pointed to her bag. "Judging by your accessories, I assume you're staying here."

"Looks that way. You don't mind, do you? I could stay at Charlie's place, but I wouldn't feel right about it." She couldn't stay there when her sister was—Casey swallowed—wherever she was.

"I couldn't stay there either, not now anyway. Of course, you can stay here," Alex said, patting Casey's hand.

"I didn't tell you how much I like what you've done with the place. You did a good job, Alexandra. Granny Vaughn would have loved it," Casey said, remembering their grandmother. She had been a sneaky southern broad, and Casey had loved her. Everyone had loved the woman. "And I love that you named it after her."

"I'm glad you like it. And yes, I know Granny Vaughn would have loved it too," Alex said with a sad smile.

"Do you remember the time Pops tried to buy Mabel?" Casey asked pouring a glass of iced tea. Mabel had been Granny Vaughn's blue-ribbon milking cow.

"How could I forget? She wouldn't sell her."

"What did happen to that cow?" Casey asked as she reclaimed her seat.

"You don't remember? It got loose and started running around town. Everyone tried to corral the animal, but they couldn't and she got away. Never to be seen or milked again."

"It was an accident, damn it!" Both Casey and Alex jumped when Fletcher spoke. They hadn't even noticed she'd come back in.

"What are you talking about?" Alex asked, her eyes wide. "What?"

Casey started laughing.

"I didn't mean to let the damn thing out! It just sort of happened," Fletcher admitted.

Alex looked at Casey and then Fletcher. "You're the one who let Mabel out?"

"Obviously! And I told you it was an accident." Fletcher dropped into the chair next to Casey. "Don't look so innocent, big sister. Were you or were you not the one who took the spark plugs out of Mama's jeep all those years ago?"

Casey squirmed. "I don't know what you're talking about."

"I know what she's talking about! And yes, I knew about that, Casey McKay," Alex said smiling when Casey nudged Fletcher. "Granny Vaughn figured it out and gave me a lecture about respecting other people's property. Like I would have messed with Mama's jeep."

"She wasn't our Ma then, I'll have you remember, and don't act like you never did anything wrong, Alexandra McKay. We all know you were the one who put purple hair dye in Marylou's showerhead at school." Casey snickered when Alex raised a brow.

"That goes to show what you know, Case. Charlie was the one who put the dye in Marylou's shower, didn't you, Charlie?" Fletcher asked. They all looked to the empty chair.

They'd been so caught up in reminiscing, they'd forgotten Charlie wasn't there. They looked at each other. Alex started picking at her manicure, Fletcher started playing with one of her braids, and Casey got up to look for one of the beers she'd picked up at Dot's market.

Fletcher cleared her throat and gave a small smile when Casey handed her a beer.

"Don't worry about it, honey," Alex told Fletcher. "We'll find them."

Fletcher exhaled a deep breath. "I know." She

looked at Casey, who was sipping her own beer. "What do you think we should do next, Case?"

"I don't know, Fletcher. We need all the help we can get. The FBI will be called in. They always are on missing person cases, right?"

"Jasper might not reach out."

"What do you mean? You don't think Jasper will call them? It's his job to call them!" Casey shouted.

"I know that, and believe me he knows, but Jasper likes to keep what happens in this town in this town," Fletcher said, poking the table for emphasis.

"Dad was an agent, so he'll make the call if Jasper won't."

"Don't be so sure, Alex; Pops knows if we involve the Feds, we'll be out of the loop. And that's one place Pops can't abide being," Fletcher said. "We can't afford to put Charlie's life in some stranger's hands. We're McKays; we fight our own fights."

Casey lifted her beer. "Damn straight!"

Chapter Twenty-One

Ryan was tired, hungry, and frustrated as hell. His cell phone had died, and without the GPS, he'd made a wrong turn; it had taken him over two hours to fix it. Shaking his head, he pulled into a parking space at the B and B and turned off the engine.

Ryan hoped nothing important had happened while he had been out of reach. He'd stopped at a rest stop along the way and tried using the pay phone, but no one had answered his call. Not that he had expected they would.

It was darker in the parking area than it had been before, and he couldn't see a damn thing. He needed a shower, some food, and a good night's sleep. In the morning, he would try to put more pieces of the puzzle together.

He unlocked the kitchen door with the key Alexandra had given him. The place was quiet. He toed off his shoes and headed up the stairs to his appointed room. Hitting the light, Ryan started undressing and went into the adjoining bathroom to start the shower.

He let the spray engulf him. Closing his eyes, he relaxed his muscles and leaned against the stall for a few minutes. With some reluctance, he started washing and then turned off the water. Taking the towel from the rack, he patted himself dry, stepped out of the stall, and ran smack dab into Casey.

"Shit," he grunted. Casey stood in front of him with her hands on her hips. She had on one of her tank top and shorts ensembles under her robe. She inspected him from head to toe, her eyes simmering with something Ryan couldn't name. Realizing he was naked, he quickly wrapped the towel around his waist.

"Don't cover up on my account, Keller," Casey said with false sweetness.

He crossed his arms over his chest. "What're you doing here? What if I'd been someone else?"

"First of all, Miss Priss wouldn't have gone to bed if she was waiting for a legitimate guest. And second, I'm quite sure I belong here and you don't. As I recall, you were supposed to leave town. Obviously, I was mistaken. Just answer me this one question. Have you been here the entire time?" she asked with narrowed eyes.

He sighed. "Basically." He wanted to tell her he was here for her, and that he cared. But he didn't think she would appreciate or reciprocate any of those things. Instead, he stayed where he was.

"That's what I thought," she whispered, then walked out of the bathroom and yelled for her sisters. She turned back to Ryan. "Will you please get dressed and meet me downstairs?"

Ryan nodded. She gave him one last look before shutting the door behind her. He got dressed in record time and hustled to the kitchen. He came to a halt when he approached Alexandra and Fletcher, who were sitting at the table. They were both in their night clothes, Alexandra in a nightgown and Fletcher in a T-shirt and what looked like men's boxers.

"Please have a seat," Casey said. She was pissed.

"Didn't you get my messages?" Alex hissed, while Fletcher's gaze darted between them.

"The cell died," he told her. Casey slapped her hand down on the table, and he turned to her; that's when he noticed the bruise around her eye. "Who the fuck hit you?" he demanded standing up and shackling Casey's wrists with one hand in order to inspect the damage. He lightly traced the bruise with the fingertips of his free hand.

Casey stared at him dumbstruck. Ryan was acting like he still cared and that threw her. She'd treated him like shit—not that she would ever admit it out loud—and he was being protective. Her gaze met his; the emotion in his eyes made her stomach drop, and she yanked her hands out of his grip.

"Fine," he said, stepping back, then taking his seat. "Don't tell me."

"I hit her, Ryan, so don't worry about it," Fletcher said. She patted his hand and pointed to her split lip. "See, she got me back."

"Now we've given Ryan the play-by-play, can we get on with this, Casey? I would like to get some sleep tonight," Alex said, sounding bored. Casey narrowed her eyes, and Alex sighed. "It was my idea for Ryan to stay."

"Everyone agreed," Fletcher said. "Including Charlie."

"And what? You didn't think I'd find out?" Casey asked. She wouldn't let herself focus on Ryan, or how happy she was to see him—how relieved—so she paced around the table.

"Of course, we knew you'd find out...eventually," Fletcher mumbled.

"Casey, what's done is done. You may as well sit down and listen to what I've found out in the past twenty-four hours," Ryan said.

She took a seat, knowing he was being the rational one. "I'll forget about you all going behind my back; for now, anyway. I want to know what you know. Finding Charlie and Mack is the top priority." She could be pissed later. She ignored the disbelief in her sisters' eyes. What? She was exhausted. She sat back in her chair while Ryan and her sisters told her what they uncovered.

"...I called Jasper the minute I got off the phone with Marty," Ryan finished.

"You know the rest, Casey. Even with Ryan searching the farmhouse, we're still no closer to finding Charlie," Alex said getting up to rummage around the kitchen.

"That may be true, Alex, but we do know a few things," Casey said. Now she knew how here parents felt about being left out. Not knowing was definitely worse.

She finally glanced at Ryan, who was staring back at her. She gave him a small smile. He'd been here helping them, helping her family and her; the knowledge put her at ease. Casey looked at Fletcher, who was rubbing her temples. "What is it, Fletcher?"

"The note. I was thinking about the last note I got. I was the one to go crazy; you were the one who was supposed to die in the fire. We've guessed Alex is the one who was supposed to be covered in blood. Thanks," Fletcher said when Alex handed her a glass of tea then sat down next to her.

"But you found your sanity, Casey didn't die in the

fire, and, of course, I took care of myself," Alex said.

"Yeah, but what about Charlie?" Casey asked sitting up straighter in her seat. "Didn't the note say something about shame?"

"Exactly! 'One in shame.' How is Charlie shamed?" Ryan asked.

"I, uh, might have left out a small piece of information," Fletcher said.

"What didn't you tell us now?" Casey shouted and shoved away from the table.

"It ain't like nobody asked me about it."

"Fletcher, what didn't we ask you?" Ryan asked. Casey was surprised when he took her hand and had her sit on his lap. She closed her eyes for a second, enjoying the feel of him, until Alex spoke.

"Yes, little sister, enlighten us."

"No one wondered why someone would want me to lose my mind. Nobody asked me what I'd been doing to get a sicko after me."

Casey rolled her eyes. "Okay. So what had you been doing?"

"I was, ah, looking into the identity of Mack's father," she said and had the decency to look ashamed.

Casey stared at her little sister. She couldn't believe Fletcher would go behind Charlie's back like that. But then again, she probably would have done the same…eventually.

"How could you, Fletcher! That was Charlie's secret, one she didn't want anyone to know. You should have respected her privacy," Alex said.

"Fletcher paid dearly for her mistake. And if we're all perfectly honest, any one of us would have done the same. In fact, knowing you all as I do, I'm surprised it's taken this long," Ryan said. Casey twisted on his lap.

"Why is it you're always coming to Fletcher's defense?" Casey wanted to know. Shouldn't he be on her side? Hell, yeah, he should. But he was right, Fletcher had paid dearly.

Ryan shrugged. "Why is it you don't?"

"He's got us there, Casey," Alex said and sighed. "What's done is done. So, I'll ask what we're all wondering? Who is Mackenzie's father?"

"And why would finding out send someone into psycho mode?" Casey added.

"I…" Fletcher hesitated.

"You better tell us, Fletch, or I won't be responsible for my actions," Casey said.

"Oh, all right. You're not gonna believe this, Alexandra. I didn't at first, so don't go fainting on me or anything."

"Agreed."

"It was Rick Randle."

"Holy shit," Alex whispered, eyes wide.

"Wait a minute. Wait just a damn minute. Rick Randle?" Casey shifted in Ryan's lap to look at him again. "Didn't Charlie tell us about Rick Randle marrying Marylou Thomas and then taking her for all she had? She said Marylou was twenty-one when he divorced her."

"She's Charlie's age, isn't she? That would mean…" Ryan didn't finish.

Alex finished for him. "Charlie slept with Marylou's husband."

"Shitty, isn't it?" Fletcher said.

"Didn't he get killed in a robbery or something?"

"Ryan's right. Charlie told us he was murdered. I

told you she was holding something back," Casey said to Ryan. "Charlie said it had been poetic justice. Very un-Charlie-like."

"What I don't understand is why finding this out would make someone angry. Other than Charlie, of course." Alex glanced around the table. "She has always said it was her sin."

"Yeah, well, that's not all I—" Fletcher cleared her throat. "That's not all I found out."

"Well, spit it out, young lady."

Casey jumped to her feet. Alex and Fletcher both got out of their seats to face their father and Jasper.

"Best be speaking up there, girl, 'cause you have an awful lot of explaining to do," Jasper said, nodding at Pops, who motioned for them to take a seat.

"How did you two sneak in?" Casey asked.

Alex sighed. "The passageways."

"How long have you been here?" Ryan asked.

Casey hid her wince by staring at Alex as her sister began making coffee. How much had they heard?

"I thought you left town," Pops said, and Casey's gaze darted to his.

"You and me both, Pops. But he never left." She pointed to Jasper, whose complexion was a little ruddy. "You knew, of course."

"There ain't much I don't know, missy. Best you don't forget it. I'll take some of that coffee, Alexandra."

"What brought you out here tonight, Jasper?" Ryan asked.

Casey turned. That was a damn good question.

Jasper grunted and pointed to Pops. "I was on the phone with McKay when I drove by checking on things here. I saw the light and figured something might be going on."

"That's convenient," Casey said.

"Ain't it just," Jasper said and took the cup of coffee Alex handed him. "Now, everyone sit down. I believe Fletcher was about to tell us something."

Fletcher sat up straighter. "Before I finish it, I want it understood that nothing said here goes outside this kitchen. It's Charlie's business, and I shouldn't have stuck my nose in it in the first place. But, like Alex said, what's done is done. Can I get everyone's word that nothing will leave this room?"

"I'll tell your mother, but otherwise I agree," Pops said.

Casey and Alex nodded.

"Jasper?"

He huffed. "You're pushing the limit here, girl. But as long as it's not breaking the law you have my word."

"All right, good—"

"Already knew about Randle, anyway." Jasper smirked at the shock on Fletcher's face. "What?" he said and pointed to Fletcher. "You should have dug deeper, young lady, because you missed an important piece of information."

"What did I miss?" Fletcher asked.

"If you'd looked harder, you would've known what the Thomases had kept very secret," Jasper said with a hushed tone and sly smile. "Rick Randle had divorced Marylou a year before anyone knew about it. He sued Marylou for damages and won; that's how he got all their money."

"So he wasn't married when he knocked Charlie up," Casey said, wincing when her father glared at her.

Jasper cleared his throat. "No. I see no need to

dirty Charlie's good name. I'm only happy to clear things up." He turned to Fletcher. "Now, what else did you find out?"

Her little sister had gotten herself into a heap of trouble with both their father and Jasper. Casey bit her lip when Fletcher squirmed. Her sister knew she was screwed.

"I had this feeling I should look into Rick's murder. I think the robbery was a cover-up; someone wanted Rick dead. I sent for the case files and started looking them over," Fletcher began, and Jasper choked on his coffee.

"What'd you find?" Ryan asked.

"I don't know. I kinda lost my mind in the process," Fletcher said.

"When exactly did you start feeling different?" Casey asked, sugarcoating what happened.

"I guess it was when I started looking into Rick."

"Doesn't Rick have a brother and sister?" Ryan asked.

"Yes, Dana and Daemon," Alex said.

"It isn't Daemon," Fletcher insisted.

"How do you know?" Pops asked.

"I just do."

"What about their sister, Dana? Where is she?" Casey asked.

"I'd be the first to tell you Dana isn't all there, but she worshiped Rick. I don't think she's got the mentality to pull something like this off. If anything, she's a gossip," Alex said, rubbing her arms.

Ryan sighed. "Look, we're not going to figure this out tonight. I think we should all get some rest and meet up in the morning."

"I concur. Everyone get some sleep and be at the house at ten," Pops said, shocking the hell out of Casey by agreeing with Ryan. He got up, kissed Casey and her sisters, shook Jasper's hand, and headed out the door. Casey knew he had to go tell her mother what they'd found out, and she wouldn't be pleased.

Casey helped Alex clear the table and put the dishes in the dishwasher. Ryan headed to his room. Fletcher was right behind him when Jasper called her name.

Fletcher stopped. "Yeah?"

"Walk me out," Jasper said, holding the door.

"Want me to wait for you, Fletcher?" Alex asked.

"No, this might take a while." Fletcher sighed, then went out after Jasper.

"Are you going to talk to Ryan?" Alex asked, following Casey up the stairs.

"Yeah," Casey said.

Chapter Twenty-Two

Ryan turned on the light and stripped down to his boxer-briefs the minute he entered his room. He'd been up for almost twenty-four hours, and he was beat. Tomorrow would be a busy day, and he needed to rest. He brushed his teeth and went back into the bedroom only to find Casey leaning against the door.

"Don't you ever knock?"

"No," she said, pushing away from the door.

"What can I do for you?"

"It's later," she said, and Ryan crossed his arms over his chest. He knew her well enough to know it was an argument she was after, but he played dumb.

"What's that supposed to mean?"

"I remember, quite specifically, asking you to leave town."

"And I would have obeyed your command if I hadn't been reminded I'd given Fletcher my word I would help her."

Casey circled around the room to stop in front of him. "You"—she poked him in the chest—"are always coming to my little sister's rescue." She poked him again, harder. "What's that about?"

"Will you stop that!" He took her hand before she could do it again.

"Will *you* answer the question?"

"No, I don't think I need to. Why are you always

picking fights with me?"

"Why do you always piss me off?" she asked, getting close to him again. He put his hands on her shoulders to keep her at a distance. She shrugged him off and backed away, but her gaze never left his.

"Why are you always trying to hurt me?"

"What?" Casey whispered, backing up farther.

"You heard me. Oh, let me put it in a way you'd understand. Why are you fucking with me?"

"I'm not," she said almost at the door. She turned and took hold of the knob. Ryan pressed himself against her from behind.

"Aren't you?" he whispered in her ear. She elbowed him in the stomach, but he turned her so they were face to face. He bent at the knees, bringing them nose to nose. "Aren't you?" he asked louder this time, still holding her arm. She settled beneath him, and he let her go.

"What is it you want from me?" she asked.

"I could ask you the same thing," he said, then snatched her off her feet and deposited her on the bed. He came down on top of her and held her wrists above her head with one hand.

Casey licked her bottom lip. "What're you gonna do?"

"What do you think?" With his free hand, he pulled down her tank top, exposing her lush breasts. Ryan molded one in his free hand and squeezed. Hard.

Casey gasped.

"Do you want me to stop?" He rubbed his erection against her thigh, and her eyes flashed.

She arched her back. "No."

Ryan took the invitation and latched his mouth

onto the other breast. Still not letting go of her wrists, he used his other hand to explore the valley between her thighs. He could feel her heat through the fabric of her shorts. He groaned.

"Ryan?" She squirmed beneath him, then put her lips against his ear and whispered what she wanted.

He let out a strangled moan and kissed her. She opened her lips to him, sucking his tongue into her mouth. He released her hands, and she dug her nails into his back. He nipped at her bottom lip and opened his eyes to her lust-filled gaze.

Lifting up and off her, Ryan repeated the words she'd whispered in his ear, then said, "Is that really what you want?" Uncertainty flitted across her face when she sat up, but she nodded. "Strip," he told her and stood by the edge of the bed.

She got up on her knees, never looking away from him, and pulled off her tank top. She then stood on top of the mattress and shimmied out of her clothes. Ryan motioned to her with his finger.

He circled her waist with his hands and pulled her off the bed and down his body. He reached up and released her hair from its bun. It fell down her back, and he brought a strand to his nose, closing his eyes as he inhaled. Casey trembled.

"My turn," he said, letting go of her hair.

Casey nodded. Her hands slid down his chest, plucking at his nipples as she went. She put her thumbs in the waistband of his boxer-briefs and yanked them down. Ryan stepped out of his underclothes, gauging her reaction to his throbbing erection. He couldn't remember ever wanting someone so much—so completely.

He pulled her back against his front. His arm held her captive while his other hand ran roughly to the juncture of her thighs. He closed his eyes when he made contact with her damp heat. There was no doubt she wanted him. The knowledge egged him on, and he slipped two fingers inside her. She sucked in a breath.

He worked quickly, bringing Casey to the brink, and she moaned, moving faster against his hand. He nibbled his way along her neck, nipped at her shoulder, then bit down tenderly and sent her over the edge.

Ryan bent her forward, not able to wait another second, and pushed into her. He held himself still, trying to get control. He wanted it to last. Casey rubbed her hands up and down his arms.

"Do it, Ryan," she whispered, moving her hips. "Let go."

He took hold of her hips and began to move in a primal rhythm. Her inner muscles squeezed him as he rammed into her again and again. He couldn't get enough of her...it would never be enough. The only thing clear in his mind, before it went blank with his release, was that he loved her.

Casey was still dazed when she finally got her breath back. They had somehow made it onto the bed, and Ryan had landed on top of her. His labored breaths danced across her temple. She didn't know how to process what they'd done, but she had more pressing matters at the moment.

"Let me up," she said. She wiggled, and he moved off her. She got up, not ready to meet his eyes, and went to the bathroom. When she came back in, she turned off the light.

She wasn't sure if she should leave or if he'd want

her to stay. She felt so damn good, she didn't know whether to laugh or cry. He had given her what she'd wanted, but it was more than that. It was more powerful than anything…

"Will you stay with me tonight?" Ryan asked.

"Are you sure?" She wanted him to be.

"Of course." He stood, took her hand, and pulled her toward him. He kissed her then, a slow meeting of lips and tasting of tongues. He took his time, then stepped away from her, pulled back the covers and guided her in.

Casey made herself comfortable on her side, while Ryan got in behind her. He slid next to her, and they spooned together. Wrapping one arm around her waist, he moved her hair out of the way and kissed her neck.

"That was incredible," Casey said around a yawn.

"Yes, it was," Ryan said, then snuggled closer and whispered, "I've fallen in love with you, Casey McKay."

Casey's heart squeezed, and her breath hitched. Part of her was in awe, but the other part wished she hadn't heard his words. Ryan Keller loved her. Now what the hell was she supposed to do?

Chapter Twenty-Three

The banging on the door woke her. "Hold the hell on," Casey yelled. She peeked over to where Ryan lay next to her, still sleeping. She leaned down and kissed his forehead. He loved her. It was…it was… The banging continued. She took the blanket off the bed, wrapped it around herself, then answered the door.

"What?" Casey asked her sister. Fletcher stopped mid-knock. Her eyes went as round as saucers when she noticed what Casey was wearing.

"What do you want, Fletcher?" Casey asked, amused. "Haven't you ever seen someone the morning after? Oh, sorry, I forgot. You haven't." She didn't laugh at the incredulous expression on her sister's face.

"Sure, you're real sorry," Fletcher said rocking back on her heels.

Casey didn't budge when Ryan started moving on the bed behind her, and her sister got an eyeful. Ryan must have figured it out too, because he swore and then the bathroom door slammed shut.

"Something wrong, Fletch? You're looking a bit red."

"I, uh, umm, well…are you's coming—" Fletcher cleared her throat. "Are *you* coming to the house or not?"

"What time is it?"

"Nine thirty."

"Shit. Yeah, we'll meet you there," Casey said and shut the door before her little sister could say anything else. The shower was running, and she made an instant eco-friendly decision. Conserving water was a great idea.

****

She made it downstairs before Ryan did. They needed to hurry. Casey smiled to herself. She hadn't been this relaxed in years. Hell, she hadn't been this satisfied since...well, ever. Guilt reared its ugly head. She frowned and ran right into a petite blonde.

"Sorry, I didn't see you," Casey said when the woman jumped up.

"That's okay," she said and held out her hand. "I'm Kim, and you must be Casey."

Casey shook the woman's hand. "You're Alex's cook?"

"Chef," she said with a wink.

Casey smiled. "I'm surprised we haven't met before, but I'm sure I've seen you around somewhere."

"More than likely. Everything's been kind of hectic lately. Between the B and B and the diner, I've been up to my eyeballs in work." She sighed dramatically, her blue eyes twinkling.

"I know what you mean," Casey said. She glanced over her shoulder when Ryan came into the kitchen.

"Hi, Kimberly," Ryan said.

"Hi! It's Ryan, right? I'm sorry, I didn't realize you were still here."

"Yes, it's Ryan, and yes, I extended my stay." He looked at Casey. "We need to go."

"Right! It was nice to finally meet the famous Kim," Casey said, heading for the door.

"Likewise," Kim said. "Have a good day, you two."

****

They arrived at the McKay house with minutes to spare. Ryan couldn't help the stupid grin on his face. Casey had joined him in the shower, and she'd had her way with him. She was a goddess, truly. She hadn't said anything about his declaration of love. Not that he was surprised. She'd flinched after he'd told her, but she hadn't commented. Putting the car in park, Ryan cupped her cheek and brought her mouth to his.

"What was that for?" Casey asked after he let her go.

"Because I won't be able to do it again for a while." He smiled, then followed Casey up the porch steps and through the screen door leading to the kitchen.

All eyes were on them when they walked in. Ryan reached up to straighten his tie and then remembered he wasn't wearing one.

"Hi, Ryan," Jebb said from his perch on the kitchen counter.

"Hi, Jebb, how are you?" he asked, while Casey poured them both a cup of coffee.

"All right, I reckon," Jebb said with a nod, then left the room when his mother told him to.

"Ryan and I are sleeping together, and if anybody has a problem with that, then get over it," she said, and Emmit choked on his coffee.

"Casey," Ryan hissed, heat creeping up his neck. He didn't move out of the way when Emmit took a swing at him, but he realized he should have when the other man's fist impacted his nose.

"EMMIT!" Savannah yelled at her husband, who shook his hand loose and banged out of the door.

"Good job, Casey. Maybe you could say something else, and Jasper here would have reason to put Ryan out of his misery," Fletcher said from her seat next to the sheriff.

"Don't worry none, boy... I, ah, mean Ryan. I wouldn't shoot you," Jasper said, trying to hide his grin behind his coffee cup.

Ryan blinked and held his nose. It wasn't broken, but it was bleeding. He thanked Savannah when she handed him a towel and some ice. The apology was clear in Casey's eyes. He went over and kissed her forehead. "Don't worry about it."

"I never thought Pops would actually hit you. I'm sorry. I guess I better go talk to him."

"No," Savannah said, shaking her head. "I'll deal with him later."

"I think it would be best if I spoke with him," Ryan said and ignored everyone when they told him not to. He found Emmit on the porch steps. Ryan sat down next to his attacker still holding a towel to his nose.

"Do you really think it's a good idea to sit next to me?" Emmit asked.

"I know why you felt the need to hit me. I don't have a clue why Casey said what she did, but I don't understand Casey completely yet. I do love her, though," Ryan offered and controlled his urge to flinch when the other man swung around to look at him. "I know it seems fast—trust me, I know—but I am in love with her, Mr. McKay."

"You can call me Emmit if you want."

Ryan nodded.

"Does she love you?"

"No, I don't think she does. Which makes me either stupid or a glutton for punishment. I don't necessarily care for either, but there it is," Ryan admitted. He folded the towel and laid it on his thigh.

"I felt like that once too."

Both men looked at Savannah when she sat down on the steps behind them.

"When was that?" Emmit asked.

"The first time was when I realized I loved the girls and later when I fell in love with you," she said.

"At least I'm in good company," Ryan said. He smiled when Savannah playfully smacked the smug grin off Emmit's face.

"Yes, you are," Savannah said rising. "Now let's go inside and start trying to find out who has Charlie and Mack." She took the folded towel from Ryan.

Ryan followed Emmit in and tripped over something, He had to catch himself.

Fletcher snickered. "Whatcha do now?"

He bent down and picked up a stuffed animal, a character he recognized. "I tripped over a frog," he said holding it up.

"It's Mack's," Savannah said, taking a seat on her husband's lap.

Fletcher took the toy out of Ryan's hands. "He's her favorite."

Smiling at the sentiment, Ryan mentioned his favorite character from the same program when he was a kid. He regretted it when he caught the smirks on the faces of the other men in the room.

"Really? That's interesting," Alex drawled. Ryan turned to her, but her attention was focused on Casey.

"Correct me if I'm wrong, Ryan, but wasn't that particular character a *rat*?"

Ryan almost missed what she said. He was too busy trying to figure out why Fletcher was leering at him like he had grown two heads. "What? Oh, yes, a rat, but a fun-loving one, if you remember."

"Well, don't that just beat all. Don't you think that just beats all, Casey?"

"Shut up, Fletcher," Casey snapped.

Ryan didn't understand. "I'm not sure I follow."

Casey slapped a hand over her mouth. "HOLY SHIT!" She jumped up, startling everyone and making Jasper spill his coffee.

"I didn't think it was that big a deal," Ryan said, embarrassed.

"No, no, it's not that," Casey said. She was shaking. "I can't believe it!"

"What's wrong?" Emmit asked, removing his wife from his lap and standing.

Casey prowled around the room, muttering "Damn it," under her breath.

"Casey, you're scaring Jasper," Fletcher said, winking at the sheriff.

"Alexandra, you were right! I hate to admit it, but you were right," Casey said going around the table to give Alex a quick kiss on the lips.

"Naturally," Alex said with a nod. "About what exactly?"

"It all goes back to the rats," Casey shouted, rubbing her face.

"What are you talking about?" Ryan wanted to know. He was taken aback when Casey kissed him hard and told him she'd tell him later.

"What goes back to the rats? What rats?" Jasper asked, then banged his fist against the table. "Let's get some order to this insanity!"

"I knew I'd seen her before... I knew it!"

"Knew you'd seen who before?" Savannah asked.

Casey pointed to Alex. "Your cook."

Alex brows knit. "Kim?"

"Kimberly Williams?" Jasper seconded.

"Yeah, but that wasn't her name before," Casey said and paused for a moment. "It all makes some kind of sense."

"I hate to sound redundant, but what *are* you talking about?" Ryan asked.

Casey squatted down next to Alex and took both her hands. "Think back, Alex. We were just talking about it the other night. Think back to the home."

Fletcher jumped up. "Oh, fuck me!"

"Fletcher," Savannah scolded.

"Sorry, Mama. Alex, don't you remember?"

"Obviously not," Alex said in her haughtiest tone, which Ryan had come to figure out meant she was annoyed.

"How the hell do you remember?" Casey asked Fletcher as she let go of Alex's hands.

Fletcher tapped her finger against her temple. "I have a mind like a steel trap. Except for when people are fucking with it," she said and did a small dance. "It makes sense."

"Would someone please enlighten the rest of us?" Emmit demanded.

"Little Lee, Alexandra...remember?" Casey asked, backing up when Alex stood up quickly.

"Kimberly is Little Lee. Oh. My. God," Alex said,

covering her mouth with her hand. "I hired her. I brought her here. She's got Charlie."

Everyone stood up and began talking at once. Ryan tried to put the pieces together in his head. He was remembering everything he had heard about Kimberly Williams—or Little Lee, as it were. "Fletcher, the powdered creamer? Where did you get it?" he asked, shouting above the others.

"Exactly!" Fletcher said, and everyone quieted. "That's what I was trying to say. Kim always picked it up for me when she went to the store. I thought the little bitch was being friendly. She must have dosed the powder, then resealed the container so I wouldn't suspect. *And* she could have followed me to the cabin."

Ryan didn't notice Jasper had left the room until he came back in pocketing his cell phone. "I put out an APB on Kim, and I have one of the other deputies going to her apartment. But if she had any idea you recognized her, she's probably long gone," Jasper said, grabbing his hat. "I'm going to help locate her." He looked at Fletcher, then must have thought better of it because he pointed to Emmit. "You call me if you think of anything else." He left as soon as Emmit agreed.

"Do you remember Lee's last name?" Emmit asked.

"Not all of us came equipped with last names, Pops, and Lee was no exception," Casey said.

"All right, we need to find out everything we can about this girl," Savannah said.

"I can ask Noah," Emmit said, taking his wife's hand and heading for the door. "We're going to see if Noah can help us. You girls call us if anything changes."

"And keep an eye on your brother," Savannah added before the door closed.

"I don't give a fuck where Kim is. What we need to know is where she took Charlie and Mack," Fletcher said, twisting her braids.

"I can't believe I didn't see it," Alex said shaking her head again. "I'm more perceptive than this."

"You were only three, Alexandra. Don't beat yourself up," Casey said.

"I didn't see it either, Alex, and I'm a cop," Fletcher said. "But wait till I get my hands on her."

The look on Fletcher's face made Ryan uncomfortable. Kim had done a lot of damage where the youngest McKay sister was concerned, and he figured Fletcher was ready for a little payback.

"I have an idea." They all turned when Jebb walked in the room.

"Bullfrog, this doesn't concern you," Casey said standing in front of him.

"Bullshit! Charlie's my sister too. Mack's my niece too. I have as much at stake as you do."

"He's right, Case. We wouldn't have sat around with our thumbs up our asses at his age either," Fletcher said.

"What's your idea, Jebb?" Alex asked.

"Well, I've been reading these true-crime books, and the bad guys usually return to the scene of the crime," Jebb said.

"That may be, Jebb, but there wasn't a crime committed," Casey said.

"Hells bells, Casey!" Fletcher shouted. "The basement at the home; that's the scene of the fucking crime." She turned to Jebb. "You're a genius, little brother!"

"How far is this place from here?" Ryan asked, finally getting a word in. He high-fived Jebb, who puffed out his young chest.

Casey moved toward the door. "About an hour."

"What the hell are we waiting for? We have to save Charlie and Mack," Fletcher said, following her sister.

"Hold your horses! We need a plan," Alex said and left the room.

"Where is she going?" Ryan asked.

"God only knows," Casey said, then pointed to Jebb. "Are you okay here alone?"

Jebb crossed his arms over his chest. "I'm not a baby, Casey."

"Ready," Alex said, coming back into the kitchen.

Ryan gaped at her. Alexandra had a rifle slung over her shoulder, a revolver in one hand, and a nasty-looking knife in the other.

"You have your own weapon, don't you, Ryan?" Alex asked, handing the revolver to Casey.

"Yeah," he choked out.

"Good."

"That would be mine," Fletcher said, grabbing the knife from Alex.

"Now we're ready to kick some ass!" Casey said. "Keller, you look a bit pale…are you coming or not?"

"I'm not letting you go without me!" Ryan said and leaned down to press his lips to hers. Someone cleared her throat. Ryan let her go and backed away as she blinked up at him.

Casey straightened. "Let's go get our girls."

Chapter Twenty-Four

It took over an hour to get to the old home. Casey's stomach churned as she walked around the back of the house. It was the same. Sure, it was run down and had a big condemned sign on the front lawn, but it was the same.

"Are you okay?" Ryan whispered from behind her.

Casey nodded. She had told him about this place on the way over, every little detail. Hell, she'd even gotten teary. He had held her hand, kissed her fingers, and told her he loved her, again. She glanced at Ryan over her shoulder to remind herself he was there with her. He had her back.

She took a deep breath when they came to the back door. Fletcher had climbed up the porch and was going in through the attic. Alex was keeping a lookout in her hatchback across the street with her rifle trained on the front of the house.

"Ready?"

Ryan nodded.

"Now or never," she said, then reached for the door.

****

"This place stinks," Fletcher complained when she met up with them in the downstairs hallway. "No sign of Kim or Lee or whatever the hell she's calling herself now."

"None here either," Casey said, walking down the hall. The door to the basement was in the pantry closet, and that's where she was heading.

Other than dust and spiders, the old home was empty. No rats, she reminded herself. But the memories of life here remained in her mind. The heat and humidity seemed to be causing the decaying structure to sweat. The odor was disturbing. Fletcher was right, the place stank.

She didn't know whether she was happy Kim wasn't here or if she was disappointed she couldn't kick the woman's ass. Casey stopped at the pantry door.

"Do you want me to go down first?" Ryan asked, reaching for the knob.

"No, I'll do it." She smiled at him when he handed her a flashlight. Taking a deep breath, she opened the pantry door and then the small one in the bottom of the floor. The latch squeaked, and Casey winced. She guided the light down into the darkness. The smell hit her, and bile rose in her throat. It still smelled like shit, rat shit.

Shaking off the memories, she made her way down the rickety steps. "Charlie? Mack?"

A figure huddled in the corner. It moved.

"Casey?" Charlie sobbed.

"She's down here," Casey said, running the rest of the way. Mack was in her arms first, and she hugged her niece tightly. She shone her light on Charlie and passed Mack off to Ryan. Casey and Fletcher went to their sister.

"You look like hell," Casey said around the lump in her throat.

"Yeah, you smell bad too." Fletcher sniffed,

helping Charlie up. They hugged each other.

"Well, what took you so long?" Charlie huffed, then giggled. "Where are we anyway?"

"You don't know?" Ryan asked.

"Hi, Ryan, thanks for coming. And no, I was knocked out when she brought us here." She reached for Mack and kissed her. "We were in one of the rooms upstairs; she had me all tied up like Dabney Coleman in *9 to 5*."

"We's was having an adventure," Mack said.

"Yes, sweetheart, this was all an adventure," Charlie said, then turned to them. "We haven't been down here long, wherever here is."

"We're at the old home. This is *the* basement, Charlie," Casey said.

"Oh…well, how about we leave it once and for all?" Charlie started up the steps.

"Are we's gonna go home now, Mama?"

"We sure are, sugar." Charlie squinted at the light when she got upstairs. "Alexandra!" she screeched and ran for her sister.

Fletcher nudged Casey when they came out of the pantry. "You ever see Alex run?"

"Only when there was an after-Thanksgiving sale," Casey said, grinning as her two sisters and niece hugged and kissed each other. Ryan put his arm around her shoulders, and she leaned into him.

"I'll warn you, Dad's outside," Alex said, motioning to Casey. "And he's upset."

"I can speak for myself, Alexandra. But you're wrong; I am royally pissed," Pops said without heat. He picked Charlie up off her feet to hug her.

"We were so worried about you," Pops said, giving

Charlie a squeeze and making Casey's eyes prickle.

"Grandpop! What's about me? Isn't you happy to see me?" Mack asked, giggling when Emmit swept her up in the air, then hugged and kissed her.

"Figured you were hogging all the hugs," Ma said, coming into the room and grabbing Charlie. "Oh, sweetheart, I—"

"I'm no worse for wear really, Mama," Charlie said.

"Grandma!" Mack shouted and clapped her hands.

"Was Kimberly here?" Pops asked, handing Mack over.

"No, but Charlie said she moved them to the basement not long ago, so we must have just missed her," Casey said. Right this second, she didn't care. Her sister and niece were safe; that was what mattered.

"All right. Jasper and Noah are on their way. We'll tell them when they arrive." Her father took in the scenery and swallowed. "Let's wait outside."

Fletcher nodded. "Great idea."

Casey and Ryan were the last ones out. She was surprised there weren't any neighbors out on their lawns looking to see what the hell was going on. But then again, they weren't in Blue Creek anymore.

She went to her truck and placed both her revolver and Ryan's sidearm in the glove compartment, more to stop herself from putting a few holes in the condemned home than for necessity. Casey squeezed her eyes shut and exhaled a shaky breath. She didn't want to think about the reality of what had just happened. Sighing, she walked back over to her family.

"Mama, my teddy's inside. I want my Mr. Teddy." Mack pouted from the front seat of Pops's truck.

"I'll get it. Where'd you leave it, sweetie?" Casey asked.

"In the baseboard," Mack said with a sniff.

"You mean the basement?" Charlie asked and Mack nodded.

"I'll go, Casey," Ryan offered.

"I can go," Charlie said. "As long as I know I can leave, I don't mind."

"I think I can handle it. Thanks." Casey turned and headed back inside, but she wasn't alone. She glanced over her shoulder and rolled her eyes when Ryan shrugged and Charlie stuck her tongue out. If they wanted to come, that was fine too.

Taking the flashlight out again, she headed back down. She directed the beam on the floor and spotted Mr. Teddy.

"I'll get it," Charlie said and passed Casey on the steps. She picked up the bear and shook her head. "I swear Mack would forget her head if it wasn't attached… Uh, Casey?"

"Come down the steps and shut the hatch," Kim said.

"Kim—or should I call you Lee—hiding, were you?" Casey asked, nodding at Ryan to close the latch. She felt around the wall on her left. If she remembered correctly…yep, there it was. She flipped the switch and shed a little light on things. Kim didn't look like the bubbly broad she'd been this morning. She looked like what she was…a nutjob.

"Figured it out, did you? That's what I thought. Everyone said you have a photographic memory—"

"It's not photographic," Casey clarified. "Just really good."

"Nevertheless, I figured it was only a matter of time before you put two and two together."

Ryan moved to stand in front of her. "Kimberly, we can work this out. Let Charlie go, and we'll sit down and talk," he said, moving past Casey and down the steps.

"You are without a doubt the strangest man I've ever met." Kim shook her head and looked at Casey. "What man do you know wants to talk?"

"Don't!" Casey shouted when Kim aimed the gun at Ryan and pulled the trigger. Ryan staggered, then crumpled to the floor. Casey rushed toward him. "Ryan, are you all right?"

He rolled onto his back and grunted.

"Leave him be, Casey! It's his own fault! If he'd left when you told him to, he'd be fine. But did he listen? No! So typical of a man." Kim shook her head and giggled. "I swear, though, you two are something else between the sheets. But that's what whores are good at."

Casey ignored her and snuck a peek at Ryan, whose breathing seemed steady.

"Who're you calling a whore?" Charlie said.

"Oh, now, now. You, my dear, have no room to talk. Sleeping with a married man is a very big no-no," Kim said, laughing when Charlie took a sharp breath.

"It's okay, Charlie. We know Rick wasn't married when you were with him. Not that any of us would have thought less of you if he had been," Casey said.

"How do you know?" Charlie asked, then sighed. "Fletcher."

Kim nodded. "She should have known better than to go sticking her nose where it didn't belong."

"Fletcher's never been good at staying away from a mystery," Casey said.

"Given the price, maybe she will be from now on. You know, I'm glad you didn't die in the fire, Casey. Setting a trap is what cowards do," Kim admitted and extended the arm holding the gun toward Casey. "Here, now, face to face, this is something else entirely."

Charlie snorted. "Oh, yeah, kudos for your bravery."

Casey stared at her sister for a moment. Okay, Charlie got snarky when she got scared. But it was a stupid thing to do when being held by a gunman—gunwoman?

Kim returned the barrel to Charlie's head. "You think so—"

"Why'd you do it?" Casey asked to take Kim's attention away from her sister. "The rats? Is this some revenge against me? What, because I was adopted and you weren't?"

"Those filthy things attacked *me*. I had to go to the hospital. I could have died. But *you* got away."

"What a baby! Had to go to the hospital. I tell you, Case, we're dealing with a sniveling sissy for sure," Fletcher said, coming out of a darkened corner.

"I detest whiners," Alex said, coming from behind Fletcher, "almost as much as I detest liars."

"How did you two get in here?" Kim screeched, moving the gun between the sisters.

"The question is, how did you get in?" Alex asked.

Kim smirked. "The deputy didn't check one of the closets upstairs."

"I don't do closets," Fletcher mumbled, then took a breath. "Kimberly Williams, you are under arrest for the kidnapping of Charlie and Mackenzie McKay, the attempted murder of Casey McKay, Alexandra McKay, and Ryan Keller, not to mention attempting to murder me, Fletcher J. McKay, an officer of the law, and, well, a whole bunch of other shit. You have the right to remain silent—"

"*Shut up!*" Kim shouted, while Fletcher persisted in reciting the Miranda warning.

"—do you understand these rights?" Fletcher asked, inching closer; she stopped when Kim cocked the gun. "Drop your weapon."

"Shut up and stay where you are, or I'll kill her," Kim said, tightening her grip on Charlie.

"I wouldn't kill my sister if I were you," Casey said.

"You and your sisters. They're no more your sisters than I am," Kim spat.

"You're wrong. Charlie *is* my sister," Casey said, speaking the words which had turned her life upside down all those years ago. She snuck another peek at Ryan, and his eyes met hers. She wanted him to hear this too. "Charlie and I share the same father."

"Oh, Casey," Charlie whispered, tears filling her eyes.

"I don't believe you," Kim said, shaking her head. She pointed her gun at Alex when she moved forward. Charlie bit her arm, and Kim howled and let go of her hold. A knife pierced her chest, and Kim screamed, dropping her gun.

Fletcher shrugged. "I told her to drop her weapon."

None of them gave a second glance to Kim after Fletcher kicked the gun out of her reach. Casey knelt next to Ryan, and Charlie stood beside her.

"Ryan?" Casey whispered, shaking him gently. "Can you hear me?"

"Heard every word, sweetheart," he assured her.

Fletcher hovered over them. "How bad is it?"

"She got my shoulder, I think," he said, and Casey released the breath she hadn't known she'd been holding.

"Looks like you and I may have matching scars. You can get a tattoo to cover it up, like I did," Fletcher said.

"I wondered about that," he said with a gruff laugh. "How did you two get in here anyway?"

"Fletcher and I came here a while ago," Alex began.

"We came down to the basement to look the place over," Fletcher said, glancing at Casey, then pointed behind her. "Found an old cellar door outside. I didn't think about it before." She waved her hand in the air for a moment, then grinned. "Slipped my mind."

"Mind like a steel trap, my ass," Casey said.

Charlie snorted.

Fletcher shrugged. "Remembered it in the nick of time, though, didn't I?"

"When you didn't come back after a few minutes, we went around back to see what was taking so long."

"This is one time I'll appreciate your impatience, Alexandra," Casey said.

"Is that woman dead?" Pops asked as he made his way down the steps. Jasper and Noah followed him. "I see your aim is a bit off, Fletcher."

Fletcher shrugged. "I wasn't trying to kill her."

Pops nodded. "Well, then it's a good thing we called an ambulance."

"Better make it two," Noah said and turned to make the call.

"The first one should be here any minute," Jasper said as he gave Charlie a quick hug. He looked down at Ryan. "How're you doing there?"

"I'll be all right, Jasper. If Fletcher can handle getting shot, so can I."

Casey shook her head. "Here we go—"

"When was Fletcher shot?" Noah asked. He pocketed his cell and nodded to Ryan. "Detective Noah Reed. Nice to meet you, except for the circumstances, of course."

Ryan smirked. "Of course."

"Hey, Casey, c'mere," Fletcher said from the other side of the room where Kim lay writhing.

Casey glanced down at Ryan, who winked at her. The instant Kim had shot him, Casey knew she cared for him more than she had wanted to admit to herself. She bent down, pressing her lips to his ear, not wanting anyone else to hear. "I think I'm developing some *very* strong feelings for you, Ryan Keller."

"I had to get shot first, huh?" he joked with a grimace. "Go see what your sister wants."

Casey walked over to where her sister sat on the floor next to their would-be killer.

"Come on, Kim. You may as well spill it," Fletcher taunted.

Casey stared at the knife sticking up from Kim's chest. Fletcher had missed the heart on purpose, but that didn't make the scene any less gory.

Kim's gaze followed Casey's, and she reached for the handle of the blade.

"I wouldn't do that if I were you," Fletcher warned.

Her hand dropped to her side. "Am I going to die?"

"More than likely." Fletcher sighed. She turned to Casey and mouthed, "She'll live."

Casey's brows pinched.

"Your adoption records were destroyed, and it took a while to find the social worker who handled your case. After some finagling, she gave me Alexandra's information. I did some digging, and hey, what were the chances? Alexandra needed a cook, and I was a cook."

"But why?" Casey wanted to know.

"You're right, my name used to be Lee, and after you were adopted, I had to take your place. That's not why I hate you. You see, my mother went crazy when you left."

"Miss Tina?" Casey croaked.

"Shocked, are you?"

"I'll be damned," Fletcher said. "Miss Tina was your mother?"

"Yes! She was a wonderful mother…until you came along. You were her greatest achievement, and when you left something in her snapped. She made me deal with the rats, but I got bit, and—they sent her to the mental institution. She died there."

"But you lived here with us," Casey said.

"I was Mom's spy. It's how she kept an eye on everyone. After she was arrested, I had to go into the system." Kim closed her eyes.

"I just don't get it," Fletcher began. "If you were only after Casey, why bother with the rest of us?"

"So many questions," Kim wheezed. "I hired Sean, but he was incompetent." She coughed and nodded toward Casey. "I wanted you, that's true enough. The rest, well…"

Casey moved back. "That's enough, Fletcher."

"No!" Fletcher shook Kim. "You stole my locket, didn't you?"

"In...inspired i...idea," Kim hissed.

"And the laugh?"

"Fletcher, that's enough," Noah said, coming over to stand next to them. "You can question her more later."

"Kiss my ass, Reed!" Fletcher shook Kim again. "Was it you in my cabin?"

Kim opened her eyes and licked her lips. "Someone y...yes, but not m...me." She laughed on a breath of air. "You M...McKays have a l-lot of enemies. Just happy I made their acquaintance." She took a deep breath and glanced down at the knife in her chest, then passed out.

Casey stared at Kim's body, then looked at her sister who was shaking out of Noah's hold. "Fletcher, stop it. Come to the hospital with me and Ryan," Casey said.

"Okay, Case," Fletcher agreed after she'd elbowed Noah in the stomach.

Chapter Twenty-Five

Ryan woke up sore. He was on his second day in the hospital, and he wanted to go home. Wherever home was. He looked to his left and jumped a little. "Please tell me that's you, Jake, and not some funhouse mirror."

"Funny, little brother. Real fucking funny," Jake said, dropping the newspaper he was reading. There was at least two days of beard growth on his brother's face.

Ryan smiled. "I thought it was."

"Am I laughing?" Jake sat back in his chair. "I really can't leave you to fend for yourself, can I? You have to go and get shot!"

"Yes, Jake, this is my idea of fun." Ryan looked around and noticed Fletcher peeking in the door. She mouthed, "Jake?" and he nodded.

"It must be, bro. Here I left you to take care of a little girl I—"

Ryan tried to keep his face passive as Fletcher held a pen to his brother's throat.

"There now. Take back the 'little girl' part, Jake, and we can be friends again," Fletcher said, winking at Ryan while he shook his head.

"Kid?"

"Take it back, Jake."

"Fine, I take it back." Jake grunted when Fletcher

hopped in his lap. "Deputy Do-Wrong! How are you, kid?"

"I'm happy I didn't get shot this time," she said, then stiffened when the door opened. She stood. "Detective Reed, did you get lost?"

"No, Deputy." Noah sneered. "I came to get Mr. Keller's statement. Everyone else has given theirs."

"Jake, meet Detective Reed. Noah, this is my big brother Jake," Ryan said, knowing it annoyed his brother.

"Oooh, just like the old show," Charlie said, coming into the room with Casey behind her.

"I'll just come back later," Noah said and turned around.

"Good riddance."

"What's your problem, Fletcher?" Casey asked.

"I don't have a problem. Meet Ryan's brother, why don'tcha?" Fletcher said.

"At least you two aren't armed like the kid," Jake said, then looked at Ryan with a raised brow. "Which is yours, bro?"

"That would be me," Casey said, taking a seat on the mattress. She leaned over and kissed Ryan, who groaned. "Miss me?"

"Yes." He smiled when she smirked. Charlie was shaking her head; she looked damn good for a woman who'd been kidnapped. "Where's Alexandra?"

"She's searching for a new cook, but she said she would see you later," Charlie said.

"Wait a minute, there's more of you?" Jake asked.

"Jake, I wouldn't go there if I were you," Ryan warned, but Jake grinned. Ryan sighed. His brother would never change. "Why is everyone here anyway?"

"Fletcher didn't tell you?" Casey asked.

"I just got here, but I'll tell you now." Fletcher put her hands on her hips. "We're busting you outta this joint."

Ryan sat up. "Really?"

"Be careful, damn it. You might hurt yourself," Casey hissed, then fluffed his pillows.

Ryan took her hand and kissed it. "Worried about me?"

"Someone has to," she grumbled.

"Thanks, sweetheart. Am I really able to leave?"

"Yep."

"This is one hell of a Hallmark moment, but if he's been cleared, I'm outta here," Jake said, standing. "I just stopped by to make sure you were going to live, bro."

"Thanks for taking time out of your busy schedule."

"You're welcome. Looks like I'm leaving you in good hands." Jake picked up his newspaper and headed for the door. "It was nice meeting you," he told the women, then pointed to Fletcher. "Kid, I'll see you around."

"Nice meeting you too," Charlie called after him.

"Let's get you the hell outta here. I hate hospitals," Fletcher said.

****

Two weeks later, they were all gathered around the kitchen table of the McKay home. Ryan had spent the last two weeks being pampered, but now that he was back to himself he had things he needed to take care of. Casey had spent her time with him doing everything she could to make him feel better. They woke up

265

together and had breakfast before she went to work. The garage was coming along, and Ryan could see how happy she was.

Either Savannah or one of the sisters would come by at lunchtime to check on him. Jasper came in the afternoons and took him to the gym at the sheriff's station, where Tiny would meet him to oversee his workouts. He spent his nights in bed with Casey; he couldn't agree more with her theory that making love was great physical therapy. His body was rejuvenated.

He smiled at her sitting next to him now. He didn't know how he was going to leave.

Casey winked at Ryan. He looked great in the casual clothes she had made him wear. The man could fill out a pair of blue jeans. She shivered. Ryan Keller could do a lot of things with that body. She put her hand in his under the table. She had talked to him about tonight. It was time to tell the truth. Taking a deep breath, Casey turned to Fletcher, who was fidgeting with her coffee cup.

They were all nervous. Charlie had asked Jebb to take Mack upstairs, and now she sat watching everyone; she looked sweet, but Casey knew different. She'd broken up the fight between Charlie and Fletcher three days ago. Casey had forgotten Charlie could fight, but it probably helped that Fletcher had only blocked punches instead of throwing any. Charlie was pissed that Fletcher had gone behind her back to find out who Mack's father was. Not that Casey could blame her.

Alex was sitting next to their mother. She appeared calm on the outside, but her eyes were weary. Casey pursed her lips. How long did it actually take Alex to get ready in the morning? She always looked perfect.

Alex frowned. "What?"

"Nothing," Casey said and shifted her gaze back to Fletcher. "Did you bring it?"

Fletcher sighed. "Yeah."

"Why did you call this family meeting, Casey?" Pops asked.

"I'm trying to figure out where to start," Casey said. Ryan gave her hand a reassuring squeeze, then Alex spoke.

"I may as well start. The night Uncle Evan died, Fletcher and I...well, we..."

"Alexandra, just tell us, honey," their mother said, patting Alex's hand.

"Charlie and Casey ran to get help, and Alex and I stayed behind. There's something about that night we didn't tell you," Fletcher said.

Pops rubbed his hands over his face. "Seems to me, here lately, you're always leaving something out, Fletcher."

"Yes, well, she left it out because I made her," Alex said.

"True, she did, but the reason why is Uncle Evan gave us this letter"—Fletcher pulled the old bloodstained envelope out of her overalls—"before he died."

Both of their parents sucked in a breath.

"I read it first, and then Fletcher read it," Alex explained.

"We promised not to tell anyone for ten years." Fletcher shrugged. "We're a little late on that deadline."

"I was looking for an old picture in the attic, and Jebb noticed a cut-out floorboard in the closet. He found the note, and I read it," Casey said.

"That's why you left? Because of this letter?" Pops asked.

"Yes." She looked at the letter in her sister's hand. "Read it."

Fletcher looked around the table and took a deep breath. She unfolded the old paper carefully and read.

"Dear Emmit, By the time you get this letter, I will be far away from Blue Creek. I'm leaving the only home I have ever known because I can't face the truth. I'm a coward, my friend, not the hero you thought I was when we were boys. Unfortunately, we can't go back to those days of our youth. I slept with—"

"We know this," Pops said.

Ma rubbed his back. "Let her finish, Emmit."

"Just skip that part, Fletch," Casey said.

Fletcher nodded and continued. "...I have kept something even more damning from you. Casey and Charlie are mine, Emmit."

"What!" Pops jumped from the table. "You had no right to keep this from me—either of you! Do you hear me?" No one moved as he went to the trashcan and threw up.

"Emmit, sit down," Savannah said after he'd rinsed his mouth out in the sink. "You didn't know either, did you?" she asked Charlie.

"No, I found out after Casey went ballistic." Charlie tugged at Pops's hand so he would sit down. "They were only eleven and nine, Dad. They were children. What's done is done."

"I think I understand why you left, Casey," he murmured.

"I wish I hadn't, Pops. But Fletcher...finish it," Casey said, giving Ryan a small smile when he kissed her cheek.

Fletcher cleared her throat and started to read again. "Casey and Charlie are mine, Emmit. I found out about Casey and went to the orphanage. Something about that place didn't sit right with me, and I wanted her out of there. The problem was, she had two little girls with her and I couldn't take them too. I didn't even know if I could be a father. Then I thought about how you had always wanted a large family, and I brought you to meet them. You did what I was unable to do and took all three of them. I'll be forever grateful.

"I found out about Charlie a couple of years later. I knew I couldn't be a father, at least not as good as you. I introduced you to Charlie, and once again, you did the right thing by my daughter. I was able to watch them grow up and participate in their lives. You're better for them than I could have ever hoped to be.

"Now you're probably wondering who their mothers were. Charlie's mother died giving birth, and Casey's mother gave her up at the hospital when she was born; she died in a car accident about a year ago.

"My father knows all of this. He was pretty shaken up, but we agreed I'd done the right thing. And giving my girls to you was probably the best thing I've done in my life.

"If you have any questions, ask Dad. He doesn't know I'm leaving, but he'll understand.

"I know you probably hate me right now, and I can't blame you. I know you feel betrayed, and I'm sorry for that. I've always considered you my brother, and I love you. If you never want to think of me again, that's fine. But take this last piece of advice and marry Savannah. She loves you and the girls.

"I'd ask you to please take care of the girls, but I know you will and already have. Yours truly, Evan."

Savannah was crying, and Emmit looked like he'd been shot.

"I'm sorry," Fletcher whispered and hurried out of the room.

"I don't know what's worse, that you kept this from me or that you kept it from your sisters," Pops said, taking the letter from where Fletcher had dropped it.

"Emmit, I think Alexandra and Fletcher know what they've done," Ma said, wiping her eyes. "Evan's been dead for quite some time. He was your friend and…and mine. You might not want to admit it, but he gave you the best gift he could ever give." She cupped her husband's face in her hands. "He gave you our girls."

"I'm glad he did what he did," Charlie said. "We wouldn't be who we are today if not for him, and I love who we are. I love our family, and it doesn't matter what that piece of paper says." She smiled at Casey. "It didn't matter six years ago. I love knowing Casey is my sister by blood, but Alexandra and Fletcher are just as much my sisters. I love them the same as I did before."

"It took me longer to come to grips with this. I ran instead of facing the truth." Casey reached across the table and took her father's hand. "I think I'm mature enough now to admit it wasn't really Alex and Fletcher keeping this secret that made me run." She waited for her father to look at her. "You remember, aside from Fletch, Uncle Evan was my best friend."

"Oh, Casey," Ma whispered.

Casey turned to her mother. "It's okay, really."

"Go on, sweetheart," Ryan said. He had helped her

navigate her emotions until she finally understood them for herself and could explain them.

"I loved him, Pops," she said. "And for a split second I was happy he was the one; part of me belonged to him. It was just a second, but I felt that those feelings betrayed you—let you down—and I'd fought so hard to earn your love."

Pops half stood with tears in his eyes. "Casey—"

"No, don't say anything, not yet, okay. Just let me get it out."

"Okay," Pops said and took his seat.

"Coming home, I've realized what I've been running from was the fear that if you knew the truth about who he really was to me—about that split second—then you would only see me as his, you *and* Ma. In the back of my mind, I've always been afraid this life you gave me would unravel, and one day I'd wake up alone in the basement again, a scared little girl unworthy of your love...so I ran."

"You don't have to run anymore," Pops said. He pulled her into his embrace and a sob slipped from her throat. "I don't think I'm capable of *not* loving you, Case."

"Yeah, I know that now." She smiled through her tears when he put her down.

Her mother stood. "I shouldn't even have to remind you I love you. You and your sisters are *my* girls, and I'll have words with anyone who says otherwise," she said, wiping the tears from Casey's cheek.

"I always said you were crazy as a loon," Jasper choked out from where he stood in the doorway. He blew his nose into his handkerchief.

"Jasper, how much did you hear?" Charlie asked.

"All of it, but I've known for a while about who Casey and Charlie's biological father was."

"How could you possibly have known?" Ryan asked.

"Ward Jessup told me on his deathbed. Like I've said, there's not much goes on in this town that I don't know about." Jasper jerked when Fletcher came in behind him. "Done with your secrets now, girl?" he asked her, but she ignored him.

"You two knew this," Pops said motioning to Alex and Fletcher. "Did you look for your biological parents?" All eyes turned to Fletcher, who blanched but remained silent; then the focus settled on Alexandra.

"Alex, did you?" Casey wanted to know.

Alexandra got up from the table, hugged their mother and their reluctant father, then opened the screen door. She turned and said, "My biological parents are dead." Then she walked out.

Chapter Twenty-Six

"How does Alexandra know her parents are dead?" Ryan asked.

"Fletcher probably knows," Charlie said, crossing her arms over her chest. "She knows everyone's business."

Fletcher squirmed. "Jeez, Charlie, I said I'm sorry. I even let you hit me."

"Do you know or not?" Casey asked, annoyed.

Fletcher told them what she knew. "There now...happy?" She turned beet red when Jasper gave her a half hug.

Pops sat down hard. "Oh Lord."

"Alexandra never said a word," Ma said, taking a seat on Pops's lap.

Casey shook her head. What other secrets was Alex keeping? She turned to Ryan, but his attention was on Jasper.

"What brought you here tonight, Jasper?" Ryan asked.

"Hell, I almost forgot. I came because I have some news, and it ain't good neither." He removed his hat and sat down on the window seat.

"Go ahead, Jasper. I'm not sure I can handle any more suspense," Pops said.

"Seems 'bout an hour or so ago, they found Kimberly Williams dead." Jasper shook his head.

"How?" Fletcher, Pops, and Ryan asked at once.

"Someone smothered her with a pillow."

"What happened to the guard Noah had stationed at her door?" Pops asked.

"Someone knocked the man out. And before you ask, the security cameras didn't catch a damn thing. Glitch in the system."

"Jesus," Ryan murmured.

"Someone didn't want Kimberly to talk. More than she already had, I mean," Casey said.

Jasper nodded. "That's the consensus."

"What about her apartment? Did you find anything there?" Ryan asked.

"We searched her place and—"

"Did you look in the bed?" Fletcher asked. "There was something funny about that bed."

"Never gonna hear the last of this," Jasper grumbled. "Yes, you were right, missy. The headboard had been built with a secret compartment. That's where we found the things stolen from the Thomas home. We also found several letters, none of them sighed, which indicate that Kim wasn't working alone. In fact, the handwriting expert who works with Noah said one was male and one female; neither were Kim's."

"What did these letters say?" Casey asked.

"I'll just tell you there was a lot of hate," Jasper said. "A whole hell of a lot of hate."

"Great," Charlie said as she topped off everyone's coffee. "So there's still someone out there who wants to kill us."

"Not necessarily. By eliminating Kim, their secrets are safe and they can go about their normal lives. I think they'll back off because they know we're watching," Jasper said.

****

"Do you think I should go talk to Alexandra?" Casey asked Ryan for the second time since returning to the cabin. She set her keys on the kitchen counter and grabbed a beer for each of them.

"If you want to, Casey."

"I asked if *you* think I should." She crawled up in his lap after he sat down on the couch.

"I don't know. If it was Jake, I'd go and talk to him. But with Jake, it's more like talking *at* him."

"Let's not talk about your brother," Casey said.

"What's your problem with Jake? Every time I've asked you what you thought of him you change the subject."

"I don't really know him."

"Casey, you've obviously formed some sort of opinion."

"Fine, I don't like him." She got up to pace. She knew she'd hurt his feelings. Why did he have to be so sensitive?

"Why?"

Casey huffed. "I don't know… I don't like the way he treats you."

Ryan sighed and rubbed his eyes. "It's just his way, Casey. I got all the emotions in the womb." That made her smile, then frown.

"You were shot, and he's here for a couple hours? I mean, come on. I hardly left Fletcher's side either time she was shot, and we're not twins."

"What was that look for?"

"What look?"

"I don't know; it was like a grimace or something,"

he said, taking her hand in his.

She shrugged. "Fletcher isn't even my blood, and everyone knows I like her best."

"You love Charlie just as much as you love Fletcher and Alexandra. But when it comes down to it, you relate better with Fletcher. Why, I have no idea."

Casey snatched her hand away. "What's that supposed to mean?"

"Nothing against Fletcher—you know *I* like your sisters—but she is an odd duck."

"You know I'm only letting you get away with that because it's true, right?" She grinned and kissed him, then groaned when there was a knock on the door. Casey went to answer it while Ryan finished his beer.

The McKay sisters were all standing there with various drinks in hand.

"Hey, Ryan! Got your luxury ride back, I see," Charlie said smiling.

"Yes, they dropped it off yesterday; looks great too. What brings you all out here?"

"We're kicking you out for a while," Alex said, handing him a key. "No one's at the B and B right now, so you can stay there."

"You don't have to go if you don't want to," Casey said.

"I don't mind," he said and went to grab his keys.

She turned back to her sisters. "What's all this about?"

"We're gonna have us an old-fashioned pow-wow," Fletcher said, smirking when Ryan came back.

"I'll see you later then?" he asked Casey.

"Absolutely," she said and kissed him. "Can't wait."

"Me either." He turned and saluted her sisters. "Bye, ladies."

They waited for Ryan's vehicle to be out of sight before they went inside and made themselves comfortable. Casey grabbed another beer and sat down next to Charlie, handing her sister a wine cooler.

"Are you okay, Alexandra?" Casey asked, using the name her sister preferred.

"Why wouldn't I be?"

Casey shrugged. "Okay, let's get this over with." The sooner her sisters left, the sooner Ryan would come back.

"Jeez, what's your problem?"

"Fletcher, Casey wants to get her groove on," Charlie said with a little shimmy.

"Oh." Fletcher wiggled her eyebrows.

Alex gave a ladylike snort. "Grow up, Fletcher!"

"Casey's getting impatient, so I'll hurry it up," Charlie said after Casey grumbled. "We wanted to know if you're going to stay?"

"Of course, I'm staying. Why the hell wouldn't I?"

"What about Ryan?" Alex asked, sipping the wine she'd brought.

Casey pulled at the label on her beer bottle. "What about him?"

"Is he staying here or, or not?" Fletcher asked.

Her heart pinched. "I don't know."

"You need to discuss it. But since you are staying, we need to talk about our next steps," Charlie said, nodding to herself.

"Next steps for what?" Casey asked.

"For how to handle any other fuckheads who're stupid enough to come after the McKay sisters!"

Fletcher said.

Casey rolled her eyes. "Oh, that plan."

"Yes, that one," Alex said and clinked her glass against her sisters' bottles.

****

It was late when Ryan came through the door. Casey was sprawled across the couch watching TV. She sat up, hit the remote, then stood.

"Hi," she said, standing on tiptoe to kiss him.

"Hi, yourself."

"When are you leaving?" she asked, pulling away so she could read his face.

"I hadn't really thought that far ahead... Do you want me to leave?"

"No, I mean, do you *want* to leave?"

"I've got to eventually. I have a home and a business, which I've been neglecting, Casey," he said, rubbing his temples.

"I forgot about your business. Sorry." She didn't know where to go from here. Sex she could handle. This emotional shit? Well, she was out of practice. Okay, okay, she'd never been good at it.

"With everything that's been going on, that's understandable."

"I guess." She started to pace, then stopped in front of him. "I love you."

A slow grin spread across his face. "I love you too."

"No, I mean, *I love you*." She shook her head; she was messing this up. "I've never loved anyone outside my family, Ryan. Not ever. I—you..." She stomped her foot.

"I've never loved anyone like this either, Casey,"

Ryan said in that way that made her knees threaten to give out.

"That's sweet," she said with a grin. "I mean, I've never loved someone so much, never cared or wanted or—oh, screw it—just plain needed someone as much as I need you. And that scares the shit out of me."

"I feel the same way, Casey." He kissed the top of her head and then bent so they were eye to eye. "It scares me too."

"Yeah, well, you're leaving." She pulled out of his arms. She didn't know what she was feeling. She didn't want to lose him.

"Well, yes, but not for long. I have an idea," he said, and she stopped pacing.

"What?"

"You could marry me... I mean, would you marry me, Casey? Would you be my wife?"

She stared at him. "Y-you want to marry me?" She pointed to her chest.

"I know I'll end up in a straitjacket eventually, but yes, I want to marry you, Casey no-middle-name McKay."

She stood dumbstruck as he went over to his briefcase and pulled out a little pouch. Ryan walked back to her and emptied it into her hand. Casey stared at the ring. It was white gold with a diamond in the shape of a star. She blinked and blinked again. "You're serious?"

"As a heart attack!"

"And you don't think it's too soon?"

"It's true we've only known each other for a short while, and there's a lot we'll need to figure out, but I know I want to spend my life with you. We can have a long engagement if you—"

"Screw that!"

He laughed and tilted her chin so they were eye to eye. "I love you, I need you, and I don't think I would be living without you. Will you marry me?"

"Hell yeah!" Casey shouted, and Ryan kissed her. "What are you waiting for? I said yes, put the ring on my finger." She wiggled the finger in question and stared while he slipped the ring on. "Do you always carry a ring around with you?"

"That one, yes. It belonged to my mother; my grandmother gave it to me after our parents died. She told me to keep it with me because I'd never know when I'd need it."

"I…thank you." Emotions choked her; he'd given her his mother's ring. "But Ryan, I already promised my sisters I would stay here."

"We *are* staying." He grinned when her eyes shot to his. "I like it here. Apparently, the mountains suit me. I can move the business here and sell my condo."

"You'd do that?" Casey shook her head.

"For you and for us, yes." Ryan laughed. "I can't believe you said yes."

"Well, I can't believe you asked." Then her eyes went huge. "Holy shit! I've got to tell Pops."

"Right now?" Ryan asked, checking his watch. "It's late."

"Please?" she asked and grabbed her keys when he sighed.

"Let's take my SUV," he said when they got outside.

"Okay, but I'm driving."

****

Casey hurried into her parents' house, with Ryan behind her. She hollered at the top of her lungs for her parents. Finally, she had good news to share.

She had called Fletcher and told her to get her scrawny ass over here and bring her sisters. She looked out the window as Fletcher pulled up. Casey smiled. Her little sister ran in the grass barefooted along with Charlie. Alex was taking her damn time though.

"Jeez, Casey, what's going on? Hi, Ryan," Jebb said, scratching his chest. Ryan waved at him. Jebb grabbed an apple and hopped up on the counter.

She ruffled his hair. "Don't worry about it, Bullfrog."

"Okay, I'm here, scrawny ass and all; brought them too. I'll have you know Jasper's not happy with either of you." Fletcher eyed Casey, then Ryan.

Casey frowned. "Why'd you call Jasper?"

"Someone had to stay with Mack," Charlie said, rolling her eyes.

"Why didn't you just bring her?" Casey asked.

"Wake up a three-year-old and try putting her back to sleep," Charlie mumbled. "Duh."

"What in the hell's going on? Why's everyone here?" Pops asked, coming into the kitchen.

"What is it, Casey?" her mother asked.

Casey held out her hand. "Ryan asked me to marry him, and I said yes. I'm getting married!" she said in a rush, then beamed at Ryan when the place erupted in chaos.

"Hold the hell on!" Pops shouted. Everyone stopped talking. "I don't remember you asking me if you could marry my daughter."

"Dad!" Casey said, surprised.

"No, sir, I didn't ask you," Ryan said.

"No," her mother said with a smug smile. "He asked *me*. And there's nothing you can do about it."

Pops shook his head and hugged Casey.

Casey turned to Ryan. "When did you ask Ma?"

"This evening, after you and your sisters kicked me out," Ryan said.

"Wow." Charlie sighed. "It's just like a movie."

"Congratulations," Alex said, hugging Casey, then Ryan. "I can't wait to start planning the wedding."

Fletcher shook her head, then shot to her feet. "I ain't wearing a damn dress!"

Epilogue

"I said I wasn't wearing a dress and I meant it," Fletcher grumbled.

They had reclaimed the attic in their parents' home as a base camp for the wedding preparations. The place looked like a bridal boutique thanks to Alex's insistence on handling every detail.

"I didn't order you a dress, Fletcher." Casey rolled her eyes. "You're wearing the pants."

"They're too short to be pants," Fletcher whined when Casey handed her the garment. "I hate lavender," she said under her breath.

"Do you want to be in Casey's wedding or not?" Alexandra asked as she slipped into her bridesmaid dress.

"Course I do."

"Then stop your whining. You sound like Mack." Charlie winked at Casey.

"Yeah, well, Mack likes dresses and girly shit like that," Fletcher said.

"News flash, Fletcher. You *are* a girl," Casey said, but she didn't mind. She was too happy; today was her wedding day. It had taken months getting ready, but it was time.

Everyone had finally agreed with Jasper that whoever held a grudge against them had backed off. They were all still being careful, but for the most part it was life as usual. Unless you counted the fact that she was getting married. That was definitely not usual.

"Will the house be ready when you get back?" Alex asked.

"Yeah, it will." Their house. Hers and Ryan's together. Casey was more ecstatic about the house than she ever would have expected herself to be.

Charlie plugged in the curling iron. "I still can't believe Ryan's filthy rich."

"The designer clothes didn't give it away?" Alex shook her head.

"I saw that look, Alexandra. And he isn't 'filthy rich.' He's just made some really good investments," Casey said as she finished painting her toes.

"I'm just glad he and Pops are getting along better," Fletcher said.

"Yeah. I think it's safe to say Pops likes him now."

"Oh please, Dad gave you and Ryan two acres of land on the McKay property as an early wedding present. I say he more than *likes* Ryan."

"What are you complaining about, Alex?"

"I'm not complaining, Casey, only stating the facts," Alex said as she slipped into her shoes.

"O*h*, before I forget." Casey grabbed an envelope from the side table and handed it to Alex.

"What's this?"

"Just open it."

Alex unsealed the envelope and pulled out a document. Her brows pinched as she scanned the page. Casey smiled when Alex looked up at her. "You're giving this to me?"

Granny Vaughn had willed her home to whichever of them got married first. Casey had no problem handing the deed over to her sister. "Granny Vaughn would have changed her will in a heartbeat if she'd known what you wanted to do with the place. It's already yours."

"Casey, I...thank you," Alex whispered.

"You're welcome. But it comes with the condition that Ryan can stay there whenever he's been bad and I have to punish him."

****

Outside, everyone was scrambling around to get things done. The wedding was being held at the McKay home. They'd set up tents along the property and had enough seating for all of Blue Creek—just in case.

By the time the wedding march started, Ryan was a bundle of nerves. Jake, his best man, walked down the aisle with Fletcher. Ryan almost didn't recognize her. Someone had fixed her hair and put makeup on her. He grinned at her when she rolled her eyes.

Jasper escorted Charlie and Alexandra down. The sheriff had been speechless, probably for the first time in his life, when Ryan had asked him to be in the wedding. Jebb, the ring bearer, walked down with Mack; she made an adorable flower girl.

The music began to play, and Ryan looked up. His heart stopped.

Casey looked like a goddess. She wore a white gown with a long skirt that trailed behind her. Her shoulders were bare, and she sparkled. He heard Emmit say that he gave his daughter to Ryan, and then Ryan had her hand.

"I love you," he whispered to her, and she glowed. They turned to the preacher.

****

"Can I take off this damn thing yet?" Fletcher asked once the reception officially began.

"Go change if you want to. I'm just glad you kept it on as long as you did," Casey said, snickering when Fletcher raced away.

"That was nice of you, Mrs. Keller," Ryan said.

"Huh? Oh…sorry." She laughed. "The name thing's going to take some getting used to. When the preacher called me Mrs. Keller, I thought I'd faint. I've never been anything but a McKay. What you just saw was Fletcher running to change."

Ryan smiled. "I barely recognized her."

"I know. Mama talked her into the makeup." Casey turned to him. "Ma's a miracle worker and undeniably sneaky."

"Not as sneaky as her oldest daughter," he said and caressed her cheek.

"What's that supposed to mean?"

"It means, you snuck right into my heart and didn't let go." He kissed her after she told him how cheesy he was.

"Great answer," Emmit said as he walked up.

"I thought so," Casey said, kissing her father's cheek.

"Are you enjoying the festivities, Emmit?" Ryan asked. Casey said he should just call her father Pops, but Ryan didn't think that would be wise.

"I am. I heard a rumor that Shmittie was thinking about selling the bar."

"I'm sure Fletcher and Jasper will find out everything about it if it happens," Ryan said.

Casey snorted. "If they haven't already."

"Duty calls," Emmit said after Jasper called his

name. He kissed Casey's temple and patted Ryan on the back.

Once it was only the two of them, Casey said, "I love you, Mr. Keller."

"And I love you, Mrs. Keller."

"Good. Great."

"I know that look in your eyes," Ryan said. "What are you up to?"

"Do you think the chauffeur would let me take the limo for a spin?"

A word about the author...

W. L. Brooks likes to write like she reads with a bit of mystery, romance, suspense, and to keep it interesting, the occasional dash of the paranormal. Living in Western North Carolina, she is currently working on her next novel.

~*~

Learn more about W. L. Brooks at
http://www.wlbrooks.com/index.html
https://www.facebook.com/authorwlbrooks/